Jade Enclave

Blue Moon Boston Book 7

Justin Herzog , Steve Higgs

Text Copyright © 2025 Justin Herzog & Steven J Higgs

Publisher: Steve Higgs

The right of Justin Herzog and Steve Higgs to be identified as authors of the Work has been asserted by them in accordance with the Copyright, Designs and Patents Act 1988

All rights reserved.

The book is copyright material and must not be copied, reproduced, transferred, distributed, leased, licensed or publicly performed or used in any way except as specifically permitted in writing by the publishers, as allowed under the terms and conditions under which it was purchased or as strictly permitted by applicable copyright law. Any unauthorised distribution or use of this text may be a direct infringement of the author's and publisher's rights and those responsible may be liable in law accordingly.

'Jade Enclave' is a work of fiction. Names, characters, businesses, organisations, places, events, and incidents either are the product of the author's imagination or are used fictitiously. Any resemblance to actual persons, living, dead or undead, events or locations is entirely coincidental.

Contents

1. What Comes Next. Thursday, July 24th 2355hrs — 1
2. Child's Play. Friday, July 25th 0540hrs — 11
3. Let the Bodies Hit the Floor. Friday, July 25th 0837hrs — 31
4. Turning A Blind Eye. Friday, July 25th 1012hrs — 43
5. A Jolly British Sailor. Friday, July 25th 1036hrs — 53
6. Forensics. Friday, July 25th 1036hrs — 62
7. An Inconvenient Plea. Friday, July 25th 1112hrs — 77
8. The Missing Roommate. Friday, July 25th 1143hrs — 86
9. Chinatown. Friday, July 25th 1300hrs — 103
10. The Lotus Garden. Friday, July 25th 1300hrs — 116
11. Jade Moon Rising. Friday, July 25th 1327hrs — 134
12. Unexpected Allies. Friday, July 25th 1402hrs — 146
13. MIT. Friday, July 25th 1530hrs — 162

14.	An Unexpected Offer. Friday, July 25th 1549hrs	175
15.	Satoru Doku. Friday, July 25th 1555hrs	184
16.	The Gray Fox. Friday, July 25th 1559hrs	197
17.	Encroaching Shadows. Friday, July 25th 1630hrs	204
18.	Sacred Pine Temple. Friday, July 25th 1724hrs	215
19.	The Jiangshi. Friday, July 25th 1749hrs	241
20.	Old Harbor Storage. Friday, July 25th 1842hrs	254
21.	Someone is Lying. Friday, July 25th 1907hrs	268
22.	The Lives We Leave Behind. Friday, July 25th 1953hrs	284
23.	Prepare for Battle. Friday, July 25th 2153hrs	299
24.	The Meeting. Friday, July 25th 2355hrs	311
25.	The Battle for Chinatown. Saturday, July 26th 0005hrs	325
26.	The Aftermath. Saturday, July 26th 0800hrs	349
27.	What is Next for Chloe?	353
28.	A Note from the Author	355
29.	More Books by Justin Herzog	357
	Free Books and More	360

What Comes Next. Thursday, July 24th 2355hrs

"Why don't I just go up there and snuff 'em?"

Yang Jei sighed and glanced at the dashboard clock. Only five minutes to go. That was good. Much longer and he'd end up slitting this orange fool's throat.

The smell of gasoline lingered just above the street, acrid but still preferable to the cheap cologne exuding from his passenger. On the roadway's surface, streaks of motor oil intermingled with the remnants of the late afternoon rainfall, their muted colors reflecting the glow of the overhead streetlamps.

They'd parked in front of an auto repair shop, camouflaging themselves among the broken-down vehicles awaiting service.

The last mechanic had left hours before, a handful of bills convincing him to leave the gate unlocked before heading home for the evening.

"I'm just saying, man, there's no reason for us to be sitting here when we could be home watching the Patriots. I put some serious money down on this game. If we hurry, we can still catch the tail end of it."

"You were not brought here to snuff anyone," Yang Jei reminded him.

"Says who?"

"Says Satoru Doku."

Marty O'Sullivan's mouth tightened involuntarily at the name, but he shook it off a moment later. "So why am I here?"

"To observe."

"Observe, what, man? We been staring at this same broken-down old building for the past two hours."

The "broken-down old building" was a six-story apartment complex on the edge of Boston's Chinatown. Red brick with pale shingle accents and narrow balconies, it was virtually indistinguishable from the dozens of others that lined the surrounding block. Just another aging structure in need of renovation, its units filled with men and women struggling to keep their heads above the poverty line.

The building itself held little interest for Yang Jei. It was the occupants inside, specifically those in the third-floor, western-facing apartment, that had brought him here. In the time they'd been parked, he'd caught only brief glimpses of them, silhouettes flashing from behind the drawn blinds.

"I'm just saying, man. This is not my first rodeo. If we're going to do this, then let's do it already."

"We will do nothing."

"Look, Stir-fry, I don't know what your deal is, but I did my time playing lookout. I'm what you call a made man."

"Good for you."

"Yeah, it is. I've shed my share of blood to get where I am, so how about we stop pussyfooting around and make something happen?"

Yang Jei sighed. In fairness, the orange fool was not actually orange. It was just his hair beneath the streetlight. The rest of him was pale, even for a New Englander, with discolored splotches along his face indicative of too much whiskey and too many cigarettes. The markings would become more prominent as Marty aged, assuming he lived that long, which Yang doubted.

In addition to the splotches, a prominent tattoo adorned Marty's neck. An unfamiliar slogan, the letters interspersed with symbols and numbers that would serve to readily identify him for the rest of his life. Stupid, but, in its own way, appropriate.

Yang Jei knew the value of anonymity. A criminal's greatest strength was his ability to blend back into the population. Tattoos, excessive jewelry or flashy clothing were all means leading to a man's undoing. It was a truth he had learned at an early age.

Evidently, no one had explained this to Marty O'Sullivan. Which was why he sat there, his soft, doughy body filling the seat even as his cheap cologne spread throughout the car, and peered carelessly out the window, his tattooed neck serving as a beacon to any who might pass.

Foolish.

Careless.

American.

Prior to his arrival in Boston, Yang Jei had spent years working in the factories, and the experience had given him a unique insight into American culture. These people were slaves to excess, their goods and products of the cheapest quality, designed to wear out and break quickly.

JADE ENCLAVE

Once, when he was young, one of the factory foremen had taken it upon himself to suggest an alternative means of production that would ensure product longevity. He was fired the same day, his family forced to retreat into the country, where they became little better than slaves working in the neighboring rice farms. That was when Yang Jei had realized a fundamental truth.

American companies preferred inferior products.

It was madness, but with a consistency that led to only one conclusion. Their companies trusted that people would simply repurchase what inevitably broke rather than demanding the producing company be held accountable for their poor practices.

Why then, would they not hold to those same beliefs when it came to their young? They were a temporary product, to be used up quickly and cast aside into the perils of the American Justice System, where, if they were lucky, they might be repurposed and, if not, discarded.

"Look, I can't take any more of this sitting here. You said there were three of them inside, right? No problem." His hand dipped down into his pants and reappeared a moment later gripping a snub-nosed revolver. "You kick in the door, and I'll take it from there. *Bang, bang,* baby." He jerked the pistol, mimicking shooting the dashboard. "In and out, no one sees nothing."

"Their lives are not ours to take. They belong to the Jiangshi."

"Who's Jiangshi?"

"The Jiangshi has no name. He is Jiangshi."

Marty shook his head. "I don't know what you're talking about, Stir-fry. He's a guy? Some kind of heavy hitter?"

Yang Jei frowned. "You could say that."

"Yeah, well, I'm something of a heavy hitter myself. This guy may be an alpha where you're from, but this is Boston, and you mention the O'Sullivan name here and people straighten up real fast, you know?"

"I do not know this."

"Well, now you do." Marty stared at him, awaiting some sort of reaction. When it didn't come, he snorted and leaned back in his seat, tapping his pistol against the side of his leg for several seconds until the silence became too much to bear. "So, what's his deal?"

"Deal?"

"Yeah. I mean, you got guns in Chinatown, right? What makes this clown so scary? He some sort of Jackie Chan type?"

"Jackie Chan?"

"Yeah, you know." He raised his hands and mimicked several strikes through the air, punctuating the last with a screeching '*Hi-ya*.' "He know karate or something?"

"Kung fu. And yes."

"Yeah? I took some boxing classes back in junior high. Coach thought I had real promise. Might be if I hadn't dropped out I could have gone that route. Heck, I'd probably be fighting in the Garden right now if I had. Sold out arena."

"You think so?"

"Darn right. But so what if this guy is some sort of ninja? He can't dodge a bullet." He raised his gun, sighting out through the windshield toward the building. "Ain't nobody that fast."

Yang started to answer, but a sudden chill swept through the air, pushing him back into the car. Instinctively, he snapped his arm out, striking Marty's forearm and knocking the gun down below the dashboard.

It was possible he hit harder than he intended, but the cry that escaped Marty's mouth should have brought more shame than he could bear. "Ow!" he screamed, seizing his forearm. "What's the big idea, Stir-fry?"

"Silence!" Yang hissed. "Open your fat eyes and look!"

Marty blinked, spots of anger rising in his cheeks. "What did you say to me?"

Yang Jei brought his hand up, pressing one finger firmly against his mouth before motioning toward the outside.

Marty stared at him for a long moment, then turned and squinted out into the darkness. "I don't see anything."

"Keep your gun down or they will kill you."

Marty cast an uncertain look his way. Then he leaned forward in his seat, rubbing the windshield with his sleeve before pressing his face against the glass. "Uh, news flash, Stir-fry, I still don't see what you're—"

A figure swept over the vehicle's roof, a shadowed ghost, seemingly appearing from thin air. He wasn't alone either. Yang Jei counted six of them, clad in midnight garbs that cast off the moonlight as they surrounded the apartment building.

"What the heck?" Marty whispered. "Who are those guys?"

JADE ENCLAVE

Yang Jei shook his head. Across the street, the lithe figures secured handholds and perches along the building's edge. Then they began to climb as one, scaling the walls and closing in on the western apartment from all sides.

When they were halfway up, a new figure appeared. He strode past the car on the passenger's side, and a sudden cold appeared, cutting through steel and cloth and chilling Marty to the core.

The light seemingly bent to avoid touching the figure as he walked out into the street, and for the first time in his life, Marty understood fear. His snub-nosed revolver slipped from his numb fingers and his lips moved of their own accord, uttering fervent prayers to a God he had spent no small amount of time mocking. He prayed that the figure would not turn around. He was afraid of what he might see, afraid of what might happen when their eyes met. Afraid of having his world beliefs torn asunder in front of him, leaving him cold and defenseless.

"You understand now why we brought you?" Yang Jei asked.

"W-what is he?" Marty asked, as the figure crossed onto the sidewalk toward the building.

"It is best that you do not ask any more questions. Instead, you must carry word back to your people."

"What word?"

"Tell them, the Jiangshi has come to Boston. Tell them, that if they value their lives, they will not interfere."

"Interfere with what?"

"With what comes next."

Child's Play.
Friday, July 25th
0540hrs

I HADN'T THOUGHT ABOUT Tommy McGinty in years before his warrant came across my desk.

He'd been the boy down the street. Not *that* boy. Just another kid who lived on my block. We'd gone through most of elementary school together. Our parents, which is to say my mom, had even organized a couple of play dates. They were fun, at first, but Tommy had a predilection for fairy tales. One in particular. I'd played along the first few times, but by the third visit it became pretty clear Tommy was sporting something of an obsession.

To my mother's credit, she stopped scheduling playdates without me having to ask, and the following year Tommy's father had gotten a job offer in Malden, just outside Boston proper. They'd moved during the summer.

Running into Tommy all these years later was a bit of a fluke, but to his credit, he'd stuck to his guns, literally and figuratively, and found another girl who was all too willing to play his games.

"Darn it, Tommy, pull over!"

My vehicle's tires screeched on the damp streets, and the roar that came from the engine was more akin to the polite cough of the environmentally conscious as I pulled my car up alongside him.

For most of my time with Blue Moon, I had driven a hand-me-down clunker literally held together by duct tape. It was a hard car to love, but considering we had no budget and no goodwill with the upper brass, it was all I could get.

That all changed two weeks ago when I walked outside to discover a brand-new vehicle waiting for me. A gift from Code Enforcement, who had more vehicles than they could use. Their sudden generosity had nothing to do with me and everything to do with our new public relations officer, my sister, who'd been assigned to Blue Moon last month.

My new car was electric. Better for the environment, my sister informed me, and less likely to burst into flames should a stray bullet pierce the gas tank. I thought the last part was a little extreme, but kept my mouth shut for fear that fate might conspire to prove me wrong.

The car accelerated forward with the sound of a child's whistle, the red and blue emergency lights on my roof casting their reflections across the storefront windows lining Newbury Street. It didn't take long to catch Tommy's attention. He glanced over through the open window, then did a double-take at the sight of me.

"Chloe?" he asked.

Time and a long-running methamphetamine addiction had hollowed out his features, but not to the point that I couldn't recognize him. Even his gray hooded sweatshirt, made to resemble the top of a wolf's head, couldn't hide the boy I'd once known.

I raised my hand, flashed my police badge and yelled, "Pull over and turn the car off."

"Baby?" a woman's voice asked from the backseat. "Who is that?"

Tommy started to answer, but we'd reached the next intersection, and he was forced to swerve around a white BMW stopped at the light. A startled curse tore past my lips, and I hit my brakes before dropping back and following behind him.

A chorus of startled horns rang out as we passed through the intersection, and a flash of movement to my left snapped my head around. I caught a quick glimpse of the other driver's startled face as I swerved onto the opposite sidewalk, nearly smashing into the Church of the Covenant's entryway before maneuvering back onto the street.

In front of me, Tommy's vehicle, a battered green Jeep Grand Cherokee that had seen better days, slowed and allowed me to pull back up beside him.

"Chloe?" he screamed out the window. "What are you doing here?"

"What does it look like I'm doing? Pull over!"

"Baby, who *is* that?" Again, the woman's voice rang out, followed by her appearance a moment later when she crawled over the center console and stuck her head out the driver's side window.

Destiny McGinty's picture had been attached to the accompanying felony warrant I'd received for Tommy. Four years younger than us, her records indicated she and I had attended the same high school, though I couldn't recall ever meeting her. She was semi-tall and semi-pretty, with a squarish face and make-up that suggested she was trying too hard. I couldn't see much of her hair on account that it was hidden under a bright red hooded cloak, but she wore jeans and a white blouse lined with frilly lace.

Attached to their warrants were a series of police reports detailing multiple break-ins of local jewelry stores. Smash and grab jobs, mostly. Store surveillance cameras had recorded their looting, and local news stations had homed in on their gimmick pretty quick, but it was a torn glove and stray fingerprint that had allowed the police to finally identify them. That was two weeks ago. Since then, Tommy and Destiny had been laying low, likely holed up somewhere smoking the last of their stash. Once they reached the filters, they'd had no choice but to venture back out into the streets.

Unfortunately for them, word had gotten around by that point, and I'd utilized my contacts within the Fenway Knights, a local group of medieval re-enactors and melee fighters who'd sworn their allegiance to me (long story). They'd agreed to keep an eye on some of the nearby jewelry stores.

I was at the tail end of a two-week night shift, a practice I'd begun implementing once a quarter in order to keep our resident paranormal bad guys off-balance, when the call went out. I'd hauled butt to the scene just in time to see our star-crossed lovers fleeing with their stolen haul shoved into an old pillowcase. From there, I'd given chase.

"Chloe Mayfield," Tommy said, shouting to be heard over the rushing wind. "We grew up together."

"Oh, yeah," Destiny said. "I remember you. How you been?"

"Busy. Mind pulling over? I need to talk to the two of you."

Tommy shook his head. "No can do, Chloe. You made it clear when we were kids that you weren't into our game."

Destiny's expression turned surprised. "Wait, is she the one who refused to play with you when you were little?"

"Yeah," Tommy said. "Not only that. Her mother told the other parents what happened. All of a sudden, everyone was too busy to come over."

Destiny's eyes flashed, and she shot me a venomous look. "You did all that? Where do you get off? He was just a little boy."

"He bit me!"

"*Pfft*, so what? It was just a kid's game. What, do you think you're too good for my Tommy? You think you're better than us?"

"I think you're going to jail."

JADE ENCLAVE

"Oh yeah? We'll just see about that."

She disappeared down between Tommy's legs, and when she came back up, she was gripping an assault rifle.

The curse that emanated from my lips would have earned me a few Hail Mary verses if any of the priests had heard it, but I was too terrified to care. I slammed my foot down on the brake and jerked the wheel to the right, passing behind their car just as Destiny leaned out the window and opened fire.

Here's a fun fact about assault rifles. Most action movies tend to downplay the kickback they generate. You can blame special effects for that. Because of this, people who aren't well-trained often underestimate the strength necessary to keep them on target, particularly when firing on full auto.

Destiny was evidently not well-trained, and the muzzle flash when she depressed the trigger cut a rough, violent line upwards as she spit bullets into the street. I screamed and ducked down so fast I knocked my phone off my belt clip. It hit the center console, bounced once, and disappeared behind my chair just as a trio of rounds went through the windshield.

I'd say it was a miracle that the glass didn't shatter, but it probably had more to do with the fact that Tommy had filled the magazine with military-grade ammunition. Cheaper bullets likely would have shattered on impact. Heavier, better crafted rounds, however, packed a bit more *oomph* to them.

The first two rounds blasted through the dashboard and passed straight through my new car, tearing through the rear seats before exiting out the trunk. The third blasted apart my department laptop and radio before veering up and punching through the roof.

The jolt of fear I'd felt at the sight of the rifle gave way to a sudden wave of nausea. My stomach tightened, and the stale taste of coffee rose in the back of my throat. Warning bells were sounding in my head, and the part of my brain concerned with self-preservation was screaming at me to get off the street. I was seriously considering heeding my own advice when a voice rang out through the radio speakers.

"Warning, collision detected. Recommend driver pull over. Would you like me to alert the authorities?"

I blinked and glanced down at the scarred dashboard. A glowing golden ball with circling blue rings had appeared in the upper right-hand corner of the GPS map screen.

"Who the heck are you?" I asked.

"Salutations, Sergeant. I am Watt, your A.I. driving assistant."

"My what?"

JADE ENCLAVE

"Your Artificial Intelligence Driving Assistant. My pre-programmed name is Watt. If this name is not to your liking, or if you would prefer to change the tone of my voice, you may do so in the system settings. Would you like me to bring up the tutorial?"

Destiny fired another burst, and I flinched instinctively as her shots went wide, blasting through the windows of a boutique clothing store.

"I'm a little busy at the moment."

"Warning: emergency detected. Vehicle sensors suggest you may be involved in a road rage incident. Would you like me to alert the authorities?"

"I am the authorities!"

"Please stand by."

There was a second's silence, then the sound of a phone ringing once before a woman's voice came on the line.

"9-1-1, do you require police, fire, or ambulance?"

"Uh, no, I didn't…" I swerved left and cursed loudly as another burst of gunfire rang out.

"Were those gunshots, Ma'am?"

"Yes! That crazy nut job is shooting at me!"

"What's your location?"

"Newbury Street, heading west."

"County records show that you're calling from a vehicle. I recommend you leave that area immediately. Find somewhere safe, well-lit, and wait for officers to arrive."

"*I concur with this recommendation*," Watt said.

"You stay out of this," I told him before turning my attention back to the dispatcher. "I can't do that."

"Why not?"

"Because I'm in pursuit!"

"Ma'am, I'm legally required to advise you to discontinue any aggressive action. The Boston Police Department does not condone civilians taking matters into their own hands. You need to pull over to the side of the road and wait for the professionals to arrive."

"I am a professional! This is Sergeant Chloe Mayfield with the Boston Police Department."

"Uh-huh. Very funny, ma'am, but our officers don't call the general emergency line. They communicate directly through dispatch."

"They already shot out my radio, and my phone is in the backseat," I said. "Plus, I didn't call. My stupid car did."

"Your car?"

"Yeah."

Ahead of me, Destiny's rifle ran dry, and she yanked the magazine free, letting it drop into the street before reaching her arm back and angrily snapping her fingers.

I'll say this for Tommy. He knew what his woman wanted. No sooner did she ask then he pressed another magazine into her waiting palm. She slapped the magazine into the rifle, but chambered too hard, her finger grazing the trigger and sending a three-round burst into the roadway. The bullets hit the pavement and ricochetted, striking against my hood and blowing out my passenger's side headlight.

"Was that more gunfire, Ma'am?"

"Yes! I already told you. Little Red Riding Hood and the Big Bad Wolf are shooting at me."

"...I'm sorry, who?"

"Warning. Multiple collisions detected. Excessive swerving suggests you may be operating under the influence. My safety-first

initiative programming requires me to pull over to the side of the road until a law enforcement official can verify your sobriety."

My eyes widened. "Don't you dare—"

The wheel shifted under my grip, and the acceleration pedal went limp, the engine slowing as Watt maneuvered us toward the curb.

"Override!" I screamed, as Tommy and Destiny's Jeep pulled away in the distance.

"Warning: Overriding my safety-first initiative programming will result in a report being electronically transmitted to the Department of Motor Vehicles for a state safety officer to review. Based on the data collected, you may receive a citation or possibly a summons to appear before a judge. Do you still wish to override?"

"Heck yes I do."

"Override accepted."

The wheel came back under my control, and I punched the pedal to the floor, the whirling whistle ringing out from my exhaust as we accelerated forward.

"Ma'am, are you still there?"

JADE ENCLAVE

I blinked, having momentarily forgotten the dispatch officer. "Still here. Now listen up. This is Sergeant Chloe Mayfield, Blue Moon Division. I'm in pursuit of a green Jeep Cherokee heading west on Newbury Street." I rattled off the license plate. "Are you getting this?"

"Blue Moon Division. Aren't you the ones who... oh, God."

"That's us." I blew through the next intersection, catching sight of the fleeing Jeep in the distance. "Vehicle is being driven by two suspects dressed as Little Red Riding Hood and the Big Bad Wolf."

"This is so weird."

"You should see it from my angle."

"I'll bet." She exhaled. "Okay, the call's gone out and officers are already responding. What else do you need?"

"Tell the officers to push west. We need to cut them off and force them north toward the river."

"Roger that, Sergeant."

"Thank you. Watt, discontinue call."

"Call discontinued. Driver warning. Given the structural damage we have already incurred, I would recommend falling back until additional officers arrive."

It wasn't a terrible suggestion. Help was on the way, and I was under no illusions as to what would happen if Destiny got lucky with one of those rounds. If I was smart, I would take the next turn and follow from a distance until more help arrived. With luck, they might even bring out the helicopter. I could guestimate how the story would unfold from there.

Tommy and Destiny's face would end up plastered all over the morning news. The chase might go on for a bit, but eventually their car would be disabled, and they'd be forced to exit with their hands in the air. I saw it all play out in my head. Just another morning news story that ended with the bad guys in handcuffs.

Then I saw another story. The one where we weren't fast enough. Maybe Tommy and Destiny got away, or even worse, they got out and fled on foot. Maybe they ended up somewhere they could take hostages. There were plenty of stories just like that one as well. Ones where innocent people died, and newscasters look out onto the public and expressed their sympathies for the victim's loved ones.

Did I really want to roll the dice as to which story would play out?

My heart knew the answer before my brain, and I shifted in my seat, angling my hip so that I could draw my pistol. I laid it barrel first into the cupholder and let out a long breath.

"Sergeant?"

"Like I said. We are the authorities."

"Clarification: I am a community police vehicle designed to assist our civilian support force. My body design and programming are not suited for high-speed chases involving sharp turns or pit maneuvers."

"Yeah, well, I was a journalism major who somehow found her way into the police academy and was subsequently assigned to Neighborhood Watch. So what? We're here now. Let's make the best of it."

Watt lapsed into silence, and I pushed the accelerator hard, weaving between the early morning traffic before drawing to within three car lengths of Tommy and Destiny's fleeing Jeep.

They saw me coming. The red and blue lights made it difficult to hide, and Destiny brought the rifle around, but this time I was ready for her. As soon as she leaned out the window, I drew my pistol from the cupholder, pressed the barrel against the windshield, and fired three times.

I couldn't aim, not really, but that wasn't the point. This was about sending a message. Let them know there was lead coming from this direction too.

My bullets flew more or less straight, and the Jeep's back windshield exploded. Destiny squealed, and Tommy jerked the vehicle so hard I thought for a moment she was going to fall out.

He caught her at the last moment, one hand seizing her arm, and jerked her up so hard that she smacked her forehead on the doorframe. Her head snapped back, the red hood falling back a split second before he yanked her back inside the Jeep.

Tommy couldn't shoot and drive, so he took the next right turn onto Fairfield Street. I hit my brakes and maneuvered behind him as we rounded the corner. His vehicle might have been faster, but mine was lighter, and I came through the turn and tapped my bumper into his rear.

It wasn't a clean shot, but it proved enough to send him fishtailing through the next intersection. His vehicle swung back and forth across the road as he struggled to bring it under control. For a second, I thought I'd done it, but he recovered at the last minute, maneuvered through the black wrought-iron gates and across the small strip of grass along the roadway divide before coming out onto Commonwealth Ave.

Where the other officers were waiting.

People think law enforcement's greatest strength is our ability to kick in doors, followed closely by our weapons. But the truth is, it's neither of those things. What sets us apart is our ability to communicate. There's an old saying: you can outrun the squad car, but you can't outrun the radio.

The patrol officers angled their cars to block the roadway, and Tommy swerved up onto the sidewalk. He cut around the patrol cars, clipping the wrought-iron lamppost before swinging back out into the roadway.

I followed closely on his heels, angling around the patrol officers and the broken post before pulling back onto the road. In the distance, the first rays of sunshine peeked over the horizon.

"Sun's coming up," I said aloud. "The roads are about to get more crowded."

"Statistical data from the Department of Motor Vehicles suggest we have twenty-seven minutes before rush hour begins."

"That's for the state. The city proper is something else." I exhaled and bit down on my lip. A quick glance in my rear-view mirror revealed the two patrol officers following closely behind me, but the roadway was narrow enough that neither would be able to get around me. "We need to end this before someone gets hurt. I've got an idea. Are you with me?"

"You have overridden my safety-first initiative programming. I have no choice."

"I'll take that as a yes. In which case, we're going to take them at the next intersection."

"Warning: this vehicle's structural frame is not designed for—"

"Too late for second-guessing."

I slammed the accelerator down, and the car sped forward, propelling me straight toward Tommy and Destiny's Jeep. This time, I didn't try to angle my vehicle around to strike their side. My front hood went right up their tailpipe, and the sudden force of impact lifted their tires off the street. The sound of broken glass and crunching metal filled the air, but I waited until the moment I saw their backend rise before violently jerking my steering wheel to the left.

It was a move they taught cadets not to do in the academy.

Had we been on a highway, their wheels would have come back down to the roadway, and they would have continued on their way, while I would have succeeded only in disabling my own vehicle.

JADE ENCLAVE

This wasn't the highway though. This was downtown Boston, filled with winding and, more importantly, *narrow* streets.

My front hood ripped its way free from underneath Tommy's vehicle, shifting his direction of travel by approximately thirty degrees before his back tires came down with a heavy *thump*.

Thirty degrees might not sound like much, but in Boston's streets, it can make all the difference.

The sudden shift in direction caused his Jeep to accelerate off the roadway. He went up onto the sidewalk, the angle sending him momentarily airborne before he crashed headfirst into the side of a three-story brownstone.

I didn't see the moment of impact, but I heard it as my vehicle spun. I did a full hundred and eighty-degree rotation before my back tires struck the curb and jerked me to a halt facing the direction we'd just come.

From there, I watched through my broken windshield as the two patrol officers pulled in behind the ruined Jeep. They came out with their weapons drawn and approached the vehicle from opposite sides before dragging a semi-conscious Tommy and an unconscious Destiny from the vehicle's wreckage. They laid them down, handcuffed them, and secured the rifle as more emergency sirens sounded in the distance.

It was a wonderful sound, like music to my ears, and I exhaled and laid my head back on the headrest.

"Drive Alert: the structural integrity of this vehicle has been compromised beyond safe driving protocols. Override no longer available. All data has been transmitted to Fleet Division, who will be enroute shortly to collect this vehicle. Extensive repairs are necessary before this vehicle can resume its duties within the department."

"In other words, you'll be taking the next few weeks off?"

"That is correct."

"Enjoy your downtime, Watt. You've earned it."

Let the Bodies Hit the Floor. Friday, July 25th 0837hrs

THE SUN WAS WELL into its ascent when we pulled into the Government Parking Garage that housed our division headquarters. I'd spent the better part of two hours helping the patrol officers secure the scene in the wake of the crash, then bummed a ride back with the last one to leave. Sleep was calling, but I was determined to hand in my report before heading home for some much-deserved shuteye.

Stepping out of the vehicle, I found Cambrie waiting for me. She had her arms crossed and was glaring at me as if I'd stolen the last of her shampoo and tried to cover it up by filling the bottle from the showerhead.

"Morning, sunshine," I said.

She snorted and stomped her way over until we were standing face to face. "Don't 'sunshine' me. I just got off the phone with Fleet Division. What did you do to Watt?"

My younger sister stood a foot shorter than me, with a petite frame and shoulder-length hair styled into a chaotic mess of blonde curls. When we were younger, people used to say we looked alike, but they'd stopped pretending that was the case long before we ever reached high school.

It's not that I was unattractive or anything, although shaving my head last month probably hadn't done me any favors. Most men didn't subscribe to the G.I. Jane look, but a surprising number of women had expressed interest.

My hair had started to grow back in the weeks since I brought an end to the war with the United Fairy Commonwealth, but I still wasn't sure what I was going to do with it. Not having to worry about blow-drying and styling had been a welcome relief these past few weeks, and the extra half hour of sleep I'd gotten as a result had done me a world of good.

Whether I was bald or sporting long, flowing locks made little difference if I was comparing myself to Cambrie. She was something else. Dressed in a cream-colored blouse and mini skirt with her police badge hanging from her neck, she could have easily doubled as a stripper gram. Even at this time of the morning, I could smell the scent cloud surrounding her. Bergamot, lavender, and rose, intermingled with the freshness of clean clothes and a slight vanilla fragrance that was just her.

She'd always been the pretty girl in her group, and she'd bet the farm, metaphorically speaking, on her looks buying her a ticket into a better life. Unfortunately, she'd misplayed her hand in college, devoting all her attentions to the would-be doctors, lawyers, and engineers, none of whom had ever come back with a diamond ring in hand. As the years went by and she continued to delay graduation, little cracks started to form in her veneer, wispy wafts of desperation slipping through no matter how hard she tried to hide them.

In a moment of drunken despair, she'd turned to me for help, and my half-hearted response had convinced her to abandon the idea of becoming a trophy wife and follow me into law enforcement. At the time, I'd thought it was a horrible idea. Especially after she started dating our boss, Deputy Bulwark.

I'd watched her party her way through the academy, telling myself that it would all catch up with her eventually, but at the last moment, I'd found myself in a bind, and I'd traded away the answers to the state certification exam in order to save people's lives.

It was a fair trade, and I couldn't bring myself to regret it, even though it led to Cambrie immediately getting hired on with the Boston Police Department. From there, things had gotten tense between us. I'd stayed away during her training period, but she'd gotten sucked into the war with the United Fairy Commonwealth, and we'd stumbled in on my boss, Deputy Bulwark, making time with another one of the academy cadets.

Things had only gotten worse from there.

The Redcap had attacked Song Grove, and although we'd defeated him in the end, it had forced me to go head-to-head with Deputy Bulwark. I'd come out on top, but it wasn't a knock-out blow, and he'd rebounded by taking credit for our operation. Then, just to add insult to injury, he'd torpedoed my sister's career by transferring her to Blue Moon Division.

To her credit, Cambrie had pulled herself together and bounced back, throwing herself into her new job. She'd done good work so far, but it would take time to convince people that our division was anything other than a convenient dumping ground for the cast-offs and screw-ups of the department who, for whatever reason, couldn't be outright terminated.

"Oh, that." I rolled my shoulders, already feeling the tension from the car crash. I was sure it would be worse come morning.

"What can I say? Duty called. I'll need the keys to the clunker back."

"Seriously?"

My expression told her I was, and she sighed and handed over my keys. I stuffed them in my pocket before descending the stairs to where our division headquarters lay.

In many ways, Blue Moon had acted as a series of firsts for the Boston Police Department. We were the first division assigned to combat the paranormal, as well as the first to be evicted from the headquarters building. I suspect the brass had hoped that by exiling us across the street, they could simply forget about us. Fat chance of that.

Our damp little Hobbit hole was barely livable, yet for all that it lacked modern amenities, it was growing on me. In many ways it was like a mascot to our little group, and while I never thought I would say this, being apart from the other police divisions had begun to feel… right.

Pushing through the door, two familiar faces glanced up to meet me. The first belonged to Robbie Rutledge, our resident juvenile delinquent and computer-slash-IT expert. Dressed in a loose plain shirt and khaki pants, the splattering of scruff along his face would never qualify as an actual beard, and the dry patches of skin around his forehead suggested he'd begun experimenting with acne treatment pads.

Robbie had come to us as an underage offender, allowed to work for us in lieu of spending time in a juvenile detention facility. Much as I hated to admit it, his expertise had come in handy on more than one occasion, and even though he still had some time left on his bid, I needed to start thinking seriously about how we were going to function once he was no longer here. It might be that I would need to frame him for something and get his probation extended. Like until he turned eighteen.

The second face in the room belonged to Officer Pongo, whose real name was Elmore Dwyer. Pongo was just a little peanut of a man, only managing to tip the scales into triple digits if he wore combat boots and a duty belt. He kept his hair short and wore dark-rimmed glasses balanced atop his pronounced nose. He'd come to us as a patrol officer, and it had quickly become apparent that he was a hazard to himself and others in the field.

Despite his limitations, Pongo had a passion for justice and a keen analytical mind. For the past several months, we'd had him acting as our division's legal advisor. Essentially, he was responsible for making sure we didn't get sued, or, when necessary, ensuring that none of the upper brass could throw our division under the bus, legally speaking, without a fight.

JADE ENCLAVE

Technically, Pongo wasn't a licensed lawyer, but you'd be surprised how easy it is to work around that. At the moment, we had a couple of lawyers on standby that we could hire on the cheap, provided Pongo agreed to do all the necessary legwork ahead of time. It was detailed and complicated work, but so far Pongo had performed admirably.

Although I did sometimes worry about his stress levels on days like today.

"Give it to me," I said as I came through the door.

Pongo cleared his throat and rose from his chair, peering down at his iPad. "It's hard to say. Reports are still coming in. There's some good news, and a whole lot of bad."

"What's the good news?"

"Plenty of street cameras caught the chase. It's clear that, once the woman wearing the red hood began firing, you had a legal duty to continue the chase. That 9-1-1 call will come in handy if the department tries to allege professional negligence."

"You can thank Watt for that one. Not that he'll necessarily appreciate it."

Pongo blinked. "Watt?"

"Long story. What's the bad news?"

"The amount of property damage is off the charts. Thankfully, no one seems to have been injured, but given how much damage there is…" He shook his head. "Well, suffice to say, somebody's going to be getting sued for all this."

"Just as long as the somebody isn't us."

A handful of steps carried me over to my corner and I dropped my bag down onto my desk without looking, the same way I had every day since I'd first arrived.

Except this time, something was different.

My bag missed the desk and hit the floor with a heavy *thud* that snapped my head around. I narrowed my eyes, then took a hard look around the office, the indentions in our cheap carpet serving to tell a story in less time than it takes to describe.

Someone had moved my desk.

A good two feet, if I wasn't mistaken.

It says something about my professional life that my first thought was that someone might have planted a bomb, but I forced myself to exhale and run through a mental list of all the reasons why that couldn't be.

Our division headquarters might have been shabby on the inside, but our security was not. We'd learned from our predecessor, Tempest Michaels, who'd lost his first office in an arson fire. Whatever weaknesses had remained, we'd shorn up over the past few months with the kickoff of the Fairy War.

There was only one way in or out, and we had cameras and motion sensors running twenty-four hours per day. Not the sissy kind that allows for a fifty-pound allowance either. We'd sprung for the real thing. If a large rat had gotten near the doorway, we'd have known about it.

Which meant that whoever moved my desk had done so without tripping any of the alarms, suggesting they'd managed to get inside without alerting suspicion.

Peering around the room, Pongo and Robbie's desks had been shifted as well, but it wasn't until I noted a new addition sitting in the west corner of the room that I realized why.

I raised my hand and pointed. "What is that?"

Pongo and Robbie exchanged glances and shrugged.

"No clue," Pongo said. "It was here when we came in."

I frowned. Up until now, our office had consisted of three cubicles. We'd talked about adding a fourth when Cambrie came on board, but she spent so much time on the phone she worried it would disturb us. Plus, she was a pacer. Instead of a cubicle, she'd set up in our conference room, and we'd continued on just the three of us. Until now.

The appearance of a fourth desk wasn't exactly unwelcome. Or at least, it shouldn't have been. Technically, we were the smallest division in the department and were desperate for more personnel. Unfortunately, that's where it became complicated.

Blue Moon wasn't exactly flush with applications. We were widely known as the department's dumping ground, and even though I should have had a say in new personnel transfers, Deputy Bulwark made it clear I would take whoever they gave me.

We'd lucked out so far, but I'd been doing this job long enough to know that not all cops are created equal. There are bad seeds in every division, cancerous malcontents that have a way of spreading their poison throughout an entire division. A part of me knew it was only a matter of time before one of them ended up within our ranks, and I wanted to make sure we were strong enough to handle it when the time came. And that meant not showing fear to the other troops.

"Alright then, we'd best get the welcome mat out. Whoever they are, I'm sure they'll turn up sooner or later."

"Are you still taking the weekend off?" Pongo asked.

JADE ENCLAVE

"Heck yes I am," I said. "Soon as I send this report to Lieutenant Kermit, I am out the door. Five minutes and counting."

"Is this supposed to be some kind of a big deal?" Robbie asked.

I gave him a withering look, but let it go on account of his age. He might have been a boy wonder when it came to computers, but he had no idea what it was like to go seven months without a single weekend off.

"You got plans for the weekend?" Cambrie asked. "Maybe a hot date?"

No date, but I had plans. They involved catching up on sleep, ordering in a ridiculous amount of Chinese takeout, and spending at least one whole day in pajamas. "The Redsox are playing Sunday afternoon, and I scored a ticket from one of our patrol officers who forgot about his nephew's birthday party. Right field line."

"You're going to the game by yourself?" Cambrie asked.

"Well, yeah," I said, trying not to sound defensive. "Why shouldn't I?"

Her look spoke volumes, but I pretended not to know what she meant as I dropped into my chair, which had also been moved, and booted up my computer. Ten minutes later, I had my report finished, and I hit the upload button with a flourish, leaned back, and let out a contented sigh.

"Alright then," I said, rising to my feet. "That, as they say, is that. I bid you all a very fond adieu, and I will see you come Mon—"

I never got to finish the sentence, because that's the moment the ceiling came crashing down.

Not the whole ceiling. Not even most of it. Just the part directly above my desk. Three tiles, to be precise, their plyboard forms giving way with a resounding crack as the body fell through.

I glimpsed just enough to see that it was a male before he crashed down on top of my desk. He smashed my computer screen and landed face up, his head lolling just off the edge, his feet extending from the other side, not quite touching the carpet.

Silence reigned for a handful of seconds. Then Robbie cleared his throat. "Should I call the Redsox and tell them you won't be in attendance after all?"

Turning A Blind Eye. Friday, July 25th 1012hrs

It took over an hour for Forensics Division to show up.

I guess it's true what they say about police response time in the city being on the rise.

While we waited, we gathered our personal belongings and moved what we could out of the office and into the hallway. Technically, this was a breach of protocol, since my principal responsibility should have been to preserve the scene and avoid contaminating evidence at all costs, but I figured this was one of those times when practicality won out over department policy.

No one in our office wanted to risk their cell phones becoming state's evidence, and Robbie flatly refused to leave his laptop behind. Pongo felt similarly about his law books, and Cambrie was reluctant to leave her purse behind.

I set the timer on my phone for sixty seconds and turned a blind eye. Once the office was clear, I stayed behind just long enough to grab my own bag, since there was no way I was leaving it behind for forensics to root through. I slung it over my shoulder, sidestepped the fallen corpse, and joined my colleagues in the hallway, locking the door behind me.

No one said anything for several moments, and it slowly dawned on me that they were all waiting for me to tell them what to do next. A little flutter went through my chest as the weight of responsibility settled on my shoulders, but I forced it aside and took a deep breath.

The first order of business was to alert Lieutenant Kermit. He was over at City Hall, rallying support for our cause and searching for ways to supplement our meager budget. We'd long since given up any hope of overtime pay, but there were other needs. Things like replacing faulty and broken equipment, professional training and development courses, and community engagement events.

Initially, the brass had tried to keep Blue Moon under wraps, but the fame of our predecessor, Tempest Michaels, as well as our own work on a number of high-profile cases had made that impossible. Instead, we'd become something of an open secret, viewed by the public as, at best, a publicity stunt, and at worst, a shameful display of government spending that malcontents could use in their "Defund the Police" campaigns.

Bringing Cambrie on board and installing her as our public relations specialist had been the first step toward legitimizing our public image. People needed to know we were here, and that they could call on us in times of need. And yes, making ourselves more readily available to the public meant opening the floodgates to every would-be psychic and charlatan trickster in the New England area, but it was necessary if we were ever going to make any real progress in the public's eye.

I sent Lieutenant Kermit a text message apprising him of the situation, and he wrote back that he would be there within the hour. Once that was done, the next order of business was to figure out a temporary workspace.

Like it or not, our office was now an official crime scene, and if Forensics Division decided to drag their feet, we could be displaced for days, if not weeks. The cases wouldn't stop just because we were homeless.

I wracked my brain for several minutes before coming up with a suitable solution that didn't involve marching across the street into the police department headquarters. You might wonder why not, since even in exile, we were still part of the department, but there were several reasons.

Firstly, doing so would have raised all sorts of questions we weren't in any position to answer. A body literally dropping into my lap was going to raise all sorts of eyebrows. I'd already been framed for murder once during the Fairy Wars and was in no hurry to repeat the experience.

That wasn't the only reason though. Mostly, I just didn't feel like dealing with the sideways glances and muffled smirks I knew we would get from the rest of the department.

None of us had come to Blue Moon by choice. We all knew what this was, but working together these past few months had instilled in us a sense of pride. I felt good about what we were doing. Morale in the office was, I daresay, at an all-time high, and the last thing I wanted was to see my people wilt under the mockery of other officers.

With the police station out, that only left one viable choice. Thankfully, it was located just down the road. I straightened my shoulders and led the way up the stairs, pausing beside my old clunker of a car and stowing my tactical patrol bag in the backseat before exiting the garage and heading north onto Congress Street.

JADE ENCLAVE

The Union Oyster House was the oldest restaurant in Boston and had twice been classified as a national historical landmark. A four-story building made out of red brick that dated back to Pre-Revolutionary days, it had played host to multiple presidents, foreign dignitaries, military generals, professional athletes, and royal powers, including the deposed King of France, Louis Phillipe I, during his exile.

It had also served as the official headquarters of the Sons of Liberty militia, both in the eighteenth century and during their present-day incarnation. They had begun as a troupe of re-enactors, but had transformed into a legitimate fighting force last year when a group of bay-spurned cultists tried to summon a leviathan from the depths of the harbor. Ever since, the Sons of Liberty had made it their mission to safeguard the city from supernatural threats, including rescuing me from the clutches of the Headless Horseman.

Or, at least, it *had* been their mission. A couple of weeks back, we'd run afoul of a group of bloodthirsty medieval knights looking to retrieve the legendary Excalibur. They thought Titus, the admiral of the Sons of Liberty, could aid them in their search, and when he'd refused, they set fire to the place, hoping to remove him from the field rather than risk him helping any of the competition. He and the rest of the Sons of Liberty had survived, but city officials were more than a little surprised to find a fully working armory inside the restaurant, along with several functioning cannons and a horse stall.

In the aftermath of the attack, Titus, Ethel, and the rest of the Sons of Liberty had been forced into hiding. I hadn't heard from them since, and even news of the Fairy War hadn't brought about their return. I worried about them, and even worse, I couldn't shake the feeling that I had failed them somehow. Maybe if I had been smarter, faster, then they would still be here. The memory formed a lump in my throat, but I swallowed it down and crossed over the red cobbled sidewalk to the entrance.

The Oyster House opened its doors early during the summer, and a burst of warm air ripe with the scent of fresh fish, garlic, and lemon swept over me as I swung open the door. The inside was abuzz with the soft hum of conversation, clinking silverware, and the low sizzle of cooking butter coming from the kitchen. Framed portraits of long-gone sailors and sea captains lined the dark paneled walls, and soft, golden light spilled from the hanging lanterns and brass fixtures, casting their glow over the weathered wooden floors and mahogany booths, polished smooth by years of use.

The main fixture of the ground floor dining room was its U-shaped bar, where a seasoned cook with a thick gray beard and weathered hands shucked oysters onto chilled plates, seasoning them with lemon and salt before passing them along to eager patrons. In the main dining room, a rush of waitstaff weaved their way through the table aisles, balancing platters of shrimp, scallops, and chowder with steam billowing from the top. I searched among their number until I found a familiar face whose name I had never learned.

I couldn't classify her as either young or old. Both felt wrong, and whether that was a result of hard living or genetics I couldn't say, but she was seasoned at her craft, moving with practiced fluidity as she cleared away dishes with ease.

I waved my arms to get the unnamed waitress's attention, and she narrowed her eyes and motioned her head to the side, guiding me over to the far corner of the restaurant.

Some people might find the fact that I didn't know her name odd, given that we'd survived multiple battles together, but she'd never volunteered it, and asking now after all this time felt invasive. Some mysteries are better off unsolved.

"Didn't expect to see you around here anytime soon," she said, laying her tray down on the empty table. "How are the hands?"

Phantom pains flashed up my arms at the mention, but I forced them back down. During the attack, one of the knights had spit fire across the back of my hands, inflicting third-degree burns. There was no nerve damage, thank God, but I'd refused the doctor's recommendation for skin grafts, and sometimes, when

I caught sight of the scars, the memory of the flames' touch roared up inside me.

"Never better," I said, even though I had to force the words past the lump in my throat. "Has there been any word?"

She shook her head. "It's still early. Titus and his boys made off with a few dozen kegs on their way out the door. Like as not, they're licking their wounds at the bottom of a mug. Once the ale runs dry, they'll surface. You'll see."

"I hope you're right. As much as it pains me to say it, the city's not the same without them."

"Won't get no argument from me. But you didn't come here to talk about Titus and the Sons. You're wanting a meal, I expect?"

"Little more than that, I'm afraid."

She grunted and nodded back toward the entrance. "Who are your friends?"

"Blue Moon Division," I said. "Most of it anyway. I need a favor."

"What kind of favor?"

I laid out everything that had happened, starting with the car chase and ending with the body dropping from the ceiling.

JADE ENCLAVE

"We're temporarily displaced and need somewhere to catch our breath. I was hoping we could use the upstairs."

"Upstairs is still undergoing repairs."

"It's just for the weekend. We'll clear out by Monday so the construction workers can get back to it."

The unnamed waitress considered it. For a long moment I thought she might refuse me, but whatever goodwill I'd built up with Titus and Ethel seemed to sway her at the last minute, and she motioned the others to join, then led us up through a back stairway.

The second-floor dining room had been gutted in the wake of the fire damage, and construction plastic lined the walls, laid overtop bare studs and patched concrete. Sections of the floor were missing, and the woody aroma of sawdust contrasted sharply with the acidic notes of salt, lemon, and butter from below. I found us a little section over near the window and motioned for the others to help me. There were no desks, obviously, but we were able to bring down a couple of tables that had survived the fire, as well as a handful of chairs.

We pushed the tables together, and everyone selected their place, setting up their computers, case-law books, and, in Cambrie's case, a phone and some cosmetics. The restaurant didn't have any WI-FI, but Robbie was able to connect to the nearby

Bostonian Hotel, and fifteen minutes later, our division was effectively back up and running.

The unnamed waitress asked if we wanted to order anything to eat. I passed, stating that I needed to get back to the office, but the other three quickly placed orders for clam chowders served in bread bowls. My stomach gave a regretful growl as the waitress moved off, the scent of butter and garlic seemingly redoubling in my nose before I pushed it away and reminded myself that I had a job to do. I made sure everyone was settled, then bid my goodbyes and made my way back downstairs before hesitating at the door. I drew in one last breath, filling my lungs. The more pragmatic part of my brain, the part that couldn't be dissuaded by emotions, warned me to savor the aroma while I could. Because I knew that, all too soon, it would be replaced by the scent of death.

A Jolly British Sailor. Friday, July 25th 1036hrs

Lieutenant Kermit was waiting for me at the entrance to the Government Parking Garage.

A former British naval officer who'd retired from service and become a Bobbie in East London, Lieutenant Kermit had come to Boston two decades prior as part of an officer exchange program. He'd met his wife during the first year, and when his time was up and he was scheduled to return to England, he'd sold his ticket for enough money to buy an engagement ring. She said yes, and he'd shown up for work the next day daring anyone to complain.

His continued presence within the police department had thrown the brass for a bit of a loop at first, but the Chief of

Police at the time had been too polite to ask him to leave. Fast forward two decades and he'd become something of an anomaly within the department. Not technically under anyone's authority, he'd been free to investigate whatever tickled his fancy, which he did with a certain amount of regularity, regardless of whose toes got stepped on. Eventually, some of the upper brass decided the best way to deal with him was just to give him his own division, which he'd named in honor of his goddaughter, Jane, who was one of the original members of Blue Moon Investigations.

Under the right light, he reminded me of one of those movie stars. Not the popcorn, action-star kind. The ones who started with Shakespeare in the Park and worked their way up to the cinema.

In his early sixties, with silver hair parted down the side in a short-clipped executive haircut, he was dressed in a well-fitting blue sport jacket with a button-up shirt and a gold lapel pin in the shape of a police badge. So far as I knew, he was the only officer on the entire police force who refused to carry a gun, which was a trait I could respect even if I didn't seek to emulate it. He had a kind mannerism to him, and there was a twinkle in his blue eyes that always made me think he knew more than he was letting on.

He heard me coming and turned to reveal a pair of coffees in his hands, little wisps of steam escaping through the plastic lid. My stomach gave an involuntary growl at the sight of it, and a grateful sigh slipped past my lips when he handed one over.

"If I recall correctly," he said. "You were supposed to have the weekend off. Some kind of handball game with the red knickers?"

I paused just long enough to blow steam from the lid. "Baseball, and it's the Redsox."

"Of course."

"I'm holding out hope I might still make it. More fool me."

He shrugged. "You never know. A fool's hope is sometimes the best kind. Particularly on days like today. How are the troops?"

"Shaken, but they'll pull through."

"They're a good bunch. And they have faith."

"In the system?"

He shook his head. "In you."

I blinked. "Me?"

He nodded. "They've seen your tenacity. They know you're a fighter, and they trust you'll see them through this."

I opened my mouth but closed it after a moment when I realized I wasn't sure what to say. Truth be told, I'd never actively sought out a leadership position. Maybe I would have, in time, but I'd only been on the force for a short while before ending up in Blue Moon. Even then, my promotion to Sergeant had only occurred because it gave Deputy Bulwark an excuse to transfer me out of Neighborhood Watch.

I brought the cup up to my mouth and took a long swallow, savoring the flavor as it warmed my chest. "How are things at City Hall?"

Lieutenant Kermit's face tightened. It wasn't more than a fraction of an inch and I wouldn't have noticed it if not for the fact that I was, you know, a detective. Reading people comes with the territory.

"Change takes time," he said. "But each case we solve carries us one step closer."

"Lucky break then. I've a feeling this one's going to be a doozy."

"Bodies falling from the sky do have a certain cinematic appeal."

"Technically he just fell from the ceiling." I said. "Speaking of which, has Forensics Division said anything yet?"

"No. I believe the technician is still inside. I can run point for a couple of hours if you like. Give you time to head home and catch some shuteye."

I shook my head. "I'd rather get started now while everything is fresh in my mind."

"Alright then. What's your plan?"

Lieutenant Kermit didn't actually need to hear my plan. He's been in law enforcement longer than I've been alive. He was asking as a way of helping me to put my thoughts in order. Because I was going into this one tired and because speaking my plan aloud would help to prevent me from making any stupid mistakes. He was doing me a kindness, partly because he was my commanding officer but mostly because he was my friend.

"We'll start by identifying the victim. Hopefully, forensics will be able to help with that. Once we know who he is, we can start reaching out to family and friends. See if any of them can tell us anything useful. If that doesn't pan out, we can canvas the neighborhood. See if anybody knows him or has seen him around lately."

"A sound beginning."

"Let's hope so. In the meantime, I'm going to have Pongo and Robbie run down every business within a six-block radius that has a camera pointed toward the street."

"Hoping to catch a glimpse of the murderer?"

"More so whoever thought it was a good idea to stash the body in our ceiling."

Lieutenant Kermit's expression became thoughtful. "You don't believe they're one and the same?"

"No," I said, realizing for the first time that I really didn't. "Murder is one thing, but whoever stashed the body did so for a reason. Might be it was meant as a warning, or maybe to send a message. Regardless of the reason, they wanted our attention, and now they've got it."

"Questions within questions."

I shrugged. "I'm not overly hopeful it will pan out, since whoever stashed the body was careful enough to avoid our cameras, but maybe we'll get lucky."

Lieutenant Kermit nodded. "Stranger things have happened, and criminals are mercurial creatures."

He wasn't wrong on that count. This past winter we'd gotten a call about a car that had slipped into the Charles River. Turned out, the driver had been in the process of dumping a body and reversed too far down the ramp. Once they realized they couldn't get their car out, they called 9-1-1 to request a tow.

I'm not sure if the killer honestly thought no one would notice all the blood in his trunk or if he was just too cold to care. Either way, he went directly from the boat ramp to the police station and from there to the county jail. Rumor has it that the district attorney just rolled his eyes when the charging files came across his desk.

"You'll want to tread carefully on this one, Sergeant."

"And double check my corners for tripwires." I nodded. "I know the drill."

"Even so, some assistance might do you good. I assume you noticed the change in office décor prior to the body's unexpected arrival?"

"You're referring to the extra desk?" I asked.

"Indeed," he said. "It appears we're adding to our ranks. One Officer Thaysa Alves."

"Never heard of her." Which wasn't unusual. Boston Police Department was comprised of over two thousand officers among various divisions, along with another eight hundred or so civilian personnel. "What do we know?"

"On paper, she looks quite promising. High academy scores, exceptional physical fitness and defensive tactics ratings. She's attending night school, working toward a bachelor's degree in criminal justice. She's been on the force just under two years, with no performance issues or written reprimands contained within her file."

I narrowed my eyes. "If she's so great, why is she coming to us?"

"I don't know yet," Lieutenant Kermit said.

"Wait, they didn't *tell* you?"

"Only that it was a sensitive matter, and a change of scenery would be in her best interest."

I frowned. "That doesn't sound promising."

"No, it doesn't. But let's keep an open mind until she arrives, yes?"

"Any idea when that might be?"

"Sooner rather than later, I expect." Lieutenant Kermit glanced down at his watch and sighed. "Is there anything you need before I return to City Hall?"

I shook my head. "Nothing I can think of right now. I'll keep you appraised of what I find."

"As you wish. Good hunting, Sergeant. And because it bears repeating, watch your back."

"Sure you don't want to leave with something more ominous? Maybe talk about how this one doesn't feel right?"

Lieutenant Kermit smiled. "Take it from an old war dog, Sergeant. These kinds of things never feel right."

Forensics. Friday, July 25th 1O36hrs

THERE'D ALWAYS BEEN A wet aroma to our office. It came from the ice that formed along the pipes during the winters. It left mold deposits in the ceiling and inside the walls when it melted. This time, however, when I opened the door, the aroma felt different. It was cold in a way that went beyond mere temperature.

Investigating the paranormal could be redundant at times, and foolhardy, but the stakes were no less severe than any other investigation. We dealt in people, and we dealt in death.

The sight of the corpse laid out across my desk struck me hard in the chest, the image serving as a stark reminder as to why our division mattered. Whatever transgression had occurred, the figure had paid for it with his life. And if I didn't search for justice on his behalf, no one else would.

JADE ENCLAVE

There was already a forensic technician inside. Mid-forties, with caramel hair so curly it resembled a tangled cotton candy swab, he peered intently down at the body, his brow furrowed in concentration. There was a camera hanging from his neck, and a metal clipboard beside him, filled with scribbled notes.

"In or out," he said without looking over.

It took me a moment to realize he was talking to me. "Huh?"

"Get in or get out. Just shut the door."

I blinked and then pointedly stepped inside, closing the door behind me.

The forensic technician ignored me after that, staring down for several long seconds before raising his camera up to his eye. It was one of those fancy models, with an extended lens that probably could have seen Jupiter on a clear night. He aimed it just off center of the corpse's face and snapped half a dozen photographs before retreating several steps back. He checked the image on his camera's screen, then clicked his teeth and glanced up at me.

"I thought homicide said they weren't coming."

"I'm not homicide."

"Then who are you?"

His question hit me like a wiffle ball bat to the breadbasket and my mouth dropped with a surprised noise. "You don't know?"

Prior to joining Blue Moon, I didn't make a habit of assuming that everyone I met knew who I was, but I'd spent the past half year giving anyone associated with Forensics Division a wide berth. Ever since St. Patrick's Day and the Massacre Site case, when I'd uncovered a plot involving the head of their division and some stolen gold. I'd survived the ordeal. He hadn't.

To say there were hard feelings was an understatement of gigantic proportions, and ever since then, word on the street had been that they were eager for payback. To combat this, I'd become adept at not leaving any potentially incriminating evidence behind any crime scenes. A task that had been made monumentally easier by shaving my head, which was a point in favor of keeping it that way.

"Look lady, I've got a long day ahead of me, so if this is some kind of weird fetish, or if you're one of those true crime podcaster nuts, can you just move it along? There's really nothing exciting to see here."

It took me a moment to get my mouth working, and I swallowed before I said. "I'm not a podcaster. I'm a police officer."

"You just said you weren't Homicide."

"I'm not. My name is Detective Chloe Mayfield. Blue Moon Division. That's my desk."

The technician blinked, then turned to look at me with a skeptical expression. "Wait, seriously? You guys actually *work* in here? I thought dispatch made a mistake."

"Nope, this is home."

"Lord almighty." His eyes flickered up to the hole in the ceiling. "You know you have a mold problem, right?"

"Yeah, winter ran long this year. It's not as bad as it seems."

"I wouldn't be so sure about that." He drew in a long breath and let it out through his nose. "Alright, Sergeant Mayfield. I suppose you're wanting to assist?"

"Would that be a problem?"

"Long as you keep your head about you." He raised his hand and pointed toward Robbie's desk. "Gloves are right over there. I don't suppose you need a hairnet, but just in case."

I started toward the desk, but hesitated at the last second, whispers of paranoia halting my footsteps and causing me to retreat back to the entryway. "What did you say your name was again?"

The technician glanced at me. "I didn't. But it's Irving Yechiel. Nice to meet you."

"You been with the department long?"

"Long enough. You?"

"Going on a decade."

It was a bald-faced lie. I wasn't even at the five-year mark, but I wanted to see his reaction, and the split-second hesitation in his face gave truth to the paranoid whispers in my head.

"Is that so?"

I shifted my feet, not quite laying my hand atop my pistol but drawing closer just in case. "No. I'm a bad liar. But so are you, Irving."

Irving remained still for a long moment, then exhaled. "What gave it away?"

"Boston Police Department isn't small, but it's not that big either. And no division can easily survive the loss of its head. Especially when it involves allegations of illegal activity."

"Meaning?"

"Meaning you knew exactly who I was before I even walked through that door. The fact that you're playing dumb makes me think you've got some sort of ulterior motive. So what's your plan? You let me help with the investigation and then pick my gloves out of the trash when we're finished? Try to recover some stray eyelashes? Or maybe you'll just wait around to swab the door handle for some DNA you can plant on the body?" My anger rose inside as I spoke, and bits of red tinged my vision along the edges.

It wasn't the first time I'd gone down this road of thought, but repeated trips never made it any easier. Cops have enough to worry about. Being set up by our own would have made the job intolerable, if not for the support of Lieutenant Kermit and the other members of Blue Moon.

"Kind of paranoid, don't you think?" Irving asked.

"I prefer experienced enough to know better."

"I'll bet." He drew in a long breath and let it out in a huff. "Look, Sergeant, you got me, okay? But it's not what you think."

"How so?"

"Jerry Gatenbein was my boss for a lot of years, but I could count on one hand the number of conversations we had. We were professional colleagues. Not friends. And sure, I read the call ahead of time, so when you came through the door, I had my suspicions, but that's it."

"And I'm supposed to believe that?"

"This may shock you, Sergeant, but not everyone here takes their work home with them."

"Meaning what?"

He shrugged. "Not everyone who works for the department wants to play politics. Some of us, myself included, just want to show up, do our job, and be left alone."

"So much for being comrades in arms, huh?"

He raised three fingers and counted them off as he spoke. "One, we're not soldiers. Two, this isn't a battlefield, and three, the last time I checked, we weren't at war with our civilian population. I do my job well and ensure my reports are clean and to the point. I expect the same sort of professionalism from my co-workers. But we're not family." He reached inside his pocket and drew out his phone, flipping through several screens before turning it to face me. The screen showed a young blonde woman with two children under the age of twelve. "That's my family. They're my passion. Photographing corpses is just something I do to pay the bills."

I glanced at the photo on the screen. "They're a good-looking bunch."

"They are indeed. And I have no interest in putting them in harm's way or sacrificing my own career on the altar of whatever game you and Detective Mackleroy are playing."

"You think this is some sort of game? The man tried to put me in prison."

"From what I heard you started it by setting him up to get shot."

"It was a little more complicated than that."

He shrugged. "If you say so. Just seemed to me that there's more to this."

"Like what?"

"Look, I'm not one to pry into other people's business, but if the two of you seriously hated one another, one of you would have killed the other by now. Case in point, this guy." He motioned toward the corpse. "Someone really hated him. Or else they hated someone who loved him. Point is, if you were serious about settling your feud, you'd do it."

"How?"

He shrugged. "However seems best fitting to the two of you, I suppose. If you want my advice? The pair of you should go find some back alley and have an old west style shootout. Just so long as you leave me and the rest of the department out of your games."

I wasn't always right when it came to reading people. Lord knows I'd been fooled before, but there was something in the practical simplicity of his words that made me think he might be telling the truth. Law Enforcement, for all that it was a calling, was also just a job, and the types of people who were drawn to forensics tended to find just as much satisfaction in the science as in knowing a criminal had been taken off the street.

"Look, Sergeant, I'd like to finish up here. You can assist me if you like and get my notes now, or you can step back outside and wait for my official report. I should have it filed in a couple of hours. Your call."

I debated for a long moment before stepping up beside the desk and slipping my gloves on. I didn't trust Irving, and the paranoid whispers in my head hadn't subsided, but any detective worth their salt knows that the best chance of solving a murder is within the first forty-eight hours. They made a television show about it and everything.

That meant every hour I spent waiting for Forensics Division's official report was another hour a criminal remained free to wander the streets of Boston. If putting myself in jeopardy meant having a better chance of catching them sooner, then it was a risk I had to take.

Once my gloves were on, I stepped up beside the table, and even though I didn't want to, I forced myself to look down and really *see* the body splayed across my desk.

I was no stranger to corpses. They're a part of the job, but I would never be one of those cold, dispassionate detectives that could spend hours examining a fresh corpse without it affecting me. Maybe it was a result of growing up in Boston, where Catholic sentiments ran deep within the community, or maybe the storyteller in me just couldn't get square with the idea that the tales of our lives could come to such an abrupt and violent end. Either way, I struggled when it came to corpses and always would.

The man splayed out across my desk was in his mid-thirties, of Asian descent, with dark hair trimmed short and an expression of serene peace that struck me as odd. Don't get me wrong, it was better than the pained grimace or wide-eyed stare that usually adorned a corpse's face, but he looked as if he were leaning back into a hot bath, savoring the warmth that would never come.

He was dressed in dark brown robes that looked like something out of a kung fu movie, with knee-high socks and slip-on shoes with no laces. There was no jewelry or decoration to be found on his person, save for a red drawstring bag roughly the size of my fist. The contents inside consisted of a small rope of wooden beads, the ends coming together in a yellow tassel.

"They're prayer beads," Irving said, noting the way my eyes lingered on them. "Zen Buddhism, I would guess."

"Not too familiar with that."

"Not too many people in Boston are."

"Do we have an ID on him?"

"Afraid not. Just bad news followed by more bad news."

"No driver's license, huh?"

He shook his head and lifted his metal clipboard, consulting his notes before he spoke again. "I ran his fingerprints first thing, but they came back without a match, meaning there's likely no identification out there to find. No driver's license or voter registration card. Not even a library card."

"Okay, that's the bad news. What's the really bad news?"

"I can't tell you what killed him."

I blinked. Up until that moment I'd assumed that the cause of death was hidden somewhere under the robes. Some sort of gunshot, or stab wound. Not strangulation, based on the lack of bruising around the neck but *something*.

To be fair, forensic technicians weren't medical examiners, but they were good at their jobs, and it was rare that they couldn't accurately identify a cause of death while at the scene. Everything from the body's position, core temperature, and surrounding items told a story, and they were adept at figuring out the how and why.

"No injuries at all?"

"On the contrary, I'd say we're spoiled for choice."

I clearly wasn't understanding, so Irving motioned for me to watch. Moving with practiced precision, he slowly unwrapped the robes from around the corpse, revealing a bare torso that caused my breath to catch.

To say that the corpse had been beaten was an understatement. He'd been... savaged was the only word that came to mind, but even that didn't fit, because there was no blood to be seen. No cuts, lacerations, or anything. Just heavy patterns of deep purple highways traversing the landscape of his chest.

Bile rose in my throat, but I glanced away, clenched my jaw, and held my breath until it passed. Only once I was sure I wasn't going to immediately expel the coffee I'd recently drunk did I allow myself to look back and start to categorize what I was seeing.

The corpse's knuckles, forearms and shins were lined with heavy bruises. As if he'd been fending off blows from a baseball bat. They paled, however, compared to the darker, heavier patterns along his torso, where some of the blows had slipped past his guard. Like Irving said, when it came to wounds, we were spoiled for choice, but there was no way of identifying which of the blows had proved fatal. For all we knew it could have been an accumulation of damage. One thing was certain though. No one who had suffered this sort of punishment could be said to have departed peacefully from this life, despite what their expression might suggest.

"What do you make of it?" I asked.

"Truthfully, I have no idea. If I had to guess, I would say he was tortured."

"Tortured?"

He shrugged. "How else can you explain it? I've seen countless number of violent crimes throughout my years, but never anything like this." He motioned with his pen up toward the corpse's face. "Note, for example, the lack of damage to the face. If this was a fight, he should have had some markings. Head wounds and facial blows tend to bleed. But there's nothing, which makes me think that whoever did this struck with precision. You can't be that accurate in an active fight. People are moving, turning, not to mention hitting back. No one's that good."

"No human, anyway."

"Excuse me."

I shook my head. "Nothing."

He grunted. "I don't want to tell you your business, but if I were in your position and seeking advice, I would think about contacting Detective William Wei."

"Who's Detective Wei?"

"He heads up most of the investigations that involve Chinatown." He motioned toward the red bag of beads laid out beside the corpse. "I don't know if that guy was actually a Buddhist monk or if he just wanted to look like one, but that's where I'd start."

The paranoid whispers hadn't subsided in my mind, but I couldn't deny that Irving's advice made sense. Doubly so, since it was the only path I saw before me.

"Okay," I said, speaking aloud to myself. "Chinatown it is then."

An Inconvenient Plea. Friday, July 25th 1112hrs

I EXITED OUR OFFICE and ascended two flights of stairs toward the parking garage. As I walked, I started reviewing the case in my head, separating what I knew and what I needed to find out.

Starting with my victim.

Running a murder investigation on behalf of an unknown victim wasn't unheard of. It's something every homicide detective deals with at some point in their career. Usually, it comes about when the victim's sustained heavy injuries pre-or-postmortem, or else their remains come to you in an advanced stage of decomposition. That's where dental records can prove invaluable.

Less common are the cases where someone is actively trying to conceal the victim's identity. Oftentimes, this means removing their head and hands. In those instances, you're left to rely on other means of identification, such as birthmarks, tattoos, and DNA testing.

I'd heard of all of the above before, and even though I didn't have any personal experience dealing with them, I could have found other detectives in the department who had. This was different though. I was dealing with an unknown victim with no identification on file in either the state or national databases. That sort of anonymity added a level of complexity I wasn't immediately sure how to address.

A lot of people dream of living off the grid, free from the constraints of society and all its responsibilities. Those same people, however, don't always account for just how much we rely on our identification cards in order to get by. The days of being able to sustain ourselves on cash alone are largely over. State legislature requires all motels, even the sleazy ones, to verify customers' IDs. Likewise, any business that rents out a car or sells a bus ticket. Even a cell phone requires an ID, and you can forget about purchasing comfort vices like tobacco and alcohol. You can't even adopt a stray dog without one.

Assuming for a moment that Irving wasn't misleading me, and that my victim really was living outside the system, then someone was almost certainly helping them. And that same someone could identify him, and maybe even shed some light on who might have wished to harm him.

I just needed to find them.

And I needed to approach them carefully, because by and large, people don't go out of their way to help strangers. Not when it could end up blowing back on them. More than likely, I was looking for a family member or a close friend. Someone who cared about the victim. Someone who might be sheltering other people and would be reluctant to speak out for fear of exposing them. Someone who might even have a vested interest in keeping their presence here a secret and wouldn't hesitate to kill in order to protect them.

It was too early in the case to be this paranoid, but I'd seen enough to know anything was possible, and the last thing I wanted to do was underestimate either the victim or the killer.

A soft wind swept through the garage, cast along by the Charles River. It felt cold, despite the fact that we were in the heart of summer, and goosebumps appeared along my arms. I rubbed them away and told myself it was just my mind playing tricks, trying to distract me from turning the page onto the next piece of information I needed to digest.

The killer.

The memory of the victim's torso flashed across my mind, causing me to shudder. It wasn't the worst thing I'd ever seen. It wasn't even close. But there was something about it that sent waves of revulsion coursing through me. Gunshot and knife wounds were par for the course when it came to violent crimes, but they were also messy. This killer, however, had executed his or her crimes in a cold, almost systematic manner.

Beating someone to death isn't hard, per se, but rarely is it dispassionate. My killer was a special kind of sociopath, and if they were the same person who placed the victim inside the ceiling, they'd know I was on to them, and they'd see me coming a mile away. I needed to tread carefully, and like Lieutenant Kermit said, that started with watching my back.

Halfway down the aisle, that same cold sensation came over me, this time minus the wind. My breath caught, and the tingle along the back of my neck whispered a soft warning that I was being followed.

I didn't start running.

Most people would have. Those that didn't freeze up. Thing is, rarely is running a good choice of action when being stalked. For several reasons.

Firstly, it tells your follower that they've been spotted and forces them to decide on the spot if they want to capture you. The answer, more often than not, is yes.

Secondly, without prior warning, there's no way to be certain that you're not being herded. Pushed and pursued by an unseen attacker who holds all the advantages and who may not be working alone. Even if I took off and managed to reach the garage entrance, there was no guarantee there wouldn't be a car filled with three or four goons waiting to jump out.

Better to make my stand here.

I cut right and slipped between two government vehicles before coming out into the opposite aisle. A handful of steps brought me to the edge of the ascending ramp, and I started up, waiting until I was out of sight before breaking into a quick trot. At the top, I took the first right and slid between the wall and a white van before debating my next move.

I didn't know how many people were hunting me, and I couldn't watch every direction at once. The smart move was to call for backup. Not from Blue Moon. Robbie was a minor, and Pongo was, to put it gently, combat ineffective. Lieutenant Kermit would come, but his stance on guns was well known, and I feared I would only be putting him in harm's way.

I could call dispatch and request assistance from our patrol division, but they'd come in with lights and sirens blazing. My pursuers would hear them coming from a way's off, and if they fell back, it would only be so they could regroup and strike again at a later date. I might not see them coming next time. I had some friends. Rickson was the first name that came to mind. He would come if I called, but unless he was nearby, it would be too late.

Footsteps sounded on the ramp below me, ending the debate. Whoever was coming was evidently determined to see it through, and I drew my pistol from my holster and took aim, pressing my back against the wall as a young woman came around the corner.

In her early twenties, of Asian ancestry, with dark hair cut above her shoulders and dark glasses, the sight of my barrel pointed at her forehead drew out a surprised scream before she stumbled and fell onto her backside. She hit the ground with a pained cry and jerked her hands into the air.

"Wait," she cried. "Don't shoot. Oh, please don't shoot."

The part of my brain that is responsible for analyzing threat assessment cleared its throat, and I hesitated a fraction of a second more before lowering my pistol. "Who are you?"

"Hui," she said, peering up fearfully. "My name is Hui Lan. Please, I don't have any weapons."

That was good to know. "Why are you following me?"

"I-I'm sorry," she said. "I went downstairs but there was yellow tape strewn across the door. I was going to leave but then I heard people talking inside. I thought if I waited around someone might eventually come up, but then you did and I wasn't sure anymore."

"Sure about what?"

"If you were you. I mean, not you. Obviously, you're you, but are you *her?*"

"Her being?"

"Sergeant Mayfield," she said. "Chloe Mayfield? I read about you in the paper. I thought I'd recognize you from the picture, but..."

But I had hair back when that picture was taken. "So what if I am?"

"I-I need your help," Hui said. "That is, I have a case for you. That's what you call it right, a case?"

I took a moment to study her. Her eyes bore dark circles underneath, as if she hadn't been getting much sleep, and her fingernails were worn down to the quick. Not clipped either, more likely chewed. Which suggested she was either high anxiety or under a huge amount of stress. I debated for a moment, then holstered my pistol and stepped out from between the van and the wall. "I'm not a private detective, Miss Lan. I'm a police officer. We don't accept case assignments from private citizens. If you need help, then you should call 9-1-1 or just walk across the street to the police station. Talk to the receptionist in the lobby and she'll have an officer come meet you. They'll make sure you get where you need to go from there."

I sidestepped around her, and started back down the ramp, only making it a couple of steps before her next sentence stopped me.

"Please," she said, her voice coming out as more of a whimpering sob. "He's going to kill me."

My feet ceased to move, and a familiar fire rose up in my chest.

In law enforcement, we don't always talk about the fire, but most people carry it within them. It's the part of you that rises up when confronted by injustice, that seeks to help those in need for no other reason than you can. The best police officers carry a fire that's just a little bigger than most, and a few, like myself, even manage to keep it from being extinguished throughout the years by corrupt politics and bureaucratic greed.

My fire had taken a beating in the aftermath of the Mayor Cherri debacle, and again during my stint in Blue Moon. Some days it felt like the entire department had turned their back on me, leaving my fire tarnished and beset by cold winter winds. But it wasn't extinguished, and so long as the coals still glowed, I was going to make darn sure that anyone who came to me seeking help would get it, including this woman.

"Alright," I said, turning to face her. "Let's head across the street and you can tell me all about it. I won't make any promises, but I'll hear you out and help you as best I can."

"Across the street to the police station?" she asked.

"God no." I shook my head. "I've got somewhere better in mind."

The Missing Roommate. Friday, July 25th 1143hrs

We made our way over to a coffee house I frequented off New Chardon Street. It was an old school Boston cafe with red brick interior walls and dark wood tables. The inside smelled like fresh ground coffee beans, as well as cinnamon, nutmeg, and chai.

Antique leather-bound books lined the shelves behind the counter, and the lemon meringue pie called to me from inside the display case, its sweet, siren song tugging at my heartstrings. I met its custard eyes for several seconds, then reluctantly looked away, stepped up to the counter and instead ordered two medium coffees with room for cream and sugar.

"Okay," the cashier said. "That will be—"

"And the pie!" I didn't quite scream, but the noise that came out of my mouth was loud enough to startle her, and she jerked her hand back and peered at me with rounded eyes.

The low hum of conversation inside dimmed, and I could feel my cheeks redden as I cleared my throat. "That is, two pieces of pie, please."

I know what you're thinking. But Chloe, you say, how are you going to investigate a murder after that pie? Won't you be in a carb coma? The answer is probably, but as the corpse that had dropped from the ceiling recently reminded me, life is short, and sometimes, you just have to eat the darn pie. Besides, lemons contained vitamin C, and I might need that for... something. "And a chocolate cookie."

Sometimes you just have to eat the cookie too.

The cashier dutifully rang them up, and I paid and made my way back over to the booth where Hui sat. The young woman was slouched over the table, blankly staring down at the dark aged wood with her hands in her lap. I slid in opposite her, and neither of us said anything for a couple of minutes until our order arrived. The scent of the coffee, alongside the warmed chocolate cookie, stirred Hui, and she blinked, and peered down at the twin pieces of pie.

"Is that...?"

I motioned with one hand. "Help yourself."

She hesitated for only a moment. Then she seized hold of the pie and pulled the plate close to her chest. Her fork dipped and rose, and any conversation we might have had was temporarily suspended while she ate. I watched her for a few seconds before my own stomach growled, reminding me that I was buying energy with calories when I should have been sleeping.

I started in on my own pie, savoring the smooth creaminess of the lemon before reaching over and breaking the cookie in half. I took the slightly smaller piece and set the other half on the plate, which I slid across the table. Hui peered up, then gave me a thankful nod.

There is no greater feeling in the world than eating a warmed chocolate chip cookie inside a cafe, and had things been different, I would have happily taken my time, savoring every bite. Unfortunately, the specter of death loomed large in my mind, the imagined scent of the corpse lingering on my clothing, urging me to hurry. I finished my treats, then pointedly pushed the plates aside and got down to business.

"So," I said, as I drew two sugar packets from the cannister. I shook them against the table then tore the tops, dumping the contents into my coffee. "Who's trying to kill you exactly?"

Hui shifted in her chair, her eyes turning inward. Whatever she saw caused her to shudder, but she came back after a few seconds and forced herself to swallow the last bite of pie before answering. "I don't know his name."

"What do you know?"

"It is difficult to explain."

"How about you just lay it out and we'll see what we can make sense of?"

Hui nodded, and drew in a breath, steeling herself. "I was born in Pingshan, China. I came here on a student visa two years ago to study Electromagnetic Engineering at MIT."

MIT was short for the Massachusetts Institute of Technology. It was a private research university set up in Cambridge. I'd been there before, and hearing its name said aloud caused my chest to tighten as old memories rose unbidden to the forefront of my mind. A headless figure atop a midnight stallion. The sound of cannon fire ringing through the streets as the Sons of Liberty laid siege. I closed my eyes and pushed the memories away, forcing myself to focus on the girl's story.

"My roommate is named Ru Yee. She is also from China. We are the same age, and Student Housing placed us together so that we would not feel so homesick."

"Smart. Did the two of you get along?"

"Very well," Hui said. "We are not, how you would say, party girls. We like to read and to study. Family is very important in China. Our parents gave much for us to have this opportunity, and we both wished to make the most of it."

"I'm not seeing the problem so far."

"For the past several weeks, Ru has been acting strangely. She began staying out at night. Handing her assignments in late or skipping class altogether. I could see that something was wrong, but when I tried to speak with her, she refused to discuss it."

"Did she have a boyfriend? Some guy she was seeing?"

Hui shook her head. "No. I would have known if there was someone like that. This was something else."

"Like what?"

"I do not know, but it was weighing on her. We had always prepared our meals together, but she stopped eating. Then she stopped sleeping. Every day seemed worse than the one before, until, four days ago, she left the dorm and didn't come back."

"Maybe she just needed a break? Or a little holiday getaway?"

Hui shook her head again. "Ru has never behaved like this before. We do not have much money, but what little we do have, we send home, to help our families. She would not spend money on a holiday. Certainly not without telling me."

"That brings us back to the boyfriend theory." That or a drug problem, but I kept that to myself for now. No point inserting that into the conversation until we could be sure there wasn't some guy, or girl, footing the bill.

"No. I understand why you would think that, but you must believe me. There was no one like that. After the second night, when she still had not come back, I went to the Student Services Office to file a report, but they were not helpful. So I gathered some of the other girls from our dormitory and we went looking. We searched through Boston, and eventually we found her near the waterfront. She was dressed in the same clothes she had left in, and she seemed lost and confused. She didn't recognize us, and we feared she'd been attacked, but there were no markings on her body. At least none that we could see."

I stayed quiet, but inwardly I was thinking that the drug theory was sounding more and more likely. That or she'd been assaulted and was in shock. "What happened next?"

"I wanted to take her to the hospital, but some of the other girls recommended against it. We were afraid that the university might find out, and that it could affect her scholarship. She didn't seem to be in any danger, so we took her home, and agreed to take turns watching her." She shuddered and said the next part in a quick breath. "I do not know how to describe what happened next. Ru was there, but she was also not. It was like she was in a daze. She ate the food we made and drank what we offered, but she never asked for more, and refused to speak or to sleep. She just sat there, peering out the window. Always eastward. I did not know it at the time, but I think she was waiting for someone. For *him.*"

"Him who?"

Hui's face paled, and she struggled to push her next words out. "I do not know how to explain what happened next. It sounds crazy, even to my own ears. And yet..."

"Crazy is par for the course in my neck of the woods." I held up my hands, turning my palms around to show off the scars. "That was done by a bunch of King Arthur wannabe's. Whatever you've got to say, I can guarantee I've heard weirder."

Hui nodded and wiped at her eyes. "The second night that Ru was home, I was startled awake in the middle of the night. At first, I thought I was dreaming, but then I heard a man's voice. It was low and muffled, but it was coming from Ru's room. I rose from my bed and crept down the hall. As I walked, the sound changed. It became something horrid. Something monstrous. I began shaking. All I wanted to do was run, but it was as if a spell had taken hold of me. It drew me further down the hall, forced me to the edge of her room. I couldn't stop myself from opening the door, and that's when I saw *it.*"

"Saw what?"

"A demon," she said. "Wearing the guise of a man. It had pale skin and eyes like a harvest moon. It was bent over, and it was... inhaling her, I think." She was trembling, her body beating a rough, jerky rhythm against the table. "I was so scared. I slumped to the floor and laid there as it lifted Ru from the bed. It carried her into the hall and walked past me with hardly a second glance. I didn't hear it leave the dorm. I just lay there, slumped in the corner, until long after the sun had risen." Her last word came out with a sob, and she wiped her face with her sleeve, seizing her coffee cup and taking a long sip before exhaling. "I did not know who else to turn to. Ru has no family here in the states. I did not want to alert the university for fear that they would think she ran away, and going to the police, the real police, was unthinkable."

Inwardly, I bristled at the insinuation that I wasn't a real police officer, but decided to let it slide. Hui was clearly buckling under the pressure of what she'd seen. Or what she thought she'd seen. Experience, along with a skeptical nature, kept me from buying into her story. Unfortunately, it didn't matter if I believed it. What mattered was that she believed it, and I needed to treat it as factual until I could prove otherwise.

"Okay," I said, drawing out my phone. "You did the right thing by coming to me. I'll look into it."

Hui blinked, a faint glimpse of hope shining out from her expression. "You'll help me? Truly?"

"Yeah, consider me on the case. Now, I need some information from you. First off, what is your dorm address?"

Hui provided the address, along with answers to a series of additional questions. Unfortunately, she didn't know much more than she had already told me. Ru's social life mostly centered around school activities, and what few hobbies she had coincided with her major. They'd had similar schedules over the past few semesters, and Hui was able to recall most of the classes they'd taken, but she didn't know Ru's school login or password, meaning I would need to make this an official investigation if I wanted a judge to issue a warrant allowing me access to her emails or social media accounts. After about fifteen minutes of questioning, it became apparent that I'd gotten all the information I was going to get. I saved the information in my cell phone, then placed it back in my pocket before sliding out of the booth.

"How can I reach you?" I asked.

"I'll be staying with friends for the rest of the semester. You can call me here." Hui gave me her phone number, as well as the key to her dorm room. "I haven't been back inside since that night."

"I'll take a look and tell you what I find. It might take me some time though. This isn't my only case."

"I understand," she said. "Thank you, Sergeant, for everything."

We exited the cafe, and I watched her make her way down the street before I started back toward our office. As I walked, I started replaying our conversation in my mind, and what little warmth the coffee and treats had provided was gone by the time I got to the end.

Everything inside told me that Hui legitimately believed her story. But her belief didn't necessarily make it real. I'd been in law enforcement long enough to say with confidence that blood sucking demons don't just go around abducting random women from their homes. People do that. Regular old vanilla mortals. Which meant Hui was either mistaken, or she was lying. I hoped it was the first one, although, statistically, the odds were more in favor of the second.

One of the first things they teach you in the academy is that civilians will lie to you. Excessively so. More than they would to any friend or stranger they might meet on the street. There's something inherent in the human psyche that causes people to bend the truth when speaking with police officers.

It's not always meant to conceal wrongdoings either. Sometimes people just want so much to be helpful that they'll fabricate lies as a means of trying to assist officers in their investigation. I've seen it before. People will claim to have witnessed accidents they were nowhere near. Or they'll describe criminals in vivid detail, only for the officers to later learn that they weren't present at the scene of the crime.

The worst are those who have criminal records. The ones who've been through the system enough that they made the jump from criminal to informant. Some of them, you practically have to gag them in order to get them to stop spilling dirt on their friends and family. They're like puppies who just can't stop showing off.

Regarding Hui, I didn't think she was the type to do something like this for attention. She struck me more as someone who'd burned out. It happens on college campuses all across America. Kids enrolled in these prestigious universities start supplementing with prescription medications in order to help them study, either ignoring or underestimating the dangers. Couple of months go by and the next thing they know their brain chemistry is equivalent to scrambled eggs. That's when they start hallucinating things. Such as life sucking demons attacking their roommate.

I knew this girl, Ru, hadn't been taken by a demon. But I couldn't be sure she hadn't been taken. Unfortunately, I couldn't put out a missing person's report until I was certain that I had a real victim. And the only way I would know for certain was to head up to the university and take a look for myself. I'd start with the dorm room, and if something was off, I could see about involving campus authorities. Mind you, this would have to wait until after my visit to Chinatown. Like it or not, real corpses come first.

I rounded the corner on the next block and ducked in through the entrance to the Government Parking Garage, my ears perking up just as the sound of glass shattering rang out from above. I slowed my pace and frowned, glancing up toward the ceiling.

Most of the vehicles housed inside the garage were privately owned, but there were a few loaner cars, designed to be lent out to various public officials or low-level government employees when the need arose. The department sends out reminders a couple of times a year to be on the lookout for thieves, and, for the most part, everyone who worked nearby knew better than to leave their belongings out where someone might see them.

Everyone except for me.

My mind flashed back to earlier this morning, when I'd stopped by my car just long enough to shove my tactical patrol bag into the backseat before leading the troop to our temporary headquarters at the Union Oyster House.

My eyes widened at the memory, and my feet took off without conscious orders, carrying me to the end of the row and up a flight of stairs before delivering me out onto the second floor. As I rounded the corner, I spotted my old clunker, now missing its back windshield. Broken glass lined the concrete near the rear tire, reflecting the overhead fluorescent light as I peered across the garage and caught sight of a smallish figure with my tactical patrol bag draped over one shoulder heading for the opposite wall.

"Hey!" I screamed. "Police! Stop right there!"

The figure glanced back, and I caught a flash of reddish hair half hidden underneath a flat brimmed baseball hat. His eyes widened, and he took off, sprinting to the end of the aisle and descending the ramp.

I cursed and took off running as the more pragmatic part of my brain warned against the dangers of chasing after a potentially armed suspect. I thought back to the ease with which I'd gotten the drop on Hui Lan earlier and was pointedly aware of how easy it would be for the fleeing thief to do the same. I'd come around the corner, maybe catch a brief glimpse of a barrel pointed at my face. A flash of light, and then... nothing.

It had always been a danger of the job, and with police violence at an all-time high in the country, I knew for a fact that some departments had begun quietly dissuading their officers from engaging in foot pursuits. At least in cases where no backup was present. The unofficial policy was to follow from a safe distance, call for backup, try to surround the suspect and let them wear themselves out before apprehending them. It was a gentler, softer approach to police work, and one I wholeheartedly disagreed with.

I surged on ahead, pumping my arms and legs with reckless abandon. Once I reached the end of the aisle, I started down the descending ramp, catching sight of my thief as he turned the corner. He wasn't much smaller than me, but he was fast. Faster than I was at any rate. Even with the weight of my bag spread unevenly across his back, he cleared the garage faster than I could follow, disappearing out through the exit. I kept running, but the long hours and lack of sleep burned through my reserves quickly, and the coffee and heavy sugar left my stomach burning and my lungs heaving as I reached the bottom floor.

My legs started to slow and by the time I was halfway across the garage the thief had crossed the roadway and disappeared around the corner. I stumbled to a halt near the entrance, and jerked my cellphone from my belt, but hesitated as I brought it up to my mouth.

I'd been born and raised here, and I knew firsthand just how easy it was for someone to disappear in the city. My pride raged against the admission, not wanting to admit what my head already knew. I wrestled with the indecision for another few seconds, then let my arm drop and belted out a heavy groan of frustration that swiftly gave way to curses.

My expletive filled rant echoed through the garage, but if anyone heard it they didn't respond, and I turned and slowly made my way back inside the garage, my mind already running a tally of what I'd lost.

Inside the bag were my law books, my map of the city, including the old blueprints outlining the Acadians' tunnels beneath the sewers, my report forms, traffic flares, and fingerprint kit. The one silver lining, if you can even call it that, was that there was no ammunition in my bag. Not because I'd thought to take it out, but because I'd used it, first during the Fenway Knight's case, then during the events of Fairy Wars. I'd used all the rounds I had left to fill my spare magazines, which I kept on me, before putting in a request for more. Deputy Bulwark hadn't outright denied my request; he couldn't do that without risking someone asking why. So instead, he'd left it pending for a week now.

I'd finally made the conscious decision to bite the bullet and just buy my own ammunition from the sports store this weekend but hadn't gotten around to it yet. I guess I could add a new duffel bag to my shopping list. And in the meantime, I'd just need to make do and borrow what I could.

I made it back to my car and cleaned up the glass as best I could. A quick walk around the garage turned up an old cardboard box someone had discarded. I ripped a section of the side free and matched it up to the empty windowpane. I didn't have any way to seal it, but when I opened my trunk, I found an old roll of duct tape the previous owners had left. I tore a couple of strips free and used them to seal the opening. As I worked, I felt my anger rising.

My old clunker wasn't pretty, but it was *mine*, and just because I didn't have time to hunt down the thief who did this didn't mean I would forget. I was keeping receipts, and once I cleared this murder, and possible kidnapping, off my plate, you could be darn sure I would circle back around. Blue Moon might not be the most feared division in the department, but we weren't as alone as we'd once been. I had friends, even a couple of allies, and I wouldn't hesitate to call in some favors to makes sure we evened the score. You could bet on that.

In the meantime, though, I had more important things to worry about.

Like a date with Chinatown.

Chinatown.
Friday, July 25th
1300hrs

Boston's Chinatown neighborhood lay nestled between the towering office buildings of the Financial District and the suburban sprawl of the South End, in a vibrant, jade enclave where east met west.

The official entrance to the neighborhood was crowned by the China Trade Gate, located on Beach Street. A beautiful paifang archway with white pillars and a jade roof, it was the most photographed section of the neighborhood and appeared in most of the advertising brochures. Past the gate, the narrow streets were crowded with locals and tourists browsing the small markets and novelty stores.

It's been said that the heart of Chinatown lies in its food, and it was difficult to disagree. Every third storefront seemed to be a restaurant, most bearing bold colored signs and flyers advertising fresh bao, stir-fry, and bubble teas of every flavor imaginable. And the soup. Dear God, the *soup*.

I'd been hooked on Chinatown's Chicken Noodle soup since I was a teenager. It was my comfort food, my go-to when I was sad, sick, or just in a hurry. The string carrots, bean sprouts, sharp scallions and pulled chicken simmering in broth called to my soul in a way that no church had ever managed to replicate. Some girls were all about the bass, but I was all about the chicken.

Most of the restaurants catered their menu to appeal to more mainstream American cuisine, but the best eateries offered a more curated fare, hidden away on special menus for those craving a more authentic experience or just missing home.

I cracked my window as I drove, savoring the scent of incense and cooking oil before turning my attention to the street. Various conversations filtered past as I edged my way along. I knew enough to be able to distinguish Cantonese from Mandarin but couldn't speak either. I filtered them away, and focused on what English I could pick out, most of it coming from the younger crowd as opposed to the middle-aged or the elderly population.

JADE ENCLAVE

The conversations varied between local news and various griping, none of which struck me as out of the ordinary. At one time, a full ninety-five percent of the businesses in Chinatown were family owned. These days, the number was much lower, with competing corporations and high-rise condominium developers inching ever closer, swallowing the streets one building at a time.

I'd run a quick inquiry through dispatch as to Detective Wei's whereabouts before leaving the garage. Turned out he was where any good detective should be.

At the scene of a crime.

I typed the address into my cellphone and followed the directions, eventually pulling up onto the curb beside a six story, red brick building with blue awnings. It was nestled between a cake store and a second building that didn't even bother to advertise itself in English. I killed the engine and made my way inside. There was no elevator, and I followed the numbers up to the third floor and down a long hallway to where a uniformed officer holding a clipboard stood outside the door of an apartment. Yellow police tape was hung loosely to allow officers and forensics easy access.

The patrol officer perked up at the sight of me, eyeing me up and down as I made my way down the hall.

"Can I help you, miss..."

"Detective Mayfield," I said, causing him to involuntarily straighten. "I need to see Detective Wei."

He frowned and mouthed my last name but couldn't place it. After a moment he leaned forward, scanned my ID, and dutifully wrote my name down atop his form. "Do I know you from somewhere?"

"Depends. You ever been to JJ Foley's? It's an old Irish pub not far from here. Lot of officers and retired cops mingle there."

The officer shook his head. "No."

"Me neither." I motioned toward the yellow tape. "We good?"

He frowned, but a moment later he lifted the tape, allowing me to duck through. I could feel his eyes on me, or more specifically my backside, as I slipped through the door, but a couple of seconds later I forgot all about him.

The doorway led into a cramped little apartment that hadn't been cleaned anytime in recent memory. The furniture was old and mismatched, most of it second hand, smelling of the same sour tobacco that stained its corners and arms. A tilted coffee table stood in the middle of the room, its surface covered by old newspapers and discarded cups of forgotten bubble tea. The walls were yellowed with age, and the carpet beneath my feet was scuffed and threadbare, the linoleum leading into the kitchen peeling in the corners. Dust clung to the corners like cobwebs, and the stale air was suffocating, choking me with the scent of mildew, old cooking grease, and blood.

A quick peek through the first doorway revealed a narrow, unmade bed tucked into one corner. The window, which looked out onto the street below, was covered in a thick layer of grime that dimmed the natural light, making the apartment feel like it had been forgotten by the rest of the world.

I retreated from the bedroom and made my way into the kitchen. Inside, it was a haphazard mess, with a greasy layer of oil coating the sticky counters and a stack of dirty dishes rising up from the sink. An overflowing trash can lay shoved in the corner, a sea of plastic bags and old takeout containers spilling over its top, and a stack of junk mail lay strewn across the stove, creating a fire hazard if ever I saw one. The yellowed refrigerator hummed in the corner, the faint odor of spoiled milk and expired condiments slipping through the cracks where the door failed to seal properly.

Two bodies sat at the table.

The first was slumped face down in a plate of noodles. There was a knife handle sticking out of his back. Blood trails led from the wound, soaking through his shirt and down the back of his pants. Red froth had formed an airy crust around his mouth, staining the noodles nearest his face.

The second man was slumped back in his chair, his eyes staring sightless upward above a palm length cut in his throat. It was deep enough that it had severed the neck muscles and his windpipe, and dried blood adorned his front, which had congealed on the napkin he'd tucked into his shirt collar. The stains were thick along his pants, where blood had dried in the creases, and a small splatter pattern lined the table in front of him, tiny dots marring the paper plate, where the beef and broccoli had turned cold and greasy.

"Whoa there," a man's voice rang out from the back of the room. "I wouldn't come any closer unless you relish the idea of scrubbing blood out of the soles of your shoes."

I pulled my eyes away from the figures at the table as the speaker appeared from the back hallway. He was medium height, of Asian descent and athletically trim, with short cut dark hair and a boyish face that I suspected would last until well into middle age. He was dressed in a simple, discount rack suit with a light blue shirt and matching tie. Professional, but simple.

An orthopedic hinged knee brace was wrapped around his left leg, the Velcro straps ensuring it remained immobilized, and he walked with the assistance of two crutches, picking his steps carefully as he circled around the table and met me at the kitchen entrance.

"Can I help you with something?"

"Sure hope so," I said. "I'm looking for Detective William Wei."

"You found him," he said. "Are you Mayfield?" He waited for my nod before he continued. "Dispatch told me you were coming. Well, actually, warned me might be a more accurate phrase. They suggested I run, but as you can see..." He held up the crutches and shrugged.

"Guess I've garnered a bit of a reputation."

"Depends on who you ask. From what I've read, you Blue Moon folks have done some good work."

I blinked, momentarily stunned by what sounded suspiciously like a compliment. Outside of Rickson or Warman, our reputation within the department was basically mud. The idea that we might one day rise to the point where other officers would judge us based on our merit, rather than the rumors that Bulwark and the rest of the brass cultivated, was enough to make my heart speed up. Of course, the more pessimistic part of me warned that day was still far off, but I'd made it this far already, and who's to say what might happen in the future if we kept on—

"Uh, you still there?" Detective Wei asked, waving a hand in front of my face.

I blinked and came back to myself with a start. "Yeah, sorry. Long day. Been going at it since last night." I shook my head and cleared my throat, buying myself a moment with which to think. "What happened to you, anyway?"

"You mean this?" He motioned down toward his leg. "War wound. Some of my fellow officers and I were set upon by a mob of angry Irishmen."

My eyes snapped open, and my heart started pounding in my chest, my cop brain struggling to comprehend why I hadn't caught wind of this before now. "Were they part of the mob? Did you file a report?"

"Worse, we had to buy them all a round of Guinness."

"I'm not following."

"Soccer," he explained. "I play left midfield for the department's soccer team. We were playing EMS when I took a bad fall. Tore my ACL and MCL. Doctor says it will be at least a month before I can take off the brace. Then probably a few more weeks after that before I can ditch the crutches."

Soccer. Yet another perk reserved for those who actually fit in with the department and weren't viewed as black sheep. "I'm surprised the department didn't put you on desk duty."

"They tried, but I'm one of the few officers who speaks Mandarin fluently. My days of chasing down criminals might be on hold, but I figured I could still help more here than I could from behind a desk."

"That's good of you." I glanced around the kitchen, pointedly taking in the two corpses. "How's it working out?"

"No complaints so far. Way I figure, someone has to hold down the fort until Forensics arrives. Might as well be me."

"Yeah, about that. Where is everyone? I mean, shouldn't they be here by now?"

"Call went out this morning just before nine. I arrived shortly after that, and Forensics Division told me they were on the way." He made a show of glancing at his watch. "Of course, that was almost four hours ago, and since headquarters is only fifteen minutes away, it's safe to say they've placed this one on the back burner. Wish I could say I was surprised, but you get used to it after a while."

"Doesn't seem right, leaving you stuck here cooling your heels, no pun intended."

"None taken. And yeah, it's not. But that's how these things work."

I made an acknowledging sound and considered my next words carefully. "It seems kind of a waste to sit here all day. Especially now that there's two of us. We could use this time to do some actual police work."

"You want to start processing the scene ourselves?"

"Definitely not. That would be a huge breach of protocol. But there's no harm in us taking a peek around, right? Maybe doing some preliminary work, see if anything jumps out at us."

"You want to go through the drawers and the cupboards? Maybe riffle through the dirty clothes, look for any signs of violence or stacks of cash hidden beneath loose floorboards?"

"I'm guessing you had the same thought?"

He shrugged. "Like I said, I've been here for four hours."

"And?"

"Nothing's jumped out at me. Although I was able to tentatively identify our victims."

"And?"

"The one slumped over in his noodles with the knife in his back is named Haoran Hei. He owns the apartment. According to his driving record he's lived here for at least four years. The one sitting opposite him is Xuanming Fei. License has his address listed as one of the boat docks. I did a quick check. Apparently, he runs fishing charters and small cargo transportation. Both had experience working the docks."

"Better than nothing, but not exactly much to go on."

"Here's something odd. There are three cell phones inside the apartment."

"Three cell phones for two men?"

He nodded. "I can't try unlocking them using thumb or facial identification without disturbing the bodies."

"Which would send Forensics Division into a collective fit."

"And probably get me placed on suspension. But it's unusual, right?"

"Maybe. Although plenty of people have personal and work cell phones. Especially if they're required to be on call."

"That's true."

"What about the neighbors? I'm guessing it's too much to hope that any of them heard anything?"

"If they did, they're not saying. I talked to everyone on this floor and the two below. No one can recall hearing anything even remotely resembling a ruckus. Course, they also can't remember seeing either of our two victims, much less our alleged perpetrator."

"I can think of at least one person who saw something."

Detective Wei blinked. "You can? Who?"

I motioned toward his jacket pocket, and he drew out a pair of gloves and handed them over. I slipped them on, then made my way over to the trash, softly shifting the contents until I found a plastic bag sitting close to the surface. I gripped it with two fingers along the edge, then brought it up from the wastebasket and laid it down atop the counter, turning it over so we could see the receipt stapled along the edge.

"See that there?" I asked.

Detective Wei peered at the receipt, and it didn't take him long to see what I meant. "Says there it came from the Lotus Garden. It was placed last night. And there's a delivery charge added to the bill."

"Bingo," I said. "Someone was here, and at the very least they saw one of our victims."

Detective Wei's eyes narrowed, and he considered it for a long moment. "It's a bit of a long shot, don't you think?"

"For certain, but unless you have anything better to do?"

"Hate to say it but I don't."

"In that case..." I shrugged. "Seems like that patrol officer outside can hold down the fort for a couple of hours until Forensics Division arrives. Fancy some lunch?"

"So long as you're driving," Detective Wei said.

"Yeah," I said. "About that..."

The Lotus Garden. Friday, July 25th 1300hrs

There was no elevator, and Detective Wei was forced to make his way down the stairs sideways. I stayed within two steps of him, offering my arm for support when needed. Once we reached the ground floor, we passed through the front entrance and made our way over to the curb where my car was parked. I opened the passenger's door, noting the way Detective Wei's eyes widened at the sight of the interior.

"Um, wow. I knew your department was small, but..."

"Underfunded doesn't even begin to describe us," I said. "Don't worry though. I evicted anything that might bite you a few months back."

Wei considered my words for a long moment, then breathed something about being thankful for already having a tetanus shot before lowering himself down inside. He pushed the chair as far back as it would go, then carefully brought his crutches in before closing the door.

I dropped into the driver's seat and started up the engine, sending a stream of black flatulent smoke rising from the exhaust. We pulled away from the curb and headed off down the road.

The roads running through Chinatown were narrow at the best of times, but it had become common practice over the past few years for people to park along the side of the street. During peak hours, they could go two or even three rows deep. We regularly received calls from tourists who'd parked their cars only to return hours later and discover they were pinned in with no way out.

I stayed more or less in my lane as I weaved my way through the traffic, avoiding the worst intersections and those areas too narrow for two cars to fit through.

"So what is it you wanted to talk to me about, anyway?" Detective Wei asked. "You need something translated?"

The sight of the apartment had momentarily driven the memory of the corpse in our ceiling from the forefront of my mind, but it all came back in that moment, sending a shudder through me. "Not exactly."

As briefly as possible I filled him in on the corpse that had fallen from my ceiling. He listened in silence, his mouth drawing into a frown by the time I'd finished.

"Wow. Three murders in one day. Even for Boston, that's a lot."

"Hate to say it but I've seen worse."

"I guess you have." He exhaled and shook his head. "What do you think it means?"

"Which one?"

"The corpse in the ceiling."

"Right now, I'm operating on the premise that it was meant as some sort of message. If it was just a straight murder, they would have called it into Homicide. The fact that someone went to all the trouble of stashing the body somewhere I was sure to find makes me think they really want me looking into it. At least I *hope* that's the case."

"What's the alternative?"

"Blue Moon hasn't been around that long, but we've already dealt with our share of nasty characters. I wouldn't put it past any of them to murder someone just for the thrill of it. Having the corpse drop from the ceiling might just be their way of rubbing our noses in it."

"Jeez, that's a disturbing thought. I can see why your division has set itself apart."

I frowned. "What's that supposed to mean?"

"Nothing. It's just, most divisions don't have to worry about that sort of thing. Think about it. Homicide, narcotics, even gang task force units. When they go hunting, the criminals are usually just trying to get away to avoid being arrested. There's nothing personal about it, at least not on the surface."

I considered it in silence for several minutes before concluding that there might be some truth to what he was saying. Blue Moon's cases may have seemed nonsensical on the surface, filled with fairies and leprechauns and witches, but when you stripped all that away, we were ultimately dealing with people's belief systems.

Maybe that doesn't sound like much, but when you start to examine people as a whole, you'll realize that just about everything in our lives is dictated by some set of principles or tenets. Our views on morality, worthwhile pursuits, even the meaning of death.

Part of Blue Moon's job was to disprove the supernatural. For good and for bad. And for those who held such fantastical beliefs to be true, it meant stripping away their worldview and shattering the pillars that formed the basis of their lives. Having gone through and survived that, it makes sense that someone might come away holding a grudge. Would they be angry enough to kill? That depended on the individual, but I'd seen people do worse for less.

I exhaled and shook my head, concluding that it was just too much for me to digest in that moment. Maybe after I'd had some sleep and a proper meal, I could circle back around.

Detective Wei noted my reaction and seemed to pick up on my mood. "Okay, switching gears for a moment. Let's talk about my corpses. What do you think?"

"You asking *me?*"

"Why not? You're the one used to dealing with this sort of stuff."

"Says who?"

He shrugged. "I'm just saying. I've read some of Blue Moon's case files. Even the ones over in England and those offshoot branches in Sacramento and Appalachia. You guys don't mess around when it comes to your cases. You all have a habit of jumping in feet first. So how about it?"

I drew in a long breath and let it out slow, quieting my mind in order to organize my thoughts. "Honestly, it doesn't look like a straight up murder to me. It seems more like a hit job."

Detective Wei's nod made me think he'd already come to the same conclusion. "Anything else?"

"It was an expensive hit job."

His expression turned curious. "Why do you say that?"

"Think about it. The cuts were clean, relatively speaking. I've seen some knife attacks that looked like they could have been done with a chainsaw. But neither of the bodies had any defensive wounds along the forearms, and there was no sign of a struggle within the apartment. My corpse was battered to all heck. But yours? Mark my words, they didn't see it coming."

Detective Wei made a considering sound. "A murder like that is hard to pull off with a blade. Much less two. A gun would have been better. One quick draw, two shots. Take them out before they can react."

"Guns are noisy. People would have heard the shots. Knife is quiet and more personal."

"You think this was personal?"

"I think whoever wanted them dead *really* wanted them dead. And they probably wanted them to know why."

Detective Wei thought about it for a long moment, then sighed. "Crud, you might be right. But *we* still don't know why."

"Not yet we don't. Although experience says that cases like this usually involve money. Whether they lost some or stole some, it wouldn't be the first time people have hired a hitman to get back at someone who wronged them."

"Could be."

"Course, if it's *not* money then it probably means there's a jilted lover involved."

"I already checked. According to the state records, neither of the men are married. Noodles was, briefly, but he's been divorced for over twenty years."

"Doesn't necessarily have to be married. People do crazy things when they think they're in love."

"I guess." Detective Wei cast a sideways glance my way. "You ever been married?"

I shook my head. "You?"

"Yes. Just celebrated three years."

"Kids?"

"One on the way."

"Congratulations." I drew in a breath and exhaled. "Okay, let's switch to a bird's-eye view. Right now, we have three corpses, all of them men, and all of them of Asian ancestry. Whatever's going on here, it seems like it's somehow connected to Chinatown. I'm not familiar with the major players. Anyone you can think of who might be sporting a grudge?"

"By major players you mean...?"

"Bad guys."

He considered it for a moment. "To be honest, there's not too many of them running around these days. Everyone knows the Tong family ran the illegal gambling dens, but those dried up years ago. Most of the old guard have retired at this point, and the younger generation is more interested in E-sports betting than they are blackjack or poker."

"So probably not gambling related then. What else?"

"The drug trade went down when White Devil John copped a plea for twenty years in a Maryland prison. There's been some rumbles over the past year about a petty theft gang dealing in stolen electronics, but no one knows for sure who's behind it. Likewise, you'll always have your fly-by-night massage parlors dealing in sex trafficking, but those are more sporadic, here today and gone tomorrow type of organizations."

"Not much we can do about either of those right now. Anything else?"

"Well...there's always Satoru Doku."

"Who's that?"

"He's an old school Chinese gangster. Supposedly he's got ties to the Triad, but has fallen out of favor. He's had his eye on Chinatown for a while. Wants to relocate and make it his own personal fiefdom. He tried it a few years back, but couldn't establish a foothold."

"Why not?"

"Hard to say. There were rumors of skirmishes with other criminal gangs, but none of them ever stepped up to take credit for it. More likely, the Triad was worried he was attracting too much attention. They recalled him to China, and word among our informants is he's been itching to try again ever since."

"But he's in China, right?"

"Not anymore. He was able to pull some strings with the State Department and get himself a temporary visa. He arrived in New York a few weeks ago. No one's reported seeing him here yet, but mark my words it's only a matter of time."

"Consider them marked. In the meantime, we'll keep him on the back burner until we have reason to do otherwise. The last thing we need right now is to inadvertently start an international gang war." The corner of my mouth split up into a half smile when I imagined the look on Bulwark's face if I dropped that into his lap. It would certainly spell the end of my career, but what a way to go out. "Is there anyone in Chinatown who might be friendly to the police?"

"A couple shop owners, but they mostly deal in rumors. There's always the Sacred Pine Temple. It's run by a man named Brother Kim. They do a lot of charity work and community programs. Might be they could ask around for us."

"We should call them. For now, though, let's focus on the restaurant and see if we can't come up with some answers."

I turned on the next block and drove halfway down before reaching the Lotus Garden restaurant. Nestled between a hair salon and a novelty antique store, aged awnings cast their shade across tinted windows, and red pillars lined with Chinese symbols supported an archway covering the small stone stairway leading from the sidewalk to the front door.

We parked in the alleyway between the buildings and made our way around to the entrance. Detective Wei took the lead, and the door creaked open with a reluctant groan. Inside, the air was dense with the aroma of garlic, ginger, sesame oil and soy sauce. There were half a dozen tables spread around the floor, and twice as many booths, but there were only two other groups inside, both comprised of aging locals.

The walls were red brick with dark wood panels, and red lanterns with fraying edges hung from the ceiling, their bodies lined with dust. As I peered around, I noted other signs of age in the restaurant. There were scuffs in the wood floor, and tiny tears in the booth seats. The tables' surfaces were dull and scratched, and there was a wheezing hum coming from the ventilation shaft above our heads that didn't sound right.

Thankfully, there was nothing too abrasive, no rat droppings or anything that would have sent me running for the health inspector's office, but it was clear that whoever owned the restaurant either lacked the funds for repairs or had simply elected not to do so.

As we moved up toward the empty hostess stand, the kitchen door swung open and an aged woman with silver hair appeared.

JADE ENCLAVE

She was dressed in a worn, mandarin-collar shirt with a red apron. Petite, her hands worn and swollen around the knuckles, but there was a strength to her steps, and her eyes were sharp as polished amber as she moved to greet us.

Detective Wei greeted her in Mandarin, and the two conversed for several long seconds. The woman's face grew concerned by what she heard, but she eventually gave a reluctant nod and bid us to wait in the dining area before disappearing through the swinging doors into the kitchen. I could hear her talking to someone but couldn't understand what was said. As I stood there, the hairs along the back of my neck rose, and a soft bristle slipped down my spine. I turned and took a quick glance around, searching for the source of my discomfort.

I found it after only a moment, noting a pair of eyes peering out at me from underneath one of the booths. They belonged to a young boy with tan skin and darker hair. Our eyes met, and he smiled shyly, giving a soft wave that I returned with a grin.

The kitchen door swung open, and two figures stepped through. They were both in their early twenties and dressed in kitchen attire, including a dark neckerchief for the man. Something about them, possibly the shape of their jaws or maybe their matching hair, marked them as siblings in my mind. I pegged the man being a year or two older than the girl.

Detective Wei greeted them, and soon the three were conversing in quick, pointed sentences. I had no hope of deciphering what they said, so instead I focused on their body language, noting the way their stances stiffened as the female brought one hand up to cup her opposite elbow.

"What's going on?" I asked, once a break in the conversation occurred.

Detective Wei shifted, angling his body to face us all. "The man's name is Yichen Guai. The woman is his sister, Mei. They own the restaurant, sort of."

"Sort of?"

"Technically, it belongs to their grandmother, Lian, but they've taken over in all but name. The three of them will inherit it when she passes."

I frowned. "Three?"

"Apparently there is another sister. She's away at school."

"Did you ask them about the delivery?"

"I did. They don't want to talk about it. Or tell me who delivered the food."

I frowned. "Why not?"

"I'm not sure yet." Detective Wei considered it for a moment, then began speaking again. This time, the siblings' answers came more hesitantly. Detective Wei asked several more questions, then nodded and made a soothing gesture.

"I'm pretty sure the boy delivered it, but they don't want to admit it. They're scared of being cited for child labor laws."

I stared at him for a moment, then turned my gaze back to the boy crouching beneath the booth. He was maybe seven or eight. Thin, but not underfed. And there were no dark circles around his eyes or other bruises that made me think he was being abused.

Growing up in Boston, I knew a thing or two about family-owned restaurants, and most of them couldn't function without help from within the family. So long as it wasn't abusive, there were worse things kids could get up to in a city this size than helping out their folks.

"Tell them we're not interested in anything like that. We just want to know if the boy might have seen anyone else inside the apartment."

Detective Wei reiterated my words, and the answer he got back clearly wasn't what he'd hoped for. "They want to know what will happen if he did? They figure something bad must have happened. They're afraid the state will take the boy away." The woman, Mei, who I assumed to be his mother, said something. Her brother tried to stop her, but she shook her head, and the next words out of her mouth were angry.

Detective Wei translated. "She says she won't allow that to happen. That if we try to take the boy, she'll send him back to China."

"Tell her she won't have to send him anywhere. All we want is to ask him a couple of questions. After that, we'll be on our way, and, with a little luck, she won't hear from any of us again."

Detective Wei hesitated. "You sure about that? It could come back to bite us down the line. If the boy knows something and we can't explain how we got the information, it might leave a hole that a good defense attorney could exploit."

"We'll cross that bridge when and if we come to it. In the meantime, let's first find out if he knows anything."

Detective Wei nodded and said several more things to the siblings. They answered reluctantly, and he turned back to me. "Okay, they say we can ask."

He turned toward the booth, and spoke softly to the boy, who watched him with cautious eyes. His mother motioned him forward after a moment, and he slowly crawled out from underneath the booth and made his way over.

JADE ENCLAVE

Despite being on crutches, Detective Wei lowered himself down until he was at face level, and when he spoke, his voice came out soft and even. The boy answered, hesitantly at first, but little by little, more words came pouring out of him.

"What's he saying?" I asked.

Detective Wei waited for the boy to finish before he glanced up at me. "He says the order came in last night, and he rode on his bicycle to deliver it. He says a man met him at the door. From the way he described his clothes, it sounds like our victim. He took the bag and went into the kitchen to get the money. The boy knows he shouldn't have gone inside, but he was afraid they weren't going to pay him. He says it was dirty inside, and that it smelled bad."

"That sounds like our place."

"He says there was another man at the table. He had a drawing in front of him." Detective Wei frowned and said something to the boy. I got the sense that he was asking if the boy was sure. The boy repeated himself and nodded, and Wei's frown deepened as he straightened.

"Well, what was it?"

"A jade moon rising with the Chinese character for life flipped upside down in its center. It's the symbol for the Jiangshi."

"The what?"

"The undead," he said. "Specifically, a vampire."

I stared at him. Whatever else I'd been expecting, it wasn't that. "Vampire as in Count Dracula?"

Detective Wei made a sort-of gesture. "Not exactly. Dracula and his type are a Western European legend. Asian vampires are different."

"How so?"

"The Jiangshi are thought to be reanimated corpses, said to kill by absorbing their victim's chi or life force. No fangs. No need to drink blood."

"What about superhuman strength, nigh-invulnerability and immortality?"

"Those are all pretty much par for the course."

"Lovely," I said and exhaled. "Well, lucky for us, I've been around the block enough to know that vampires aren't real."

No sooner had the words left my mouth then the front door of the restaurant burst in with a sudden fury, striking the far wall as several figures came inside. The late afternoon sun cast them as shadows for the half second it took my eyes to adjust.

Once they had, I saw four men dressed in black kung fu garbs with green stitching and matching belts. Their heads were clean shaven, and their skin was pale and ashy, with dark lips and even darker circles around their eyes. They were armed, one with a slender sword on his hip. Another with a pair of nunchakus. A third bore a spear point connected to a chain, and a fourth held something in his palm I couldn't make out.

"Did I hear someone say that vampires aren't real?" The figure standing at their center peeled his lips back to reveal yellow, rotting teeth. "Perhaps we should put that to the test."

Jade Moon Rising. Friday, July 25th 1327hrs

Here's the thing about police work.

You can spend your entire life studying it. You can bury yourself in case files, criminal law, and psychological profiles, but the only way to truly understand it is to go out into the street and face it head-on. With experience comes enlightenment.

The past few months working in Blue Moon had served as a crash course in abnormal psychology and criminal behavior. I'd paid for each of my lessons in blood and tears, and they'd honed my skills and reflexes beyond what I'd previously believed was possible. I'd learned a lot about people, and I knew how to recognize a bag guy's entrance when I saw one.

JADE ENCLAVE

My gun cleared the holster before the lead figure finished speaking, my sights aligning on his forehead before the front door swung closed.

Nobody moved for a long second.

Then the lead figure pointedly stepped forward and spread his hands to either side. "Sergeant Mayfield, I presume? It is a pleasure to finally meet you. I confess, I had hoped it would come under different circumstances, but, as Sun Tzu once said, 'Within chaos lies opportunity.'"

"You know who I am?"

"Of course. Did you think we would arrive here with no understanding of the challenges we might face? Boston is not so large a place, and word of Blue Moon has spread far beyond its borders."

That was good to know, I guess. "Who are you?"

"Ah, of course. Introductions are in order. You may call me Cicuta."

"Sounds like a fancy kind of cheese," I said. "And I suppose you're going to tell me that you're an immortal vampire? The, what was it called, Jelly fish?"

"Jiangshi," Cicuta said, his voice tight. "And no."

"Then you're a peon?"

Cicuta's eyes flashed, and his anger shined out. "We are servants of the—"

"Thought so," I said, cutting him off. "Alright, how about we speed this along and you call your little chi-sucking buddy and tell him to get down here? What's his name, anyway?"

Cicuta's lips parted, and a low hiss slipped out before he answered. "The master bears no name. He has shed all traces of his mortal coil. He is Jiangshi, and we are his will given flesh. As he desires, so do we obey."

"Well, something tells me he's going to *desire* a meeting with me before long. So how about you hop along back where you came from and arrange it?"

Cicuta let out another hiss. "Such arrogance. To think that the master would rouse himself to deal with the likes of you."

"Oh I wouldn't worry about that part. I can be very persuasive, and barring that, pretty darn destructive, when I want to be."

"You overestimate your importance," he said. "In any event, we are not here for you." He turned his head, his gaze slipping past me to where the siblings stood. He held them pierced with his stare for a long moment, then his eyes dropped, his lips splitting into a cruel grin as he regarded the boy. "We are here for him."

A low, almost animalistic sound slipped past the young boy's mouth as he turned and buried his face into his mother's apron.

"Wow," I said. "Undead wannabe monsters coming out of the woodwork to abduct children? Even you can't deny that's a bit of a bad guy cliché."

"As I said, this does not concern you, Sergeant."

"Unfortunately, that's where you're wrong. Creepy, kung fu cronies looking to harm children is a solid no-go for me. Afraid I can't allow it."

He stared at the boy for a long moment, then glanced back up at me. "You lack the power to stop us."

"That's one theory," I said. "Want to hear another? If you or your little Jade Fang buddies take one more step, I'm going to blow a hole in your forehead, and we'll find out just how immortal you really are."

"Insolent cow. You are making a grave mistake, Sergeant. One you will come to severely regret."

"Man, if I had a nickel for every time I heard that, I could retire early and buy a houseboat. Alas, that doesn't seem to be in the cards. In the meantime, stay there and keep quiet. Detective Wei?"

"Yes?" Detective Wei asked.

"Would you be so kind as to escort the Guai family, as well as the rest of the diners, out through the back?"

"What about you?"

"I'll be fine." Another gun would have been useful, but I didn't know how effective he was, given his injuries. And besides, I wasn't going to send the civilians out there alone. "I'll keep them here long enough to give you time to make your getaway. But quicker is better. And if you see any of their friends lingering out back, put them down fast and hard."

"Understood." Detective Wei motioned to the diners, then herded them, along with the Guai family, through the kitchen. As they exited out the back door, the dining patrons fled in every direction. The grandmother, Lian, was the last to leave, a small flash of metal revealing the kitchen knife she had palmed.

Cicuta watched her go. "Keep your boy safe," he told her as she departed. "We will be along shortly to collect him."

"Not likely," I said, as the door swung closed "In fact, I don't think any of us are going to be going anywhere for a while. So I'd suggest you get comfy and—"

As I spoke, the Jade Fang cronies shifted, and the one farthest to the left abruptly jerked to the side and flicked his hand. I caught a brief glimpse of a shuriken's spinning edge before it struck the barrel of my pistol. Pain flashed from my hand up my arm, and my fingers opened of their own accord, my pistol slipping from my grasp and crashing to the floor a second before the closest Jade Fang leapt toward me.

He threw himself into the air, tucked one leg and kicked out with the other. Instinct took over, and I dropped into a low crouch an instant before his foot would have taken my head off. I felt the wind of his motion as he swept past overhead, and no sooner had I straightened then another Jade Fang moved to take his place.

Full disclosure, I wasn't some fancy martial artist, but growing up in New England had imparted a certain amount of scrappiness in me. Evidently, the vampire wannabe hadn't gotten that memo. He swept up beside me, his lips peeling apart into a wide, cruel grin as he brought his hands up, spreading them apart and inviting me to take my best shot.

Which I did.

Twice.

The Jade Fang clearly had me pegged as a newbie, and as such, likely expected me to attack in a straight line toward his face or maybe his torso. I'd been in my share of fist fights before now, and the past six months had taught me the value of attacking where your opponent least suspects. It also taught me the value of misdirection, particularly in the way of giving your opponent exactly what they think they want, and then pulling the rug, literally and metaphorically, out from under them.

I lashed out with a simple jab, my fist traveling toward the Jade Fang's nose. Rather than fully commit, I stopped when I was still a hand's length away, and snapped my fingers, the sudden *popping* noise causing his eyes to jerk toward my hand.

Which is when I kicked him in the knee.

I threw my weight behind the kick, and the bottom of my foot struck him directly on the kneecap. I felt his knee flex, heard the sound of something pop, and savored the scream that tore from his mouth in the second before he crumpled to the ground.

Unfortunately, any victory I may have had was short lived.

No sooner did the Jade Fang go down then Cicuta moved in to take his place. I saw him coming, and lashed out fast, hoping to overwhelm him with a three-punch boxing combination. He was expecting it though, and parried the first of my punches, then effortlessly ducked beneath the other two. I had a sudden flash of realization that none of my tricks were going to be enough to fool him, but by then it was already too late. He came up along my side, and I tried to turn, but my feet were out of position, and the best I could manage was to tuck my head a split second before his fist struck. He hit me along the side, down near the bottom of my ribs, and the blow resonated throughout my whole body. All the air fled from my lungs, and a desperate gasp slipped out past my lips a split second before he struck again. This one hit me high up on the side of the head, and the entire world went topsy-turvy in the blink of an eye. I ended up face down on the floor, my fingers digging into the hardwood in an attempt to stop the room from spinning.

Cicuta loomed above me for a split second, then reached down and seized me by the back of the neck. He lifted me from the ground and held me suspended like a limp rag before he brought his hand up in front of my face. He pressed his palm close to my face, then slowly drew it away, as if pulling an invisible sheet from my face. At the same time, he made a low, almost animalistic sound, as if he were devouring some unseen wonder.

To be honest, I didn't feel anything from the motion, although I was knocked senseless and distracted by the pain. Whether he was actually draining my life essence, I couldn't say, but regardless of whether it was fact or fiction I didn't care to watch it happen.

I turned my face away, desperate to focus on anything besides these kung fu freaks, and that's when I noticed the new figure as she slid into the room.

She was probably a head and a half taller than me, with chocolate cherry hair and dark brown eyes. And she was buff. Like, She-Hulk buff. Her department issued patrol officer's uniform fit her snuggly, especially around the arms and shoulders, which were on full display as she seized the nearest chair and lifted it into the air.

Cicuta gave me a rough jerk, snapping my gaze back around. Dimly, I realized he'd been saying something, likely gloating, but I hadn't the faintest idea what, and it didn't matter, because a split second after our eyes met the female officer brought the chair down over the back of his head.

The wood broke with a resounding *crack*, and he pitched forward, dropping me to the floor as he went down in a sprawl. I hit the hardwood and blinked rapidly, managing to clear my vision after a moment and glancing up to see my rescuer as she went to work battling my attackers.

The closest Jade Fang swept in, striking with a clawed palm. She saw it coming, and dropped the broken chair legs, ducking back and allowing the blow to pass in front of her face before she bounced back and drove her fist into the Jade Fang's mouth hard enough to send a tooth flying. Then, before he could recover, she seized the front of his kung fu garb and lifted him into the air, spinning him around like a professional wrestler and spiking him down head first as if he were a football.

JADE ENCLAVE

Something flashed past me, and I screamed a warning. It came out as more of a mewling cry, but my rescuer spun around as another of the Jade Fangs leapt into the air. He tucked one leg and made to strike with the other, but my rescuer was faster. She shot in and seized his leg before he could uncoil it. Gripping him around the ankle, she spun violently, completing a full circle before flinging him like one of those shot-put athletes you see in the Olympics. The Jade Fang flew over the booth and crashed against the wall hard enough that I feared the entire building might come down on our heads. He rebounded and crashed limply to the floor as my rescuer turned and kneeled beside me.

She seized me around the arm and started to lift, but Cicuta had roused himself, and he hissed and shot in, striking low and then high. His foot impacted against my rescuer's thigh with a heavy *thwack*, but she barely flinched, her leg remaining firmly planted as she tucked her head and deflected the second blow off her shoulder.

Cicuta went to strike again, but my rescuer snapped her arm out, seized him by the front of his garment, and slammed her forehead into his nose. Cartilage broke with a resounding *crack* and I had a sudden suspicion that he wouldn't need makeup to darken his eyes in the coming weeks.

The impact knocked him silly and left him stumbling on wobbly legs. Not wanting to give him time to recover, my rescuer raised her leg and drove her foot into his belly, sending him crashing backwards across the floor.

The room spun and my eyesight blurred, the edges of my vision going dark. I'm not sure how many seconds passed but the next thing I knew my rescuer was lifting me up off the floor. I seized her arm, and tried to protest, but all that came out was a string of garbled nonsense.

There was a moment of confusion, then my rescuer noted my empty holster and scanned the floor until she saw my gun. It probably says something about me that, even knocked silly, I refused to give the department any excuse to fine me. They'd already threatened to do just that once it came out that I'd lost more guns in the line of duty than any other officer on the force. No way I was going to give those penny-pinching jerks in accounting the satisfaction of seeing my already meager paycheck docked.

My rescuer retrieved my pistol, shoving it back into my holster before half-carrying me out through the door. The afternoon sunlight struck my eyes like a spike through the temple, and a low groan echoed past my lips as she paused by the doorway to retrieve a nylon backpack before helping me over to my vehicle.

I could barely stand as she plucked the keys from my pocket. The passenger's door opened with a rusted *creak,* and she tossed her bag into the back before she lowered me down inside and buckled my seatbelt. I leaned forward and tried to speak, but it was just more garbled nonsense, and after a moment she patted me on the shoulder, the simple motion enough to send me back in the chair.

"If that's some kind of long winded thank you, then you're welcome. But I need you to sit back right now. The sooner we're away from here, the better off we'll be."

I let out a groan that I hoped she would take for total agreement.

Unexpected Allies. Friday, July 25th 1402hrs

We drove for the better part of twenty minutes. I spent most of that time with my head back and my eyes closed. Part of me wanted to sleep, but the other part was too fueled by what had just happened to allow myself to slip into unconsciousness. The two sides battled for dominance, the latter steadily gaining ground as the world gradually came back into focus.

First things first. I did a quick self-assessment and concluded that, although I was bruised, tired, and sore, I wasn't entirely out of the fight.

I also wasn't entirely in the fight either if that makes any sense. Not yet anyway. I needed time to regroup and gather my wits.

And, more importantly, I needed more information about what we were dealing with.

Starting with the Jiangshi.

Vampires were bad enough, but at least there were common themes that veered toward predictability when dealing with them. You had your staples of power: dominance, blood drinking, and tight leather pants. Tropes and expectations that you could set your hat on and direct your investigation accordingly.

Kung fu vampires, however, were a whole other ball game. And I didn't know what I didn't know.

You know?

I let that play on words rattle around in my head for a bit before reluctantly setting it aside and focusing on what little I did know.

Starting with the Jade Fangs.

For one, they didn't actually have fangs. I'd heard it from Detective Wei, then seen it for myself when my rescuer backhanded one and sent his tooth flying. No fangs and, by extension, no blood drinking. Good to know.

Furthermore, they obviously weren't from here. Cicuta had outright said as much. *"Did you think we would arrive here with no understanding of the challenges we might face?"*

That was concerning for several reasons.

So much of law enforcement comes down to making quick decisions. The call for aid goes out, patrol officers respond, and from there it devolves into a series of snap-decisions dictated by circumstance, training, and experience.

Don't believe me? Go look up the national averages concerning offenders who flee in vehicles. You'll find that, by and large, most of them end up getting caught. Why? Not because they're not determined to evade us, but because they're making it up as they go, shifting from one decision to the next with little time to consider their overall strategy.

Meanwhile, the police pursuing them have strength of numbers and, oftentimes, better geographic knowledge of the surrounding streets. It allows them to head off the offenders, set traps, etc. Mindless fleeing from the cops gives them all the advantages, and the longer it goes on, the less chance the offenders have of getting away.

This was different though.

JADE ENCLAVE

The Jade Fangs knew my name. No one goes to the trouble of scouting out the local law enforcement ahead of time unless they're planning to come up against them. They knew me, which meant it was a safe bet they knew everyone within our division. Which, I don't mind admitting, was scary as heck.

I'll happily cling to the reputation of being stubborn and hard-headed, but I draw the line at naïve or, even worse, stupid. I believed in our division. I believed in our mission and to a greater degree, our capabilities. That being said, my experience with the United Fairy Commonwealth had shown me just how unprepared Blue Moon was to fight a war. Especially one like this. The residents of Song Grove had been fighting for their freedom, but the methods they'd employed, while annoying, had been of the less lethal variety. The Jade Fangs didn't strike me as the less lethal type.

For the first time that day, I found myself suddenly grateful that we weren't in our usual headquarters. The thought of them slinking in through the garage, pushing past the door and striking down our team one by one sent a cold shiver running through me.

Robbie, Pongo, Cambrie and Lieutenant Kermit all had their own areas of expertise. But taking on ninja vampires wasn't in their wheelhouse. I was the only one in the division who could even remotely be considered combat effective, and I hadn't lasted more than two minutes before being disarmed and incapacitated. Fact is, if not for my rescuer's timely intervention, I'd probably be bleeding out on the floor of the restaurant right now.

Speaking of which.

I opened my eyes and turned in my seat, taking a moment to regard said rescuer as she drove. She was roughly my age, give or take a few years, with naturally tanned skin that had nothing to do with the summer. Her chocolate cherry hair hung halfway down her shoulders, curling near the ends, and the curves and musculature in her arms and shoulders reminded me of a high-level CrossFit athlete. Definitive, but not so masculine that anyone would confuse her as being a member of the opposite sex.

"Hi there," I said, unsure until the last moment if my voice was going to come out as intended or if I would still be reduced to spitting garbled nonsense.

She blinked and glanced over in surprise. "Hi. You're back already?"

"Think so."

"I figured you would need a few more hours. Head wounds can be nasty that way."

"Not the first time I've been whacked upside the noggin. Probably won't be the last." I shifted as I spoke, rising up and angling myself so that my gun wasn't digging into my side. It also, sheerly by happenstance, allowed me to change positions to where I could draw my pistol if needed.

I mentioned earlier that working in Blue Moon had given me a crash course in abnormal psychology. It had also taught me the value of skepticism and how, when something seems too good to be true, then it most likely was.

For example, let's say I was getting beaten down and a total stranger came to my aid and whisked me away to safety. Most people would say don't look a gift horse in the mouth, but experience told me it was best to keep my guard up until I could ascertain my rescuer's motives.

"Help you with something?"

"Eh?" I asked.

"You're staring at me."

Crud. I probably was. Head wounds make time do funny things. Most likely I wasn't quite as recovered as I thought. "Sorry."

"No worries. Here." She reached behind her into the backseat, lowered the zipper to her backpack and dug around inside before retrieving a light blue plastic pouch about the size of my palm. She brought it forward, then tightened her hand into a fist. Something cracked inside, but I didn't realize what it meant until she handed it over, and I felt the sudden cold coming from the center.

I made an appreciative noise and brought the ice pouch up to the back of my neck, sighing as the cool sensation swept through me.

"Not bad, right?"

"Not bad at all," I agreed as I leaned back in the seat. I savored the feeling for several seconds, then forced myself to return to the matter at hand. "Ask you something?"

"Sure."

"Who are you?"

"Oh, right. I probably should have started with that. Name's Thaysa, but everyone calls me Tootsie."

"Tootsie," I said. "Who do you work for? Patrol?"

"Used to. As of this morning, I work for you."

"Eh?"

"You're Sergeant Chloe Mayfield, right? Blue Moon Division?"

"Yeah."

She shrugged. "In that case, I'm the new girl. Officer Alves, reporting for duty. Didn't they tell you I was coming?"

I thought back, recalling the extra cubicle inside our headquarters, as well as my conversation with Lieutenant Kermit. He had mentioned a new officer was coming on board, although there wasn't much information about her.

"They were a little light on the details. What are you in for?"

"In for?"

"Come on, Thaysa."

"Tootsie. Might as well get in the habit now."

"Tootsie, then. Let's not start off on the wrong foot by playing dumb. No one ends up in Blue Moon by accident. What's your story?"

"Permission to speak freely, Sergeant?"

"Granted."

"If it's all the same to you, I'd rather not discuss it right now. I'm sure you'll hear about it eventually, but for the moment, just know that it won't affect my work or my abilities in the field. Fair?"

I considered it. On one hand, I didn't like the idea of having an unknown liability within the division. That way led to disaster. On the other, she had just saved my life, so maybe I should give her the benefit of the doubt. Besides, forcing someone to discuss something they didn't want to talk about rarely led to a positive working environment.

"Alright," I said, leaning my head back and closing my eyes. "We can put a pin in the conversation. For now."

"Appreciate it," she said, and steered the conversation back to the matter at hand. "Who were those guys back there?"

"Lackeys." I felt her questioning stare without having to open my eyes. "They have a certain feeling to them. You get used to it after a while. I'm calling them Jade Fangs."

"What did they want?"

"The kid, apparently, although it's anyone's guess why."

"No clues?"

"Depends what you mean by clues." As briefly as possible, I filled her in on the corpse from this morning, as well as the two bodies we'd found back at the apartment building. She made a tight-throated sound when I described the violence inflicted on them. That was good. I was firmly of the opinion that police officers shouldn't be strangers to violence, but I also didn't want someone in our division who reveled in it. Folks like that have a way of corrupting everyone around them.

"My gut tells me that the two men inside the apartment were involved in something nefarious, and whatever it was got them killed. As for the kid, I'm operating on the assumption that they want to question him to see what he might have seen or heard while inside. Unfortunately, I don't have enough information to even speculate what that something might be. Likewise, I've got nothing to connect any of this to the corpse that fell on my head. It's all just a giant jumble that I can't make heads or tails of."

Tootsie made a considering noise. "So what are we going to do?"

"We focus on our victims. Keep digging until something rises to the surface that makes it make sense. Hopefully it'll happen sooner rather than later. Which reminds me, where are we going?"

"Back to the station. I passed Detective Wei on my way inside. He said he'd meet us there once he got the civilians to safety."

I made an affirmative sound and pressed the ice pack to the back of my neck, remaining still for the rest of the ride.

Once we reached the station, Tootsie pulled into the lot. She parked well away from the other patrol vehicles, out near the far end, which I greatly appreciated.

When I'd first been transferred to Blue Moon, I'd taken our exile from headquarters as just another in a long line of insults. As the months had passed, however, I'd grown more appreciative of the space. It was true that our division wasn't typical, and our cases required a delicate touch. There was no way we would have been able to successfully navigate our workload with Deputy Bulwark constantly looking over our shoulders. In many ways, our exile to the Government Parking Garage was the only reason we'd made it this far.

Tootsie kept the engine running, and I shifted the vent to allow the air conditioner to keep blowing on my face. We sat there for the better part of fifteen minutes before a patrol car pulled in. It parked along the curb, and Detective Wei got out of the passenger's side. He spoke a few words, and the patrol officer in the driver's seat gave a friendly wave before pulling away.

Detective Wei watched him go, then peered around, spotting us when Tootsie flashed her lights. He started our way, moving at a steady pace despite the crutches, and Tootsie and I exited the vehicle.

"Is everyone okay?" I asked. "The Guai family is safe?"

Detective Wei nodded. "Yes, and yes. They're with friends. They were reluctant to leave the city at first, but I convinced them it was for the best. They're gathering a few essentials and will be on the road within the hour."

"Good enough I suppose."

"What happens now?" Detective Wei asked. "Do we report what happened back there?"

I shook my head. "And say what? That kung fu vampires have invaded Chinatown and tried to kidnap a child who's since gone into hiding? Dispatch would just kick it over to Blue Moon and we'd be right back where we started."

I left off the second half of that thought. Even if Bulwark backed me, which was a big if, what then? I'd be lying if I said there wasn't a part of me that wanted to turn around and head back into Chinatown, but another part, the more logical side, knew that wasn't a good idea.

Firstly, sending armed officers door-to-door through a residential neighborhood should always be treated as a last resort. There's just too much that can go wrong too quickly. Especially in a place like Boston, which had a strong reputation of being a fighting man's town. Martial arts schools littered the surrounding area. Kung fu, karate, mixed martial arts, you name it. If we started rounding up anyone with a fighting background and accusing them of being in league with an immortal chi-sucker, we'd have a full-blown riot on our hands in no time.

Secondly, I knew a thing or two about gang mentality, and even if I was able to round up every Jade Fang in Boston, it wouldn't matter. My problem wasn't the Jade Fangs. My problem was the Jiangshi. He was the head. The master vampire. And if he was even half competent, he'd shed the Jade Fang cronies as easily as a serpent sheds its skin and replace them in short order. If I was going to put a stop to the killings, then I needed to put a stop to him.

Unfortunately, that was easier said than done. I didn't know anything about him. Not even his name. And granted, Chinatown wasn't that big of a place, but there was no guarantee he was in Chinatown, or even Boston for that matter. Experience had taught me that I couldn't afford to sit back and wait, not in cases like these, but I had no way of hunting him, no trail to follow beyond that of our victims.

Unless, maybe I did and just hadn't realized it until now.

As I stood there, it occurred to me that maybe I did know something about this Jiangshi. Vampires are defined by their predatory nature, whether its blood or chi. If he was in Boston, then he would need to feed. That meant bodies. Or at the very least, missing persons.

JADE ENCLAVE

And I already knew of one.

Hui Lan's roommate. What was her name? Oh, right. Ru Yee. A Chinese immigrant here attending MIT on a student visa. Replaying Hui's story in my mind, it struck me that the symptoms she'd described, the ones I'd thought to be drug related withdrawals, could have been something else. Maybe she'd run afoul of this Jiangshi, and he'd... not fed on her. That wasn't the right word. And not just because I didn't believe in vampires, no matter their nationality. But maybe he'd given her something. Gotten her hooked in order to make her play along with his fantasies. We'd seen such cases before, and considering that it was my only real lead, it suddenly seemed worth looking into.

Which led me to my next area of concern.

Running a successful police division all came down to knowing how to allocate your resources, and in this case, that meant your people. Right now, Blue Moon Division was displaced. It would take time to find our footing, and if I was going to stay focused on this vampire case, I'd need Cambrie, Robbie, and Pongo to pick up the slack while dealing with the day-to-day calls.

The neighbors casting voodoo curses on each other from the safety of their front lawn. The elderly woman who believed her cat contained the reincarnated soul of Ludwig Von Beethoven. The never-ending parade of ghosts, goblins, and boogeymen who haunted our closests and attics. None of that was going to stop just because I already had a full plate. And sure, ninety-nine percent of it was utter nonsense, but someone still had to show up and take down the report.

All that was just to say, for the moment at least, the rest of the division was going to be busy covering for me. We were on our own, and if we wanted to survive this, we would need to proceed carefully.

I exhaled and straightened my shoulders. "Okay, here's what we're going to do. Detective Wei, don't take this the wrong way, but you're not exactly field capable."

"Can't really argue with that," he said, raising his crutches in a casual shrug. "IS there anything I can do?"

"Research," I said. "This Jiangshi and his Jade Fang cronies didn't come to Boston for the lobster rolls or the clam chowder. They want something, and the sooner we can find out what they're really after, the better."

"Is that all?"

"No. See if you can't figure out the connection to our victims. They're all wrapped up in this somehow. Darned if I can see the pattern, but if you find something, anything, then it's probably worth looking into."

"I can do that," Detective Wei said. "Where will you be?"

"That all depends." I turned and fixed Tootsie with a pointed look. "I appreciate what you did back at the restaurant, but before we go any further, I need to know if you're ready for this. I know some people prefer to hit the ground running, but kung fu vampires are a tough first day for anyone. It won't hurt my feelings if you'd rather sit this one out."

Tootsie snorted and crossed her arms. "Are you kidding me? I've spent the last three months babysitting drunks at the hospital and sitting watch over nighttime construction sites while the brass tried to figure out what to do with me. Trust me, ninja vampires are a breath of fresh air compared to the sheer boredom I've already endured." She was grinning by the time she finished, and the expression was infectious.

"Okay then," I said. "That's settled. Wei, get cracking. Meanwhile, Tootsie and I are going hunting."

MIT. Friday, July 25th 1530hrs

I LET TOOTSIE DRIVE. My head was still throbbing, and I didn't have it in me to fight the afternoon traffic. "So, where are we going exactly?" she asked as we pulled out of the station parking lot.

"I told you. Hunting."

"Right. I got that part. Any particular area of the city you want to focus on?"

"Just head toward MIT."

"You think the vampire is in college?"

"No. But I got a report this morning of a missing girl. Pieces of the story weren't adding up, but in light of what we've learned about the Jiangshi, I want to take a closer look."

"Gotcha." We lapsed into silence that lasted until we were halfway over the Longfellow Bridge before she spoke again. "Is it always like this?"

"Like what?"

"Blue Moon. I mean, I read the reports, and I heard from some of the other officers, but I still wasn't sure what to expect."

"It can be a little confusing at first," I said. "Truth is, I've been here for eight months and I'm still figuring it out. One thing I do know though. What we do, it has meaning. It's important."

"Because we're enforcing the law?"

"Yeah, but there's more to it than that. Blue Moon is different from other divisions. We're a lone ray of hope for people who find themselves confronting the terrors they thought they left behind in childhood. The ghosts, the boogeymen, and, in this case, the vampires that scared us all so badly when we were young."

"It's tough to be little," Tootsie said.

"It is," I agreed. "Worse still, our bad guys aren't your everyday garden variety. Fear is their weapon of choice. They use it to manipulate and to terrorize. To make our victims feel small and alone. All for the sake of lining their pockets or gratifying their own ego. That's why we don't tolerate it. Not us, or Tempest, or any of the others following suit. We stand against that fear and stare unflinching into the darkness. We unmask the horrors and by doing so, give people back their dignity. We let them sleep at night, secure in the knowledge that those who would prey on them are safely in handcuffs."

"And after that?"

"What?"

"I'm all for the arresting part. I'm just curious what happens after? Presumably they go to trial, right? What's that like?"

It was a good question. One we'd struggled with before Pongo arrived. His legal knowledge had proved invaluable, and he'd quickly established himself as the go-between for Blue Moon and the district attorney's office.

"Usually we try to downplay the supernatural and fantastical aspects. Focus on the facts of the case. For example, those leprechauns last year? Bank robbers. Strip away the shamrocks and highlight the elements of the crime itself. How they did it. Why they did it. The evidence connecting them. Make the leprechaun motif sound exactly like what it was. A theatrical gimmick."

"What about the smaller cases? The ones that are less high-profile. More personal."

"Focus on the victim. Give the jury a reason to believe our perpetrator had motive to want to cause them harm. One strong enough to explain why they would've concocted whatever ridiculous masquerade they cooked up."

"How's our conviction rate?"

"Not perfect, but it could be a lot worse."

And that was just the god's honest truth.

The dormitories at MIT were on the southern edge of campus overlooking the Charles River. Red-brick multi-story structures surrounded by manicured lawns, their old-world New England aesthetic stood in sharp contrast to the futuristic, geometrically diverse glass buildings that comprised the rest of the campus. We parked along the side of the road outside the Burton-Conner house, and I paused to grab my flashlight and a few other investigating essentials before we made our way up onto the sidewalk. The front entrance was open, and we passed through a small entryway before taking the elevator up to the fourth floor.

"Just so I'm clear, what exactly are we looking for?" Tootsie asked. "Detective Wei said these guys aren't like normal vampires. So there shouldn't be any blood, right?"

"Shouldn't doesn't always mean won't be," I said. "And even if there's not, we still want to be on the lookout for any potential evidence that might give us a clue or provide insight into what this Jiangshi might be doing here."

There was more to it than that, but I was reluctant to voice it out loud.

This wasn't the first time Blue Moon had run up against vampires. We'd encountered them here in Boston as well as over in England. Regardless of whether they were playing Dracula or Emperor Ming, one consistency across the board was their ability to buy into the delusion that they were an immortal creature of the night.

The ones we'd tangled with before had rewritten their identities and sculpted their entire persona to align with that belief. If this Jiangshi believed he needed to feed on this girl, it would explain why he'd risked coming back for her. Even worse, if he believed repeated feedings would eventually kill her, he would follow that fantasy all the way down to its inevitable conclusion.

The elevator doors pinged open, and we made our way down the hall, drawing up beside the doorway. I pressed my ear against the door and listened for a slow ten count, but there was only silence from the other end, and when I inserted the key, the front doorway creaked open to reveal the chaos beyond.

What should have been a minimalistic living room more closely resembled a war zone. A faded old blue sofa sat at an awkward angle, opposite a recliner chair which had been tipped on its side. A mostly full bag of microwave popcorn had fallen from its perch atop the chair's arm, spilling its contents onto the floor. I sniffed the air, but there was no lingering trace of butter or salt. Which meant it had been there for a couple of days. A fact which aligned with Hui's story.

Opposite the upturned chair was a bookshelf filled with textbooks and notebooks. Its base had snapped, and it leaned precariously against the wall, half its contents spilled onto the ground. Crumpled papers were scattered across the floor.

Tootsie let out a low whistle. "Wow."

"Shut the door behind you," I said and stepped inside.

I dug into my back pocket and withdrew a pair of latex gloves. Once ready, I sidestepped my way around the living room and into the nearby kitchen. An upturned coffee cup sat on top of the counter, its spilled contents having long since dried. The trashcan was seventy-five percent full, but it was mostly papers and handwritten study notes, so the smell wasn't too bad. I started on the far side of the room, and passed through systematically, checking the cupboards, cabinets, and refrigerator.

It was the usual fare. Quick, cheap food consisting mostly of instant noodles in bags with Chinese lettering. Some canned goods and brightly colored shrimp chips. There were a handful of vegetables inside the refrigerator, but they'd long since spoiled.

I closed the refrigerator and made my way back through the living room before stepping into a narrow hallway which led to two bedrooms. The first door I came to was open. I peeked inside and saw it was in a similar state to the living room.

The bed was a tangle of sheets and blankets twisted into unrecognizable knots. One pillow, its side split and its stuffing spilling out, had been flung across the room, landing on the floor next to an overturned desk chair. The desk beside the window was a mess, lined with torn papers and pages crudely ripped from the textbooks. On the floor beneath a shattered picture frame showing Hui smiling in front of a large Chinese temple were a pair of discarded sneakers, their laces cut. A lone sock sat in the center of the carpet, with no sign of its other half.

"Something about this feel off to you?" Tootsie asked, peering over my shoulder.

It did, but it took me a minute to realize what. Looking around, the feeling that came over me was that I was looking at something staged. There was a manufactured disarray to the entire thing that my mind struggled to reconcile. I stared for a few moments longer, then shook my head and moved on to the second room.

JADE ENCLAVE

The door was closed. Glancing at the nearest wall, I noted several scuff marks right about chest level. The exact height a woman's shoes might be if she were being carried out, or so I estimated. Glancing at the opposite wall, I noted several scratch marks down near the baseboards. Three pronounced scrapes, with hints of a fourth line beside it. I turned my hand around and matched the lines up with my fingernails. As my fingertips brushed the wall, I had a flash of Hui kneeling there, her back pressed against the drywall, digging her nails into the wall so hard that she scraped away the paint.

Old memories swelled up inside, and my heart began rapidly beating in my chest. It was a familiar fear. Brought about by having experienced the terror of knowing someone had been in my home. Someone dangerous. Someone uninvited. In my case, a maniacal killer clown. In Hui's case, a vampire. Stark differences, although the result was much the same.

I drew in a breath and forced the feeling down, slamming shut the door in my mind before I was forced to relive the months I'd spent excessively checking my apartment. Every time I entered, I'd done so with my gun drawn. I'd checked every nook, every corner, and when that was no longer sufficient to set my mind at ease, I'd begun paring down my belongings, discarding any excess in an attempt to limit an intruder's hiding places. I'd traded in my shower curtain for clear plastic and wouldn't so much as take out the trash unless I was armed. Even after Bloodcuddles was caught and convicted, I still found my life had been altered by the knowledge that he'd been in my home. That he touched my belongings, likely laid his head on my pillow.

They say home is where the heart is. But knowing someone had been inside waiting to kill you has a way of draining all the romance out of that sentiment. A part of me hoped Hui would be able to get past it. But another part of me knew that was like an amputee hoping their arm would grow back in the middle of the night.

Lovely if it happened. But not likely.

Instead of holding out hope for something I couldn't control, I needed to focus on what I could actually do. And that meant finding this Jiangshi, carting him and all his little kung fu buddies off to jail, and bringing Hui's roommate home safely. It wouldn't undo the trauma they'd endured, but it was better than the alternative.

I swept open the door to the bedroom and the air that came out hit me clean in the chest. It was cold, at least ten or fifteen degrees colder than the rest of the apartment. And stale. Not stale like a bag of old bread. More like the scent of dried flowers crumbling in your hand.

A sense of wrongness threatened to send me back out to the hall, but I gathered myself and held firm until it passed. Once it had subsided, I crossed the threshold and walked two steps into the middle of the room. Then I did a slow survey.

Where Hui's room had been theatrically ransacked, Ru's looked as if it had been tossed by someone on the verge of an emotional breakdown. The closet door was open, and most of the clothes had been torn from their hangers and left in uneven piles along the floor. A similar desk to the one in Hui's room sat near the window, but the textbooks had been cast onto the floor and kicked into uneven stacks in the corner. The top of the desk was littered with scratches and small stab wounds likely inflicted by the broken pencil that lay in splinters along the desk's surface.

I allowed myself a moment to take it in. Then I turned and looked towards the section of the room I was most reluctant to view. The bed lay unmade, the blanket kicked carelessly to the floor. The sheets beneath hadn't been changed for some time, and there was a salty, sour odor coming from them. I'd encountered similar scents before. Usually when dealing with drug addicts or those freshly checked into detox. It wasn't quite the same aroma as I might have found in a cocaine or meth addict's home, but it was in a similar wheelhouse.

"No blood," Tootsie said.

For a moment I'd forgotten she was there, but then I became aware of her standing by my shoulder. Peering down toward the bed. I didn't know her well enough to know if she understood what she was looking at, but I gave her the benefit of the doubt and figured she was trying to be helpful.

And she was right.

There was no blood.

Of course there wouldn't be. Like Detective Wei said, Jiangshi had no use for blood. One could argue they were after something more intimate, but I figured I'd leave that to the psychologists and mythology students to decide.

"Want me to strip the sheets?" Tootsie asked. "We could take them with us."

"No," I said.

I couldn't give them over to forensics without giving them the full details of the case. And even if they believed me, which, let's be honest, was a big if, they would kick it up the ladder to Deputy Bulwark, who would have no choice but to treat it as a kidnapping.

That meant making the university aware. It meant seeking out the next of kin, and, more than likely, holding a press conference to ask for the public's assistance. From there, the department would start a search, and, since I was the one who'd brought this to Bulwark's attention, I'd most likely spend the next several days going door to door interviewing potential witnesses.

I would've done it in a heartbeat if I thought it would help bring Ru home, but I feared it would have the opposite effect. Letting the Jiangshi know that we were on to him would only push him to make Ru, or more likely her corpse, disappear. Even worse, he'd likely view our involvement as an open declaration of war. Given what I already knew about how he'd been researching Blue Moon, it seemed likely he would respond in kind. That meant a hit against us.

Again, I counted my blessings that there was no one at headquarters right now. Unfortunately, I knew it wouldn't take that much effort to find where we were. If the Jade Fangs attacked the Union Oyster House, we'd be sitting ducks. Especially if I was too busy knocking on doors to fight.

I didn't doubt the Jiangshi had been here. I could feel it, like a thousand tiny needles grinding their tips against my bones. There was a sense of wrongness in the room. A heaviness to the air, carrying a quiet sense of dread.

And whatever he was after, it clearly wasn't a game. I didn't want him to know we were onto him until the last possible moment. Otherwise, it would be all too easy for him to vanish into the shadows. I couldn't allow that. I needed him thinking everything was going according to plan right up until the minute we were ready to pounce.

"Come on, I said. "We're done here."

An Unexpected Offer. Friday, July 25th 1549hrs

WE EXITED THE APARTMENT, being sure to close and lock the door behind us. I took off my gloves as we stepped out into the hall, folding them inside out and stuffing them down into my back pocket. Tootsie peeled hers off and started toward the trash can, but I stopped her with a hand on her arm.

"Keep them."

"What?"

"Your gloves," I explained.

"Why?"

"Because I'm ninety percent sure that apartment is the scene of a kidnapping. And just because we can't prove it right now doesn't mean it won't matter down the line."

"Okay," she said drawing out the word.

I could tell she thought I was being paranoid, but that's only because she didn't know what I knew. "Look, if you're going to last here, there are some things you need to know. First among them, we've had something of a spotty relationship with Forensics Division. Which means that, as of this moment, you're responsible for all your parts. That includes hair, fingernails, blood, even spit. Treat them all as if they can be used against you and conduct yourself accordingly."

"Wait, you think Forensics Division would plant evidence against us?"

"I think they've already done it once, and there's no reason to believe they won't try again. Even if they don't, the last thing you want to do is leave a pair of gloves with your DNA lying around near a crime scene."

"Right," Tootsie said, stuffing the gloves in her pocket. "Consider it noted. Anything else?"

"Homicide Division. They *really* hate us. Steer clear when you can, and don't give them any reason to know your name." I sighed and pinched the bridge of my nose. "There's more. A lot more. But I'm too tired to think of it right now. Let's just focus on this and I'll catch you up when I can."

"Alright," said Tootsie as we made our way down to the elevator. She pressed the down button, and the little light came on in response. "The Jiangshi then. Suppose we're right, and he took this girl to feed on. This isn't why he's here. I mean, he wouldn't come all this way with his entire Cobra Kai clan just for one girl, would he?"

"I don't know," I said. "The Spartans and the Trojans went to war for just one girl."

"You think that's what this is?"

"I hope not. Until we find more evidence, let's assume she's more of a peripheral concern for the Jiangshi."

"Fair enough. What *do* you think he's doing here?"

"Honestly, I have no clue." I rolled my shoulders and tried to clear my thoughts. Now that the adrenaline from being inside the apartment was fading, the lack of sleep and food were beginning to take their toll. I could feel the brain fog slowly working its way through my skull. At this point I'd been on duty for almost twenty-one hours. I needed to sleep and refuel. I also needed to run by my apartment. Yosemite was probably more than a little peeved that he'd been forced to skip not one but two meals. At least I'd made sure to fill his water before going on shift last night.

"Let's assume he has a reason beyond abducting young women. There are three corpses that tell me it's somehow connected to Chinatown. Either he's here for something or for someone. If it's the latter, I don't think we've found them yet. Maybe the corpses inside the apartment knew about it, but they're not telling. Or maybe the one that fell on my head. I don't know."

"What if it's a thing?"

"Then we need to find out what it is. If it's a physical item, then we need to find it first, and use it as leverage to draw the Jiangshi out of hiding."

"So we can kick his butt?"

"Exactly. If it's more of a nonphysical entity..."

"Nonphysical Entity?"

"Power. Possession. Say he wants to rule Chinatown. It's more of a goal than a physical item."

"Gotcha. What do we do if that's the case?"

"Hopefully, we find him first and put a stop to it."

JADE ENCLAVE

"What if we can't find him?"

"Find out who stands against him and assist them as best we can. Warfare through proxy."

"Sounds rough."

"And long," I agreed. "But we can't just sit by and do nothing."

The elevator doors opened, and we stepped inside. Tootsie pressed the button for the ground floor, and I exhaled and leaned back, resting my head against the cool metal.

The elevator doors started to close, but a hand suddenly appeared between them, halting them in their tracks. I cracked open my eyes as the doors spread apart and two men got on. They were both of Asian descent, and too old by half a decade to be living in a dormitory. Dressed in black suits with crisp white dress shirts, their expressions were stern, their hair cut short and neat, and each bore an identical bulge under their suit jacket.

I knew a concealed holster when I saw one, and a soft flutter rose from my stomach to settle in my chest. A quick glance to my right revealed Tootsie hadn't noticed anything amiss yet. I considered nudging her, but caution held my hand. The elevator doors closed, and we descended, stopping at the next floor, where four more men with matching aesthetic stepped inside.

There was a shifting of feet, as they spread themselves wide, forcing Tootsie and I back against the wall. I snaked out one hand to flick Tootsie's arm. She blinked, seemingly taking note for the first time of the way we'd been boxed in. I watched her take stock of the situation, and the muscles tightened in her jaw. She brought her arms up, seemingly resting her hands on her belt, but I knew it was so she could better defend herself if things went bad.

Which, by all indications, seemed likely.

The elevator doors shut, and I drew in a long breath, considering my next move as we began our descent. Most traps, the simplistic ones at any rate, work best when the target never sees them coming. They're left struggling to digest what's happened, not wanting to believe their eyes as the net closes in around them.

The better traps are those that aren't dependent on the element of surprise. That way, even if your target suspects what's coming, they're still forced to try and fight their way out from a disadvantageous position. As I stood there, I came to the uncomfortable realization which kind of trap we'd fallen into. Which meant I needed to make a choice. Speak up or stay quiet.

"Are we going to do this now, or were you fellas waiting for more friends to show up?"

My voice echoed out through the elevator, my tired, rattled brain making the choice for me. I knew they all heard me, but no one moved, and no one said anything. As the silence stretched, I considered going for my pistol. I thought I could clear the holster in time, but then what?

There were six of them inside with us. Granted, I had enough bullets, but it would be messy, and I had no idea whether the rounds I fired would ricochet. If they did, none of us would be walking out of here uninjured.

Assuming we walked out of here at all.

I stayed my hand, and the elevator touched down on the ground floor. The doors opened, and the men inside exited first, stepping aside and separating into two lines as if preparing to toss rice onto a newlywed couple making their way to the car.

At the end of the aisle stood a man dressed in a modest yet tasteful suit. In his early forties, he wore his hair in a simple, office-friendly cut, and kept his mustache neatly trimmed. There was absolutely nothing remarkable about his face, but the bulge underneath his jacket coincided with those of the men surrounding us, although a quick glance at his hands revealed delicate fingers and soft palms, suggesting he wasn't an avid shooter.

"Good afternoon, Sergeant Mayfield." He stepped forward and folded his hands in front of him.

Cautiously, we stepped from the elevator, making our way down the makeshift aisle until we drew up beside him. "Afternoon, mister...?"

"Zheng," he said. "A pleasure to meet you."

"Likewise. Something I can help you with, Mr. Zheng?"

"My employer, Mr. Doku, would like me to extend an invitation to speak with him."

Doku. The name sounded familiar, but it took me a minute to recall my earlier conversation with Detective Wei.

Satoru Doku.

How had he described him? A triad gangster with his sights set on Chinatown. In other words, not someone that I wanted to associate with. "Thank him for the invitation, but I'm afraid I must decline. There are other matters requiring my attention."

"Of course," Zheng said. "Matters such as a murder? Or two?"

I narrowed my eyes. "What do you know about it?"

"Only what my employer has instructed me to know. He suspected you might be reluctant to meet with him, which is why he has authorized me to make you a good faith offer."

"What kind of offer?"

"Fifteen minutes of your time. The length of a short conversation."

"And in return?"

"Two men were murdered in Chinatown last evening. You know of what I speak?"

"I do."

"If you agree to meet with Mr. Doku, he will provide you with the name of their murderer."

"Just like that?"

Mr. Zheng nodded and offered me a polite smile. "Shall I have them bring the car around?"

Satoru Doku. Friday, July 25th 1555hrs

The "car" turned out to be a pair of blacked out Mercedes-Benz sedans. The one that pulled up alongside the curb had its windows tinted right up to the legal limit, and the silver grill was sparkly clean, showing none of the insect or mosquito corpses that plague the bridges at this time of year. I could see a man's figure in the backseat, but not much else.

"If you please?" Mr. Zheng said.

Tootsie and I started forward, but he stopped her after only a step, his face adopting an expression of sincere regret. "Unfortunately, the invitation does not extend to any of your associates. If Officer Alves—" I noted that he hadn't paused to read her nametag before referring to her. "—would like to remain here, I'll see to it that she is kept comfortable until your return."

Tootsie's jaw hardened, and she glanced over, waiting for my nod before reluctantly taking a step back. "Fifteen minutes?" she repeated.

"Not a second later," Mr. Zheng assured her.

"Best hope not. Because at 15:01, I'll be calling out the cavalry, and you'll have every cop in Boston hunting for you."

"I assure you, such measures will not be necessary."

Tootsie grunted and pointedly looked at her watch, noting the time before giving me a final look.

I gave her a nod. Then I climbed into the backseat alongside a Triad gangster.

To be fair, the backseat was lovely. The seats were roomy, the dark leather supple. I could feel myself involuntarily beginning to relax, drawn in by the rich aroma and gentle cushioning. Mr. Zheng closed the door behind me, cutting off the sounds of the outside world. Had I been alone, I likely would have been asleep in short order.

But I wasn't alone. And I waited until we'd pulled away from the curb, noting the identical vehicle following in our wake before I forced myself to look at the man next to me.

I'm not sure exactly what I'd been expecting. Maybe Chow Yun-Fat with a long flowing Fu Manchu mustache, like the way he'd appeared in those pirate movies.

Satoru Doku wasn't like that.

He was a few inches shy of six feet tall, and had embraced his receding hairline, adopting a short clipper cut more in line with Jason Statham rather than the full-on Bryan Cranston in Breaking Bad. His suit was nice, but not overly fancy. The kind a middle manager might wear, but not a C-suite executive. He had an outdoorsman tan, the tiny freckles and shaded blemishes evidence of ample time in the sun. His hands were scarred along the fingers rather than the knuckles. Not a prize fighter then. Maybe a farmer? Or a shadow of a youth spent climbing trees and picking fruit.

"Sergeant Mayfield," Satoru Doku said, offering me a polite smile. "Thank you for meeting with me. We have many things to discuss."

There were two men in the front seat, including the driver. Both were middle-aged men of Asian descent, dressed similarly to the ones that had corralled us inside the elevator. For a brief instant

I couldn't help but feel a little like James Bond, bandying words with the villain while his henchmen stood silently by, waiting on his word to kill me. Come to think of it, maybe that wasn't such a good comparison.

"Not too many I hope," I said. "I've got a busy day planned, and your man promised to have me back in fifteen minutes."

"Yes, of course. I will strive for brevity. Before we begin, I should apologize to you. It was never my intention to involve you in these affairs."

"Dropping corpses down onto my desk doesn't exactly scream, 'Stay away.'"

"That was a most unfortunate incident. Rest assured I had nothing to do with it. In fact, I had hoped to stabilize my position before requesting a meeting."

"Well, I'm here now. What is it you want?"

"I assume you want the name of the murderer that was promised?"

"I'd rather hear what you have to say first."

"Oh?"

I turned and regarded him for several seconds. He didn't look like the sort of man who would have me chopped up and fed to the sharks in the bay. In fact, his demeanor, combined with his suit, made him seem more like a middle manager at a wealth management firm. It was a visage that, I suspected, he'd worked hard to cultivate. Successful, but not too successful. Competent, for certain, and ambitious, but not so ambitious that those in power needed to be concerned.

At least not until they looked into his eyes. If they had, they might have noted some things. Specifically, that he was approaching the age where the last traces of youth had begun to fade. The age where men sometimes grow desperate. When put up or shut up becomes more than just a motivational slogan, and when the fear of fading away into obscurity takes hold. I wondered if Satoru Doku saw Chinatown as his last chance to carve himself out a kingdom. If so, he was going to be sorely disappointed.

"A name is all well and fine, but I still need evidence in order to win a conviction. Don't misunderstand, I want it, but I've a feeling you're about to ask for something you think is more important. I'd rather get it out of the way now so I can refuse. Afterward, you can give me the name, and we can go our separate ways."

His polite smile faltered. "Are you so certain that you'll refuse me?"

"Seems likely."

"May I ask why?"

"I'm a cop. You're a gangster. Some things just aren't meant to mix."

He made a low, considering sound. "Perhaps we can remedy that."

"I guess we'll find out. Let's hear your pitch."

He drew in a soft breath and exhaled as the driver took the next turn and began to circle the block. "Chinatown has long been considered an outside element within the city of Boston. The authorities come when compelled, but they leave just as quickly. It seems obvious to me that both sides would benefit from having a caretaker in place. A go-between, to ensure order and limit potentially dangerous misunderstandings."

"Is that what you're calling yourself? A caretaker?"

"What other term would you prefer?"

"I don't know. Drug lord. Kingpin. They all have a more accurate ring than caretaker."

"Drugs are a concern for any community. Time has proven that they cannot be eliminated. However, they can be controlled through rigorous adherence to a set of prescribed laws."

"Laws set down by the government. Not by a kingpin."

"In order to ensure the citizens' adherence, such laws must be enforceable. Without the threat of consequence, chaos seeps in and begins to threaten the very stability of the community."

I made a bored sound. "We can sit here discussing social degeneration all day, or we could skip to the part where you tell me what you actually want."

"As you wish. I want to assist you in catching a murderer."

"The one who killed those two men inside the apartment?"

"The same, although they are not his first victims. Nor his fiftieth. A hoard of bodies lay at his feet, enough to cross the River Styx were they laid atop one another."

"And does this mass murderer have a name?"

"Indeed. In China, he is referred to as the Yaojing. The onset of fog and darkness. In more western settings, he is known merely as the Gray Fox. He is an assassin, Sergeant Mayfield. A ninja of deadly skill."

I shifted in my seat and held up my hands. "Whoa now, hold on. A ninja? Like an actual ninja?"

"Mock if you wish, Sergeant, but I assure you this matter is deadly serious. I trust you know this is not the first time I have visited your fair city?"

"I heard you made a play for it a few years back but that it didn't work out too well for you."

"Indeed not. I am loath to admit it, but I found myself completely unprepared for the appearance of the Gray Fox."

"Probably should have called first before you tried setting up shop."

"It is not that simple. The Gray Fox once served as a contract killer for the Triad. He vanished decades ago, leading many to believe he had been slain. When I attempted to redistribute those I believed to be in control of Chinatown, he took matters into his own hands and waged an unrelenting shadow war upon my men."

"Shadow wars are tough. I've had some experience with them."

"So I've heard. Unfortunately for us, the Gray Fox used more than glitter."

Evidently word of the Fairy war had gotten around. I tried not to let my annoyance show on my face as he continued.

"Under such an unexpected onslaught, we were forced to retreat for fear that things would escalate to the point where the federal authorities would become involved."

"Sounds to me like you made your play and got smacked down. So far, I am not seeing the problem."

"That's because you are not viewing the situation in its entirety. You, like many, would paint this Gray Fox as a sort of mythical, Robin Hood figure, defending the poor and downtrodden. The truth is that he is far more dangerous than even I care to admit."

"If he's so dangerous, how come I've never heard of him before now?"

"That is precisely why you should be afraid. Chinatown is not bereft of leadership. It never has been. The Gray Fox rules from the shadows, overseeing the drugs, the money laundering, and sex crimes that occur within its streets. My plea is not only for my benefit, but for the benefit of all. I am offering you a choice. You can allow the people of Chinatown to continue to suffer under a faceless shadow that deals only death, or you can help me to remove him, and acknowledge me as his successor."

"Or I could slap you both in handcuffs and set you up in opposite cells where you can glare at one another all day."

"Perhaps, but if you did, another would simply move to take my place, and he may not look upon your division as favorably as I."

"I didn't realize you were such a fan."

"I am. And you should be grateful. After all, a shadow cannot be spoken to or bargained with. No favors can be granted, no compromises reached. The Gray Fox's only means of negotiation is to kill those who vex him. There is no other path. With me in his place, the two of us could make informed decisions that would allow for greater prosperity within Chinatown and its citizens. Crime will never cease, not in any neighborhood, but it can be controlled, if both parties approach it with an open mind. I'm offering you the chance to save lives, Sergeant. To put a stop to the chaos."

"Sounds more like you're wanting me to save your hide."

His smile disappeared entirely, and his face darkened. "What did you say to me?"

"Just calling it like I see it, Satoru. This is your second chance at Boston. Fail, and I can't imagine the Gray Fox is going to give you a third. To make matters worse, the Triad doesn't seem like the type of organization that hands out do-overs. From where

I'm sitting, you've gone all in and are waiting to see if your cards hold up. Now you're asking me to slip you an ace from up my sleeve. But I haven't heard one good reason why I should."

"In that case, consider what I offer. The Gray Fox killed those men. Of that I have no doubt. Likewise, I am certain there was no warning, no negotiation. Such things have happened before, and will again, unless there is a change. Ask yourself which you would prefer to deal with in the future. A blade or a handshake."

"How about instead, you answer one of my questions?"

"Regarding what?"

"I've listened to you talk about the Gray Fox. Now I want to talk about the Jiangshi. What do you know about it?"

Satoru made a low noise and brought his hands together in front of him. "That all depends. Were you my ally, I might have information to share. But as you've made it clear that you are not, I find little benefit in giving away information which I have worked to acquire."

"You might want to rethink that. Consider it an act of good faith."

"Why are you so concerned with him?"

"He stole a girl."

Satoru frowned. "What girl?"

"One of the university students. Plucked her right from her bed. That's a problem for me."

"I don't know anything about a girl."

"I sure hope not. Because I'm going to get her back. And anyone who's involved is going to pay in spades before I'm through. Regardless of if they're a vampire, or just, how did you put it, a caretaker."

Satoru's mouth tightened. "I would strongly advise caution before you begin making threats, Sergeant. Your tenacity is well known, but you are not invincible. Do not make the mistake of overestimating your capabilities or underestimating mine."

"The only thing you should worry about underestimating is—"

Something blew from below us, and the car jerked suddenly, striking the curb and ricochetting off.

Satoru Doku snarled and jerked forward in his seat. "What's happening?"

"The tires," the driver said. "They all blew out at once."

As if to lend credence to his words, the vehicle's rims touched down on the pavement, scraping their way along and sending up an arc of sparks as we ground to a halt. I shifted in my seat, one hand brushing my pistol as I reached toward the door handle. Before my fingers touched, something struck the front windshield, shattering the glass and spraying shards onto the driver and front seat passenger. The two started screaming and struggling with their seat belts while Satoru Doku barked orders.

I started to add my own voice to the commotion, but a split second later something came flying through the windshield. It was about the size of an egg, though it was black instead of white. There was a little fuse pushed into the side. The cord was no longer than my pinkie finger, and I watched as the fire burned down the length, disappearing into the ebony shell a split second before it exploded.

The Gray Fox. Friday, July 25th 1559hrs

Smoke bombs are inherently unpleasant. First, because they're *loud*. Loud enough to be disorientating even without the cloud of inky smoke that rose up to fill the car. The smell was acrid, putrid, lined with a chemical aftertaste that burned my mouth and tongue. Ears ringing, a surge of panic rose within me, but I managed to keep my head long enough to find the door handle. The door opened, and I spilled out of the car onto the street.

No sooner did I hit the pavement than strong hands seized hold of me. They jerked me around and one of Satoru's henchmen peered down at me. My face evidently wasn't the one he wanted to see, and he tossed me aside without care before reaching back into the car. He pulled Satoru free a moment later, a second gunmen seizing him on the opposite side and yanking him free as cleanly as any close personal protection detail could have managed.

They started to move away from the car, but something flashed out of the darkness, and a piece of metal was suddenly sticking out of the back of one of Satoru's henchmen. He screamed, hit the ground, and flailed wildly. I started to rise, but something struck the top of the car, and I glimpsed a flash of metal as it skidded past my face.

From within the smoke, another man screamed, and a heavy burst of gunfire rang out, the rapid explosions echoing through the streets. The lone gunman holding Satoru dropped down, covering the Triad crime boss's body with his own. Still on my knees, I suddenly found myself face to face with Satoru.

It was his expression that startled me out of my daze. Staring around wide-eyed, I realized he was even more afraid than I was. A surge of energy coursed through me, and I snarled and threw myself up off the ground, seized Satoru around the arm and pulled him up to his feet. Once he caught his balance, I turned and shoved him toward the nearest building.

The sign on the door identified it as a used furniture store that catered to the University. It was closed for the summer, and I didn't know how to pick a door lock, so I drove my boot into the side. Once, twice. Satoru's henchman saw what I was after, and he added his foot to mine, the two of us combining forces to kick the door in.

The door broke with a resounding *crack* that didn't quite drown out the screams or the gunfire of those men still in the fog. We pushed through the entry just as two more henchmen appeared and joined our party, all of us rushing forward into the safety of the building.

We traveled half a dozen paces before I remembered the flashlight attached to my pistol. I drew it from its holster, and the golden beam came alive, illuminating the store and allowing us to navigate our way deeper inside.

The building smelled of wood polish, sawdust and recycled upholstery. The late afternoon daylight filtered in through the windows, as well as from a skylight in the ceiling. Most of the furniture was second hand, arranged to mimic different sized dorm rooms. For a brief second, my mind flashed back to Hui's room, and nightmarish images of vampires rose up around me, flittering between the surrounding shadows. I shook my head, and forced the image away, pushing deeper into the store as Satoru's gunmen spread out around us.

"What's happening?" I asked.

"I told you." Satoru was crouched beside a slender kitchen table. "The Gray Fox does not negotiate. He can only kill."

As if his words had been prophetic, one of the henchmen let out a sharp scream that ended abruptly in a wet, gurgling cough. I whipped my gun around, and my flashlight beam showed me a blood red shirt, the man wearing it grasping at his throat as blood poured out from between his fingers.

Fear and shock caused my hand to flicker, and my light started to dip. I jerked it back up, but I overcompensated, sending the beam of light up over the henchmen's head just in time to see the Gray Fox swinging down from the ceiling.

He was short, lean, dressed head to toe in gray. A shinobi shōzoku, it was called, complete with a hooded cowl and ending with soft slippers lined with thin rope. A thick belt encircled his waist, and I noted the small grappling hook set among various throwing stars, and a gray leather pouch, likely loaded down with more of those smoke bomb eggs or other, similar nastiness.

He swept in from the darkness, kicking his legs forward and slamming his feet into the nearest henchman's face, knocking him senseless even as he came down into a roll.

I couldn't fire, not without risking hitting the unconscious gunmen. Unfortunately, by the time I'd figured that out, the Gray Fox had rolled to his feet beside the second Triad guard.

JADE ENCLAVE

He swept around him, encircling his body like a striking serpent before seizing hold and hip-tossing him down onto the concrete. The henchman hit hard and immediately went limp, a low moan escaping before he slipped away into unconsciousness.

Instinct seized hold as the Gray Fox straightened, and I shot forward, placing myself between him and Satoru. I adopted a shooting stance, aligned my sights and blasted three rounds into his chest.

Or, at least, that's what I tried to do.

As my finger depressed the trigger, the Gray Fox jerked down and around, casting his torso through a wide, circular movement that carried it clear of my line of fire. The flash from my muzzle temporarily blinded me, and by the time my vision cleared the Gray Fox had already closed the distance.

They say the hardest hits are the ones you don't see coming.

I didn't see any of them.

There was a flash of impact, followed by the sense of being totally and completely overwhelmed. I don't know how many times the Gray Fox hit me, probably somewhere in the neighborhood of a dozen. The first one snapped my pistol out of my hands, and the last involved driving his heel into my stomach, sending me flying back across the floor.

I hit the ground and skipped to a sideways halt, my back striking the edge of a light blue floral sofa. I couldn't move, but I could see Satoru as he sputtered and turned to run. He didn't make it far. Two steps, and the Gray Fox swept out his leg, catching the Triad boss by the ankle and sending him crashing down onto a kitchen table. The table legs broke with a resounding wooden *crack*, dropping a wide-eyed Satoru down onto the floor. He struggled to right himself and get his hands beneath him, but shock and fear had robbed him of his dexterity, and he just ended up scrambling for nothing.

The Gray Fox started forward but halted as a voice yelled "Freeze!" from behind him.

For a brief second, I thought I'd imagined it, but I fought through the encroaching darkness, clinging stubbornly to consciousness and peering around just as Tootsie moved into view. She must have been drawn by the sound of the attack, or maybe Zheng had told her. Either way, she took up a shooting position, aiming her pistol at the Gray Fox's temple.

"Turn around and put your hands on your—"

The Gray Fox evidently wasn't taking orders. He whirled around before she'd finished speaking and swung his face down toward his toes. At the same time, he whipped his opposite leg around like a scorpion's tail, smacking Tootsie in the face and knocking her flat on her back. She hit the ground hard, and her pistol slipped from her hand, skidding across the floor just out of my reach.

The Gray Fox spun back around and somersaulted atop the broken table, landing so that his feet were straddling Satoru's prone form. One hand disappeared inside his tunic and drew out a curved blade sprouting from a wooden handle. A kama, as it was known.

Satoru's eyes widened as the Gray Fox drew back his arm, suddenly seeing his end in perfect clarity. A flash of panic rushed through me, and I jerked myself forward, grabbing up Tootsie's pistol from the floor and firing twice before I had time to think.

The first bullet grazed the Gray Fox's arm, but the second one struck him in the back, just above the left shoulder blade. The force of the bullet's impact whipped him around, and he tumbled off the table. He hit the ground in a roll and somersaulted back up into the air. As he rotated, he seized something near his belt. I had just enough time to recognize the smoke bomb before he threw it down against the floor. It erupted, filling the air with a cloudy, inky darkness. For a moment I considered blind firing into the fog, but I didn't know where the bullets would travel, and my hesitation cost me, because a few seconds later the smoke began to dissipate, and there was no trace of the Gray Fox.

Encroaching Shadows. Friday, July 25th 1630hrs

THE VIOLENT MELEE ENDED as swiftly as it had started.

Then the cleanup began.

The MIT police were the first to catch wind of the incident, their dispatch flooded by dozens of emergency calls from the nearby dorm rooms. They were followed by department patrol units. Mr. Zheng, however, was already waiting, and he greeted the first officers as they arrived, explaining the situation with a quiet calm. By the time we emerged from the furniture store, he had the whole matter well in hand.

The story, as he told it, was that a blown tire had caused one of the henchmen to have a weapon's malfunction within the car.

The bullet had struck the engine and caused the brief explosion, thereby explaining away the smoke. Any reports of automatic gunfire were gross exaggerations, a theory supported by the lack of brass shell casings that should have littered the street.

I kept my distance and allowed the patrol officers to handle the affair as they saw fit. The sight of Tootsie's swollen nose earned us some sideways glances, but they likely assumed she had gotten it when the car crashed, and once it came to light what division we worked for, they were more willing to turn a blind eye. No one bothered to enter the furniture store, and Satoru's remaining henchmen were swift to see to their wounded, including the lone fatality.

Satoru Doku left quickly and without so much as a thank you. He emerged from the furniture store and was immediately rushed into a waiting car before being driven off to who knows where. Not Chinatown, I assumed, but couldn't have said much more.

Once it became clear that none of the patrol officers were going to want a statement, Tootsie and I walked back to my car and drove to a nearby gas station. I filled the tank while Tootsie disappeared inside, reemerging with two Cokes, a bag of ice, and a carton of freezer bags. "Have at it," she said, as she tore open the ice and scooped a large handful into her bag. She sealed the top and pressed it against her swollen nose, letting out a relieved sigh as I went about seeing to my own wounds.

I filled three bags of ice. The first I placed on my ribs, where the Gray Fox had kicked me. The second went on my hip. I had no clue why that was hurting. The third I placed on the back of my head. Then I leaned back in my seat and tried hard not to feel like a popsicle. Several minutes passed in silence as we sipped our Cokes, and it wasn't until the bottles had run dry that one of us finally decided to speak.

"So," Tootsie said, her voice nasally. "That was something."

"Sure was."

"What do you think?"

"I think it hurts too much to think right now."

"Oh."

I sighed after a moment and leaned forward in my seat. If the ghost of Topher were here, he's the little Jiminy Cricket that lives in my head and shows up whenever I push myself too far past the red line, he'd probably say I needed to work through the pain. As tired and sore as I might be, I was still alive, and not everybody could say the same. The fact that he hadn't made an appearance yet meant I still had more gas left in my proverbial tank, and so long as the engine was running, I had a responsibility to keep going forward.

"We've stumbled into something here. Something we didn't see coming."

"You mean you didn't plan on fighting ninjas when you woke up this morning?"

"Yesterday morning," I said. "And no I did not. But it's more than just that. Or, better said, there's more going on here than we know. Ninjas, vampires, and Triad gangsters. It's a cluster of epic proportion."

"You think they're all here for the same reason? Each one vying to be the next Chinatown boss?"

"Yeah. Or no. Maybe. I don't know."

"Is that your final answer or are you just going through all the possible response options?"

"Yes, to all of the above."

"Okay then."

I sighed again and rolled my shoulders, forcing myself to organize them in my mind. "We know what Satoru Doku wants. He was pretty forthcoming about that. And we can assume that the

Gray Fox wants things to continue the way they are." I frowned. "Or at least that he's not on board with Satoru's plan. Honestly, who the heck knows at this point. It's all speculation. Truth is, I have no idea who the Gray Fox is or what he wants."

"He's kind of a little guy," Tootsie said. "But, man, he fights hard."

I grunted, a spasm pain in my ribs agreeing with her.

"That still leaves the Jiangshi."

"At the risk of sounding like a broken record, I have no idea what he wants either." I leaned my head back, condensation from the freezer bag sending icy droplets of water sliding down my back. I'd be lying if I said they didn't feel nice.

"What if the Jiangshi is after the Gray Fox?" Tootsie asked.

I blinked and cast a sideways glance her way. "What do you mean?"

"Supposing we're on the right track and this is all a big play for Chinatown, the Jiangshi would want to eliminate the Gray Fox, right?"

I considered it a moment before nodding. "Stands to reason."

JADE ENCLAVE

The Jade Fangs had said inside the restaurant that they'd done their research. I'd assumed at the time they were just talking about Blue Moon Division, but maybe it was more than that. If so, then it was a safe bet that the Jiangshi knew what happened to Satoru the first time he tried to take over. He wouldn't want to end up fighting a similar shadow war. If that was the case, it was likely he'd built himself a little Rolodex of enemies and was working his way down the list, crossing names off one by one. I said as much.

Tootsie shivered. "God that's scary."

"No kidding."

"There's more to it though."

"What do you mean?"

"Think back to the restaurant. The Jiangshi was looking for the kid, right?"

"Yeah, so?"

"What did he want with him? I mean, he's just a kid, right? Not some specially anointed chosen one destined to be the next Dalai Lama, right?"

"Not that I know of."

"The Jiangshi sent five of his Jade Fangs to retrieve him. That seems like overkill."

She had a point, and I could feel my mind starting to rev up. "Maybe he's having trouble finding him. And he figured out the kid had been in the apartment with the two men who were murdered."

"Presumably by the Gray Fox?" she said.

I nodded. "Assuming Satoru is telling the truth."

"Is it possible the Jiangshi thinks he might've witnessed the murder?"

"Could be," I said. "I didn't get that vibe from him though. If the kid had seen a murder, much less two, I think he would've been more shaken up. At the very least, he'd have been a lot more reluctant to talk to us."

"Something else then," Tootsie said. "Something inside the apartment. Something the Jiangshi needed to know." She considered it.

"Maybe," I said, hating the word even as I said it. There were too many maybes, and not enough facts. "There's a whole other side to this that we're not thinking of."

"What's that?"

"Why," I said. "If the Jiangshi really is looking to take out the Gray Fox, why now? And why Boston? I mean, don't get me wrong, I love this city, but our Chinatown is relatively small. He came a long way just for a couple of street blocks."

"You think there's more to all this?"

"I think we'd be foolish to try to chalk all this up to one big game of King of the Hill. The pieces aren't adding up, and we need to figure out the bigger picture before more people get hurt."

Tootsie made an agreeable noise. "Hard to figure out someone's motivation when you don't know what makes them tick. Or their name for that matter."

"Doubly so when they're going around claiming to be an immortal vampire."

"Yeah," Tootsie said.

We lapsed back into silence, but it didn't last long. Tootsie's cell phone started vibrating, and she drew it from her pocket, glancing down to the screen. "It's Detective Wei."

"Put it on speaker," I said.

"Thaysa?"

"Hey, Wei. I'm here with Sergeant Mayfield."

"Are you guys all right? I heard there was some kind of commotion up near MIT."

"Commotion is a nice way of putting it," I said. "We just had a run-in with the Gray Fox. Ever heard of him?"

"The Gray... wait, seriously?"

"Yeah."

"Oh, wow," he said. "I've heard of him, but I always thought it was just an urban legend. One of those Chinatown myths. Like Santa Claus. Be good because the Gray Fox is always watching."

"He's no myth. He single-handedly dismantled Satoru Doku's entire convoy. Would've had him too if we hadn't been there."

"Wait, you met up with Satoru Doku?"

"Briefly. It wasn't a productive conversation."

"Jeez."

"It's been a busy afternoon. I'll fill you in on all the details later. For now, just know we're okay, but we're no closer to figuring out the identity of the Jiangshi."

"Well, I might be able to help with that," Wei said. "Do you remember the cell phones inside the apartment?"

I thought back. "Yeah. There were three of them, right?"

"That's right. Two of them belong to our victims. Forensics is still processing the scene. But the third one isn't registered to anyone."

I frowned. "A burner phone?"

"Exactly. I had a friendly judge write me up a quick warrant."

I bit back my initial reply. Why couldn't I ever meet a friendly judge? "And?"

"And get this: there was only one number saved in the contacts list. The Sacred Pine Temple in Chinatown. You know it?"

I wracked my memory before shaking my head. "I remember you mentioning it in the car, but I couldn't tell you much else."

"The abbot is named Brother Kim. It's a modest temple, but they do a lot of charity work and community outreach stuff."

"You got an address?"

"Sure do. You got a pen on hand?"

I didn't, but Tootsie did. I borrowed it and wrote the address out on my palm as Wei gave it.

"Also, I was able to do some more research into our two victims inside the apartment. One of them owned a boat, and I found some marina records showing where it was docked. I was going to head up that way and take a look around. Nothing official. Just a sneak and peek. But I can hold off and meet you at the temple if you like?"

I thought about it. Having Detective Wei might get us further with the locals than Tootsie or I would on our own, but we weren't going to crack this case by tracking down one lead at a time. We needed to utilize our resources more effectively. "No, stay with the victims. Let me know if anything turns up. We'll handle the temple."

"Roger that," he said.

"And Wei? Be careful. There's more going on here than we realize, and people are playing for keeps."

"I hear you loud and clear. You two take care of each other. I'll be in touch soon."

He hung up, and Tootsie slipped the phone back into her pocket before twisting in her seat to look at me. "So, are we going to see a temple?"

I nodded and dropped my icepack into the backseat. "Yeah, we're going to see a temple."

Sacred Pine Temple. Friday, July 25th 1724hrs

As it turned out, the address Detective Wei gave didn't lead us to the Sacred Pine Temple. It led us to a grocery store.

Sort of.

Officially, the address didn't exist, but two numbers up belonged to the Asian Eatery, which occupied the first floor of a four-story white concrete building that had seen better days. We parked along the edge of the street and peered up, noting the dirty windows and withered yellow awning. The gutters had splintered at some point last winter, and the snows had left a long trail of mold running down the side of the wall.

"Doesn't really seem very tranquil, does it?" Tootsie asked from beside me.

I shook my head. "Seems more like a trap."

Tootsie grunted, suggesting she might have been thinking the same thing. "Poor visibility. Not much foot traffic. Definitely no one that's going to raise an eyebrow or call for help. It's a good spot for it."

"Yeah."

"You think Wei sold us out?"

Much as I hated to admit it, tendrils of doubt had started to worm their way inside my mind, insidious whispers wondering why Detective Wei would have sent us here. Try as I might to ignore them, I had to ask myself what did I actually know about him?

I knew he was the lone detective assigned to Chinatown on account of being able to speak Mandarin, but not much else. It was difficult to try and guess where someone's loyalties might lie without knowing their background. For all I knew, he could be in league with Satoru Doku, or even the Gray Fox himself. Or he could be just as he appeared. An honest cop trying to do the right thing. Maybe I was letting my paranoia get the best of me. After all, he'd offered to meet us here, and I'd waved him off. Would he have done that if he was planning to sell us out?

Worse still came the realization that if he really was working for Satoru or the Gray Fox, he didn't *need* to sell us out. We'd been chasing our tails all day without much to show for it. With a little bit of creativity, he could keep us spinning for long after this entire affair was brought to its inevitably bloody conclusion. Heck, maybe this whole temple business was just that, a fruitless errand meant to waste our time. There was really only one way to know for sure.

"Want to go inside?" Tootsie asked.

I didn't. Not just because I was worried about a potential ambush. The entire thing just felt off. I'm not usually a fussy girl, but beyond the tinted windows I could see cramped, narrow aisles snaking their way between overstocked shelves filled with processed fare. There was a small spattering of fruits and vegetables, but they looked old, and the bins and baskets in which they rested were none too clean. Even from the street, I could smell the odor of stale produce.

"I really don't."

Tootsie grunted but didn't argue. I took that to mean she didn't want to go in either. "What about down there then?" She motioned around the side of the building, down a narrow alleyway that ran between the eatery and a parking garage. "Wouldn't hurt to take a look around first."

"Sure," I said, more so to stall having to go inside the eatery versus any desire to see what lay around inside the alley. I figured the most we would find would be some homeless or discarded trash. There was always lots of trash hidden away in the corners in a city like Boston.

I led the way into the narrow alley, the two of us taking our time. The smell was stronger back here, but it wasn't anywhere near as foul as I would have expected, especially given the summer. Mostly, it just smelled like cardboard.

The alley curved south around the eatery. As we rounded the corner, my cop brain started picking up on little oddities. There was no refuse, no human waste or food. Likewise, no needles or other signs of drug paraphernalia. There were shipping boxes aplenty, but they were broken down, then stacked in a staged manner that would have allowed them to be quickly cleared away. Something about it rubbed me the wrong way, warning that not everything was as it appeared.

"Sergeant."

I glanced back, and Tootsie nodded over my shoulder. Turning around, I saw what she was looking at. There was a doorway, built into the back of the eatery building, sealed behind a black grated gate. Its once red paint had faded to a dull orange, but there, carved into the brick above the doorway, was a circle with eight spokes sticking out. As I stared, a gentle breeze swept through the alleyway, carrying an unfamiliar, smoky scent that reminded me of incense.

"What do you think?" Tootsie asked.

In response, I raised my fist and knocked three times. The noise echoed through the alleyway but was met with only silence. "Huh."

Tootsie stepped forward and seized the grated gate, giving it a gentle tug as I peered around. "I could probably pry it off," she said. "But it would be loud."

"Let's give them a minute to figure out what to make of us first," I said.

"Them?"

I nodded my chin toward the second-story window, where a small camera sat nestled beneath a leaning awning. You couldn't see it from the street, but from directly underneath, its black, beady eye was focused in on us, and I could feel someone watching from the other end.

My hand slipped down toward my belt, and I slid my jacket aside, allowing them to see the police badge on my belt. I waited for a slow ten count, and right when I was about to give Tootsie the go-ahead, I heard the deadbolt slide back, and the door opened to reveal a young boy.

He was maybe ten or eleven, dressed in a little gray martial arts uniform with black shoes. "What do you want?"

"My name is Sergeant Chloe Mayfield. I want to speak to Brother Kim."

"You come in, you make no trouble. Yes?"

"We won't make any trouble."

"Right," Tootsie said under her breath. "Cause that's never happened before."

I elbowed her and motioned for the boy to open the door. He thought about it for a second, then nodded. "Okay."

He unlocked the grated gate, and we stepped back to allow it to swing open before following him inside.

Past the doorway was a small, dimly lit hallway. I could hear running water coming from somewhere nearby, and the smell of incense was stronger. The young boy tapped my hand twice, then motioned for me to follow. He led us to the end of the hall and through a sliding screen door into a place unlike any I'd ever seen before.

JADE ENCLAVE

The building had been gutted, the floors cleared away to create a wide-open courtyard that stretched up to the ceiling, where skylights allowed the afternoon sunshine to peer down onto the green grounds below.

At the heart of the temple stood a small pavilion crafted from dark wood and smoothed stone. Its arched ceiling beams were touched with gold, and there was a statue of a praying Buddha at its center, holding fresh orange and white flower blooms within the cusps of his upturned palms.

Around the main building sprawled an intricate garden containing every color of flower I could have imagined. There was even a bamboo forest, their bodies stretching twice the length of my height. There was a small scattering of people about. Most of them were men, dressed in simple gray robes or martial arts outfits similar to our guide. They all had clean shaven heads and wore no jewelry or adornment save for eyeglasses or, in one case, a hearing aid. Children ran amongst them, helping to tend the gardens or carrying various messages, as well as a couple of women, dutifully going about their tasks.

Our young guide led us along a well-worn walkway path that wound its way through the lush greenery, passing around the vibrant flowerbeds and over a series of reed bridges that looked down over half a dozen koi ponds scattered across the yard. As I glanced down toward the water's surface, I caught the occasional glimpse of black and orange scales as the koi fish rose to touch the surface. The sounds of the water created a gentle, babbling melody, and the smell of incense swept its way around me, containing hints of jasmine, sandalwood, and bamboo. Peering beyond the courtyard revealed a series of simple rooms lit by paper lanterns. I noted neatly made beds and prayer benches, along with the kitchens and some storage rooms.

We reached the main temple, its floor covered in soft mats that could be easily rolled up and removed. As we stepped inside, a soft calmness came over me, slowing my heart and causing my shoulders to drop. In that moment, I became keenly aware of the pistol on my hip. Never before had I viewed it as anything other than a necessity, a tool I was grateful to have. Here though, in that moment, something about it felt *wrong*. My pistol didn't belong here. *I* didn't belong here. Dimly, I wondered if that was how Lieutenant Kermit felt, then I shook my head and banished the thought from my mind.

Regardless of whether I belonged, I couldn't just turn around and leave. Not when there was a chance that my being here could end the violence and bring justice to those who'd been murdered within my city.

The young guide raced over to the only other person inside the main building. Kneeling in the center of the floor with his head bowed, he didn't stir as our guide leaned over and whispered in his ear. Several long seconds passed before the man said a single word I didn't catch, and our young guide nodded and raced off, exiting out the opposite way we'd come.

The kneeling man exhaled, then smoothly came to his feet, pausing to retrieve his mat and rolling it up before gently setting it aside. "Greetings, Officer, I understand you wish to speak with me?"

I narrowed my eyes. "I was hoping to speak with Brother Kim. I understand he's the abbot here?"

"He is. I am."

"*You're* Brother Kim?"

I'm not sure what I'd been expecting. Someone older, I suppose. A mini-Buddha, or else a Mr. Miyagi, who could deliver a few cryptic lines that would lower my blood pressure, clear my skin, and raise my self-esteem. Something like that.

The real Brother Kim wasn't much older than me, probably just on the other side of thirty, with a smooth-shaven head and soft eyes. Dressed in a gray martial arts uniform, he wore a necklace of prayer beads and had a dark sash wrapped snuggly around his waist. "Yes," he said, drawing out the word. The expression on his face suggested he was trying to decide if I was slow-witted or under the influence of something.

"Sorry," I said. "It's been a busy day. My name is Sergeant Mayfield. I need to speak with you regarding a murder that happened here in Chinatown. Three of them, actually."

Brother Kim raised his eyebrows. "Three?"

"Like I said, it's been a busy day. Is there somewhere we can speak?"

He hesitated for only a fraction of a second before nodding. "Of course. This way."

He led us from the main temple, pausing at the entrance to retrieve a bamboo walking stick. It was a simple, thumb-width staff approximately the height of his shoulders, and he clicked it lightly against the ground as he led us down the stairs and across the bridge to the first small garden. He slowed his pace once we reached the other side, silently inviting me up beside him. "I hope you do not mind if we walk while we speak. Our order teaches that movement clears the mind, and I have always enjoyed strolling these grounds."

"I can see why," I said. "It's beautiful here."

"Have you ever been to this place before, Sergeant Mayfield?"

I shook my head. "No. Truth be told I had no idea this place even existed before now. And I'm not sure I would've believed it if I hadn't seen it with my own eyes."

His mouth curved up into a satisfied smile as he paused beside a flowerbed filled with white and yellow flowers. He breathed in deeply, savoring the aroma. "I have always preferred the aroma of jasmine in the late afternoon."

"They're all nice," I said. "I can see why you hide them away from the public."

Brother Kim's smile slipped. "You are mistaken, Sergeant. We do not hide. In order to find us, one must merely seek us out."

"I guess, but you don't exactly make it easy." I raised up my hands. "Not that I'm judging. If word of this place got out, you'd be swamped with tourists in no time. By the end of summer, all your lovely flowers would be plucked, your fish would be too traumatized to come to the surface, and all your statues would be engraved with lovely little slogans like 'Timmy was here' or 'Brian and Sarah forever.'"

Brother Kim's eyes tightened, but I could tell the thought had occurred to him before now. "People do not always appreciate the beauty in front of them. Perhaps one day that will change."

"Perhaps," I said. "But not today, and I'm here to talk about something else."

"As you said. Murder."

"Not just one murder." I held up my fingers. "Three. And two of them occurred only a couple of blocks from here." I watched his face as I spoke. There was a flash of detached sadness but not surprise. He already knew. I said as much, and he didn't bother to deny it.

"Chinatown is a very small place. News finds its way even here."

"We found a cell phone at the murder site. One that wasn't registered to either of our two victims."

"Is that so?"

"It's what they call a burner phone. It only had one number saved in its contact list. And that was for your temple."

"Hmm."

I waited a second to see if he would say more, but he didn't. "Care to explain?"

"Explain what?"

I drew in a breath and let it out slowly. Darned if he wasn't right about the jasmine. "Explain how an unregistered cell phone bearing only your phone number came to be found at a double murder site."

"That is a difficult question to answer," he said. "There are, as Americans are fond of saying, many possibilities."

I nodded and turned my head away, allowing my focus to linger over a small bed of sky-blue flowers for several seconds before speaking. "Brother Kim, can we speak candidly for a moment?"

"Of course," he said. "Our order believes that deceptions, even small ones, damage not only the speaker but the listener as well. I would hear your honest words, Sergeant."

"I like this place. It's beautiful and peaceful. It shows what can be accomplished with dedication and hard work."

"Thank you."

"I wasn't finished. Just because I admire what you've accomplished doesn't mean I won't tear it apart if I think you're lying to me. Doubly so if I think you're trying to cover up a murder."

"Sergeant..."

"I'm dealing with life or death, Kim. And we can play these little word games all day, but the clock is ticking, and if even one more person gets hurt when I think you could've helped me prevent it, I'm going to call every cop I know and tell them about this place. Then I'll head straight to the fire marshal. I hope your permits and building codes are up to date."

"Sergeant—"

"And if by some miracle you come through all that and still don't want to talk to me, I'm going to stop by every bar I know and hand out flyers for an all-night keg party offering free beer. And I know a lot of bars, Brother Kim. Every drunk Irishman within a hundred-mile radius is going to descend on this place. You think the tourists are bad? I'll have them laying in your flowerbeds and pissing in your koi ponds. And all your lovely little fish? Well, they're going to end up on someone's George Foreman. And don't even get me started on the graffiti slogans. So I'm going to ask you one more time, as nicely as I can. Why was there a cell phone with your phone number at my murder site?"

I watched Brother Kim's face the entire time I was delivering my threats. There were a few twitches, but they were quickly suppressed. I could practically hear Mel Robbin's 'Let them' slogan whispering along in the background as he considered.

Eventually, he said, "You drive a hard bargain, Sergeant."

"That's because I'm not bargaining. I'm threatening. It'll break my heart to do it, but if you force me, I'll make good on it."

A full minute passed before he spoke. "There is honor in the work we do here. Honor in tilling the soil and uplifting those who look to us for guidance." He drew in a breath and then let it out in a quiet exhale. "And there is honor in placing the needs of a community above one's own desires. Ask your questions, Sergeant. I will assist you as best I am able."

A soft flutter went through my chest, but I pushed it aside and forced myself to focus. "The cellphone."

"Many who come to train at our temple seek an inner peace which has eluded them in the outside world. In order to quiet one's mind, they must be willing to sacrifice many of life's modern amenities. Computers. Video games. Romantic relationships."

"Cellphones," I repeated.

"Such things serve to distract one's focus, but we are not immune to the need for them. Sometimes, situations arise in which technology is necessary. In those rare cases, we allow for the purchase of a phone such as you have described, so that it can be given to one of our brothers in order to ensure they have the ability to communicate with our temple."

"And by chance is one of your brothers missing?"

He started to shake his head, then hesitated. "Not precisely. Brother Dai left us some days back. We have not heard from him since yesterday afternoon, but he was not expected back until next week, so we had not yet begun to worry."

"This Brother Dai. He about my age? Shaved head? Dressed in your little outfit?"

Brother Kim's face remained stoic. "Is there something you wish to tell me, Sergeant?"

"We won't know for sure until we can arrange for someone to come down to the coroner's office and give a positive identification, but I think there's a high likelihood that we found your missing brother early this morning. The details aren't good. Are you sure you want to hear them?"

Brother Kim nodded. "Brother Dai was a good man. His life will not be defined by his passing. Please continue."

"He was beaten to death. Someone worked him over good. I don't know what they used, but it wasn't pretty."

Brother Kim stopped breathing while he digested the information. Eventually, when he was ready, his shoulders dropped, and he exhaled out of the mouth as if whispering a silent prayer. "This is very sad news."

"Why did Brother Dai leave the temple? Why did he need a cell phone if he wasn't going to leave Chinatown?"

"Because there was a need."

"What kind of need?"

JADE ENCLAVE

"This temple and those of us who call it home do not exist in a vacuum. We are meant to serve the people of Chinatown. To see to their well-being by ensuring they are fed, educated, and when needed, protected."

"Is that what he was doing? Protecting someone?"

"Indeed. Some days back, two men approached the temple and requested our help."

"Who were they? What were their names?"

"The first man was named Xuanming Fei. A boat captain. The second man was his employee. Haoran Hei."

My face dropped as he recited the names, and Brother Kim was quick to notice.

"I see that you know them."

"They're my victims." Despite the serene atmosphere, my heart started beating faster in my chest. "Why did they come to you seeking protection?"

"They believed their lives were in danger. That they were being hunted by a man who had passed beyond the realm of mortality."

"You're talking about the Jiangshi?"

Brother Kim's eyebrows rose. "You're familiar with the legends?"

"Not really. But I'm learning as I go, and all the evidence I've found over the past twenty-four hours leads me to believe that this Jiangshi, or at least someone claiming to be a Jiangshi, is here in Boston."

"I feared as much. If what you say is true, he has already claimed his first victims."

"I wouldn't be so sure of that. Word on the street is the Jiangshi didn't kill the two sailors. The Gray Fox did."

Brother Kim missed a step, his mouth curving down into a speculative frown before he shook his head. "I fear you are mistaken, Sergeant. The Gray Fox would not have killed these men. Not unless there was provocation, or if they were intent upon harming the citizens of Chinatown. Of this, I am certain."

"From what I hear, the Gray Fox is less of a Robin Hood character and more of a shadowy kingpin quick to kill anyone who gets in his way."

"I fear you have been misinformed. Life has never been easy for the people of Chinatown. We have struggled hard to create a better life for ourselves. There are many who have tried to exploit us over the years. The Gray Fox has only ever acted to keep our home free from harm."

"Do you know the Gray Fox's identity?"

"I do not," he said. "I have never spoken to the Fox directly. But messages have a way of reaching me when there is great need."

"And do you have any way of sending messages back?"

"I'm afraid not."

"Figures." I sighed. "Putting the identity of the murderer aside for a moment, why did the two sailors think the Jiangshi was coming after them? What could a tiny boat captain have that an immortal being of the night would want?"

"It is not what he had, but what he had received."

"Meaning?"

"Once, a man could feed his family by fishing the waters of the Boston Harbor. But that time is gone. Those who would make their living by way of the water have been forced to seek out other avenues to avoid going destitute."

"Cargo. He had something the Jiangshi wanted." I considered it for a moment. "It couldn't have been much. I haven't seen his boat myself, but from what I understand. It's not that large.

What could he have been hauling that the Jiangshi would be willing to come all the way here?"

"I can answer that, but in order to understand, you must be willing to peer beyond the curtain into the Jiangshi's past. He may have shed his mortality, but there are those who still remember."

"Remember what?"

"Who he was before."

"You're talking about before he became a vampire?"

Brother Kim nodded. "Tell me, Sergeant, are you a practicing Buddhist?"

"No. I tried the whole meditation bit for a while. Didn't take. My bike works better."

"Perhaps a Christian faith then?"

I shrugged. "Once upon a time, my mom would've smiled if I called myself Catholic, but I've seen too much of what goes on behind the scenes to really embrace it. Way I figure, any organized religion that starts and ends their service by asking for money is only a short step away from a Ponzi scheme."

"Do you not have any beliefs which you can hold to?"

"Afraid not. These days I'm all about disbelief and disproving."

"I see," he said. "Then it may be that the story of the Jiangshi will not help you as much as you wish."

"Won't know until we try. Lay it on me."

"According to historians, his given name was Zi Ran, and he was born in China, in the year 1602. He came to manhood during the reign of Emperor Zhu Youjian, also known as the Chongzhen Emperor. It was said he was a warrior, a doctor, and a loyal servant of the Emperor."

"I'm guessing things took a turn for the worse."

"In the 1630's, he helped quell a peasant uprising and gave aid to those affected by the northern blight. For his bravery, the Emperor allowed him to wed a beautiful young woman who was said to hold the heart of many men in the Emperor's court."

"How did she feel about this match?"

"Historical texts do not specify, but by all accounts, they lived together for many years until a distant stranger came to call upon the Emperor. The words of their meeting are lost to history, but at its conclusion, the Emperor ordered his soldiers to go to Zi Ran's home and remove the woman. Zi Ran was away treating soldiers, but when news of this reached him, he fled home in haste to find his wife gone. For days, he begged an audience with the Emperor, but each time he was rejected. Having no other choice, he cast aside his official duties and gathered those who had been most loyal to him. Together, they set off across the land, hunting for the mysterious stranger."

"And did they find him?"

"Indeed, though it was said they searched for the entirety of winter and most of the new spring before they found them living in a decrepit fortress high in the mountains. Under cover of night, they snuck inside, and Zi Ran found his wife, but she was changed. The writings of those who saw her claimed she was more corpse than woman, her mind void of any thought beyond savagery and violence.

"Zi Ran took the mysterious stranger and threw him into a dark cell, where he was left for weeks with neither food nor drink. During that time, it was said he focused all his attention on his wife. He sang to her. Spoke to her. Reminded her of the children they had left at home. Nothing served to bring her back from madness, and when he had exhausted all hope, he drove his sword through her and burned her body atop a funeral pyre.

"Afterward, he collected her ashes, and ground her bones into powder, placing them carefully within a sacred vase. Only then did he return to the dark cell in which he had chained the mysterious stranger."

JADE ENCLAVE

"What did he find when he got there?" I asked.

"Although it had been many weeks, the stranger yet lived, though he was so weak he could barely lift his head up. It is said that Zi Ran kneeled beside him, seized his throat, and wrung all his secrets from him. How he yet lived. How he had convinced the Emperor to abandon honor and break his word. The stranger held nothing back, and for two days Zi Ran remained sequestered with him. Then, on the morning of the third day, he exited the cell as a ghost of his former self. His followers cried to see him so, and they fled the fortress in fear, returning to the Emperor and begging his forgiveness along with offering up a warning.

"Zi Ran was not satisfied with the death of his wife or the distant stranger. He sought revenge on all who had wronged him, including the Emperor. For many weeks, Zi Ran traveled amidst the countryside, snaring and enslaving all who saw him. He beguiled and enchanted the discontented, forming them into a rebel army that acted without need of rest. The emperor's generals sought to combat this army but were defeated at every turn. Finally, as the rebels closed in around him, the Chongzhen Emperor fled into the hills overlooking Beijing. There, he hung himself rather than face Zi Ran's wrath and brought an end to the Ming Dynasty."

"Huh," I said, unsure how else to respond.

"From there, Zi Ran fades into history, and no mention of his name is seen again. That is, until recently, when news broke of a tomb uncovered within the Kunlun Mountains. Inside, it was said to contain many historical artifacts, including several scrolls recounting the legends of Zi Ran. By right, all items inside should have been taken to the university, then distributed to the government museums, as is fitting and proper.

"Unfortunately, it had become commonplace for researchers to offer such wares first to private buyers. Treasure hunters and collectors, such as it were."

"I'm surprised the government lets them get away with that."

Brother Kim shook his head. "To sell such items in China is very dangerous. Anyone found guilty would face severe punishments. For that reason, many items are often smuggled out of China as quickly as possible, before their discovery becomes known. Negotiations and sales have been known to take place while on the ocean. It means less money for the sellers, but also less risk. Should they be discovered, they can merely dump the artifacts overboard, and claim ignorance."

"You think some of those artifacts might've been brought to Boston? And that's why the Jiangshi is here?"

"Not some of those artifacts. The most important one. A vase, described in detail within the scrolls, said to contain the ashes of Zi Ran's wife."

"You're kidding me?"

"I make no jest, though I suppose such belief would depend on whether or not one accepts the story I have just told you as true. I can tell you this much. The ship captain believed it. He claimed he had no knowledge of the artifact's significance prior to taking possession, and upon learning of its past, immediately set out to make amends. He sent word to the mainland that the vase and its contents would be returned undamaged. Unfortunately, word travels slowly, and he feared he would be slain before things could be set right."

"So, he believed the Jiangshi was coming after him. And he couldn't go to the police because it would mean unmasking his entire operation. So he came here and asked for a monk. What did he offer you?"

"Nothing," Brother Kim said. "And we would've accepted nothing from him. Look around, Sergeant. Much has been given to us, so that we can ensure the well-being of our people. To take from them in such a matter would dishonor our temple and its purpose."

"I guess I can buy that. But here's the million-dollar question for you. If the Jiangshi is here seeking his wife's remains, and the ship captain and his first mate are already dead, where's the vase with her ashes now?"

Brother Kim opened his mouth, but a series of bells started ringing, echoing throughout the grounds before he could answer. A flash of confusion crossed his face, then his eyes widened. "Oh, dear."

"Oh, crud," I said. "Tell me those bells don't mean what I think they do?"

He shook his head. "You should leave, Sergeant. Quickly. The temple is under attack."

The Jiangshi. Friday, July 25th 1749hrs

THE INHABITANTS OF THE temple had evidently prepared for this possibility, though whether they had rehearsed for something from the supposed supernatural world or for some sort of government intervention, I couldn't say. It didn't matter. As soon as the bells started ringing, the men and women scooped up the children and headed toward the eastern corner of the grounds. They disappeared into one of the rooms and didn't come out, leaving me to conclude there was most likely some sort of hidden tunnel that would deposit them on the outside.

Tootsie and I remained behind with Brother Kim and two of the other monks, the three of them arming themselves with bamboo staffs. As the crowd inside the temple thinned, raised voices reached us, screams and shouts echoing out from the same hallway we'd entered through.

Fifteen seconds passed before one of the monks came crashing through the sliding screen door, tearing through the paper and landing in a painful roll. There were bruises on his face, and his robes were torn. He skidded to a graceless halt, and Brother Kim motioned his monks forward. They raced to their fallen brother and lifted him from the ground, supporting him to stand.

"Go," Brother Kim said, in a voice that allowed for no argument. "I will see to our temple's defense."

"Not alone," I said. My pistol had cleared the holster before the monk finished rolling, and I settled into a shooter's stance and drew a bead on the hallway when—

"No!" Brother Kim swung his bamboo staff up, halting the edge just in front of my pistol's barrel. "I would not have blood stain these sacred grounds if at all possible."

I hesitated a moment, then lowered my pistol and straightened as three Jade Fangs came through the broken doorway. The Jiangshi's minions were dressed as before, black kung fu uniforms with green stitching and various weapons in their belts. I recognized the one in the center, Cicuta, from the restaurant.

"Well, well," Cicuta said. "We meet again. Sergeant."

JADE ENCLAVE

"Howdy, Peon," I said. "How's the schnoz?"

Something nasty flashed across Cicuta's face. "Still so arrogant. I look forward to watching the master break you."

I feigned a yawn using my non-pistol hand. "Funny thing, I keep hearing all about this master, but I haven't seen hide nor hair of him yet. I'm starting to wonder if he even exists."

"Fear not, Sergeant. The time will come when you will be all too well acquainted."

"I'm here now. Feel like giving him a call?"

"Alas, we have other matters to attend to." He turned and regarded Brother Kim, clearly dismissing me. "Lower your staff, monk, and bring me your abbot. We have much to discuss."

Brother Kim's staff didn't waver. "If you seek audience with the abbot, then you need only look in front of you. I am Brother Kim, and you are not welcome on these grounds. Please, leave now."

Cicuta's eyes narrowed. "*You're* the abbot?"

Brother Kim sighed. "Why does everyone always seem so surprised?"

"Don't take it personally," I told him. "You have a youthful face. It catches people off guard."

"Perhaps I should grow a beard?"

"Worth a try."

"Enough!" Cicuta snarled. "This does not concern you, Sergeant. And you, monk. You're coming with us. Do so quietly, and you will not be harmed."

"Yeah, right," I said, loud enough for them to hear.

"Do so quietly, and your people will come to no harm," Cicuta amended.

"You hold no power over my people," Brother Kim said. "And as far as your request, I must politely decline. I am, as they say, busy all week."

Cicuta's smile lacked warmth. "You misunderstand. It wasn't a request." He snapped his arms up and then out, pointing towards Brother Kim. "Bring him to me alive."

The two Jade Fangs on either side started forward. The first drew a short, slender katana from his belt. The second, a pair of trident like sai knives. They swept forward across the courtyard, and I moved to intercept them, but Brother Kim stopped me and shook his head.

"I will handle this."

He stepped forward dutifully, placed himself in the center of the small island and remained still as they circled to either side.

"Sergeant," Tootsie said from beside me, her voice low and urgent.

I shook my head, and for the first time, really looked at Brother Kim. His muscles weren't as dense as Tootsie's, but there was a leanness to him, more akin to a tiger than a lion. Something in his stance bespoke of explosive energy, and he held the bamboo staff as if he knew how to use it. A soft flutter went through my chest, cast aside a moment later when the Jade Fangs rushed forward with a shout.

"Sergeant!" Tootsie again, but it was too late.

Brother Kim and the Jade Fangs came together in a series of quick, vicious strikes, their blades catching the late afternoon sunlight as the sounds of metal hitting bamboo rang throughout the temple grounds. The Jade Fangs cut and stabbed with vicious ferocity, but Brother Kim wielded his staff with blinding speed, spinning it until it almost appeared as if he had a green force field protecting him.

The three flowed across the courtyard, shifting stances and countering footwork with every breath. The Jade Fangs leapt and ducked, striking high and low, but always Brother Kim's staff turned them back, and as the seconds passed, their strikes began to slow, their arms worn down from the effort.

That's when the momentum of the fight changed. As Brother Kim parried aside their blows, he began to add counterstrikes of his own, the tip of his staff striking against the Jade Fangs' arms, back, and hands. Within moments, every strike the Jade Fangs attempted saw them take one in return, until Brother Kim whipped his staff around his back, caught it on the other side, and slammed it against the back of the closest Jade Fang's skull. The green clad vampire wannabe dropped like a stone, collapsing into a boneless heap as his sword clattered to the ground.

The second Jade Fang's eyes widened, and he started to pull back, but Brother Kim was on him immediately. He danced forward, knocked the twin knives wide and slapped the tip of his staff down against the floor. For a moment I feared he'd missed his strike, but a second later I realized he'd merely bated his opponent. As the Jade Fang went to close the distance, Brother Kim snapped his arms up, driving the tip of his staff between the Jade Fang's legs and lifting his feet off the ground. A breathless gasp escaped from the Jade Fang a split second before Brother Kim yanked back his staff and brought it around in an overhand strike, smashing it down onto the Jade Fang's face before his feet ever touched the ground. The Jade Fang's eyes rolled into the back of his head, and he joined his fellow on the ground as Brother Kim spun round and regarded Cicuta.

"It would seem that you stand alone," Brother Kim said. "Perhaps you wish to reconsider your stance?"

Rather than being intimidated by Brother Kim's display, Cicuta's mouth broke apart into a wide, cruel smile, and he dropped low into a horse stance, drawing out the longsword hanging from his belt. It was a leaf-bladed weapon with a dark wood handle and jade-colored tassel. He brought the weapon up, laying the flat of the blade against his opposite forearm as his eyes danced in anticipation.

It was an anticipation that would never be realized.

Before the two warriors could come together, a low hiss echoed out from the hallway. It was the sound a serpent might make, a hissing lament to a distant memory of a place that no longer exists. The sound carried across the courtyard, echoing through the ponds and dancing its way among the flowers, causing them to twist and shy back despite the lack of a breeze. All eyes turned as dark smoke poured from the hallway, billowing and dancing as it rose to cast the courtyard in gray shadows.

A figure appeared, a lone silhouette against a dark gray backdrop. Three steps carried him into the courtyard, and the Jiangshi emerged from the mist without making a sound.

His face was pale, almost translucent, with sharp, angular features that gave him an otherworldly aura. His eyes were liquid black pools that spoke of eternal night, and his lips were the shade of spoiled raspberries.

His rich green robe seemed to hold to the darkness as he moved, as if imbued with the essence of shadows. Wide-mouthed sleeves hid his hands behind delicately embroidered patterns of dark vines and twisted lotus flowers. He came forward with slow, deliberate steps, surveying the courtyard in his deathless gaze as Cicuta turned and dropped into a deep bow.

"Master," he whispered.

The Jiangshi's eyes passed over him without seeing, focusing instead on Brother Kim, Tootsie, and myself. I didn't flinch or shy away, but the force of his gaze struck me low in the gut, and my hand involuntarily tightened around my pistol grip. Brother Kim and Tootsie felt it too, but it was the abbot who recovered first.

"That which you seek is not here," Brother Kim said. "To harm those under my care gains you nothing. Leave this place, and seek your beloved's remains elsewhere."

JADE ENCLAVE

The Jiangshi drew in a long breath, holding it as if tasting the air, and then let it out in a sudden whoosh. He rolled his shoulders once, then started forward toward us at an unhurried pace.

"Okay," I heard myself say. "Sacred grounds or not, I've had it up to my neck with this nonsense." I started to raise my pistol, but again, Brother Kim stopped me with a raised hand.

"Stay your hand, Sergeant. The more you fight, the stronger he becomes."

The corner of the Jiangshi's mouth twitched up into a smile, but his pace didn't increase. He crossed the courtyard and came up beside Brother Kim, who dropped back into a defensive stance with his staff gripped lengthwise across his body. The Jiangshi walked right up to him and raised his hand, extending his fingers so that his nails just grazed the monk's raised staff.

There was a long, drawn-out moment, where the two stared at one another, each taking the other's measure. Then the Jiangshi snapped his arm forward, his fingers closing into a tight fist. Brother Kim's staff snapped in two with a thunderous *crack*, and the Jiangshi's punch carried past, striking the abbot in the chest and sending him flying backward.

For a split second, I struggled to comprehend what I'd just seen. Then Brother Kim came down beside me, still holding one segment of his broken staff, and I snapped into action.

I raised my pistol and drew a bead on the Jiangshi as he sprang into the air. He propelled himself forward from a dead standstill, raising his legs like an Olympic jumper. His robes flowed behind him as he crossed the distance, and I fired twice while he was still airborne. My aim was good, and the bullets struck his torso with a dull *thud*, but the Jiangshi gave no indication that he'd felt their impact as he came down beside me.

A flash of fear went through me, and I jerked back as he swept his arm out toward my face. His hands were claws. Not literally. He wore an armored gauntlet, green metal scales running the length of his hand and down his fingers before ending in pointed claws.

His bladed hand shot past my face, sending black droplets spraying over my head onto the courtyard path. That was the moment I realized his clawed gauntlet was coated in... *something*. I didn't know what to call it, but I could assume it wasn't anything good. Those claws were a piercing weapon, and I was certain I didn't want whatever it was coating them coursing through my veins.

The Jiangshi swept forward, slicing his hands in a wide arc. I threw myself back into a roll and came up on one knee in a firing position. This time, I aimed south of center mass. Unfortunately, the Jiangshi was a step ahead, and he leapt into the air, twisting his body into a sideways spin as my bullets passed beneath him.

He came down smoothly, and I adjusted my aim again, going for a head shot and hoping like heck that third time was the charm.

It wasn't.

The Jiangshi swung his arm up, shielding his face with his heavy sleeve just before my finger depressed the trigger. The gun's report left my ears ringing, and the Jiangshi jerked, the impact of the gunfire forcing him back across the courtyard.

I emptied my magazine, blasting round after round to no avail. Each shot forced the Jiangshi back, but he remained upright against the onslaught, enduring the attack until my pistol eventually ran dry.

He dropped his sleeve and peered at me with black, dead eyes as I yanked free the spent magazine and slapped another in its place. I chambered my pistol, but a strong arm seized me around the waist before I could resume firing and spun me back toward the opposite side of the courtyard.

"Run!" Brother Kim said. "We cannot defeat him here."

The Bostonian in me started to protest, but a quick glance over my shoulder revealed that the Jiangshi was no longer fighting alone. A dozen Jade Fangs had appeared from the hallway. They swept in through the courtyard and formed up around their master, holding their weapons at the ready.

"Run!" I screamed and got no argument.

The three of us took off, with Tootsie taking an early lead. Brother Kim was only a step behind her, while I trailed behind them. Between the lack of food, sleep, and the beatings I'd already endured, my adrenaline reserves were shot, and my vision swam as I forced myself to keep moving.

Something flashed past my head, and I glimpsed a shuriken star just before it struck the concrete. A second swiftly followed, and this one would have lodged itself in the small of my back if not for Brother Kim. He whirled his broken staff around and knocked the shuriken aside, sending it spinning off into the nearest pond.

We reached the opposite end of the courtyard, and Brother Kim motioned to the closest hallway. Tootsie drew up beside the entryway, motioning Brother Kim and I through before falling in behind us. She fell back using a side step method, pistol raised to cover our retreat.

Brother Kim led us down a long, twisting hallway that cast us into darkness more than once before we reached its end. A circle of light in the distance revealed itself to be a doorway, and we came outside into a small alcove with a stairway leading up to the alleyway.

We were on the south side of the temple exterior, where a brown wooden fence lined with trash cans blocked it from casual view. Brother Kim waved me through, then waited until Tootsie appeared, her pistol raised. Once she passed, Brother Kim swept aside a pair of trash cans, revealing a heavy black grated gate. He swung the gate closed, and the deadbolt lock slid into place before he secured it with a second padlock.

Confident that no one would soon be following, he motioned us up the stairs, and the three of us sprinted down the alleyway and exited out the other side. I spotted my car where we'd left it along the curb. Tootsie still had the keys, and we piled inside as she brought the engine to life, pulling away in a black cloud of exhaust before the Jade Fangs could give chase.

Old Harbor Storage. Friday, July 25th 1842hrs

Once we were in the car and driving, I gave Tootsie and Brother Kim the once over. My new trainee seemed okay, minus the busted nose she'd gotten from the Gray Fox. The ice had helped with the swelling, but the skin surrounding the area had darkened into various shades of purple, and come morning, I suspected she would be able to do a passable racoon impression.

In the backseat, Brother Kim sat stiffly with one hand pressed against his torso. He was breathing gingerly, and every bump in the road caused him to wince. I feared he might have fractured a rib facing the Jiangshi, but there wasn't much I could do about it other than to drop him off at the hospital, and I doubted he would go for that.

JADE ENCLAVE

As for me, I took a quick rundown of myself and was relieved to note I wasn't shot or stabbed. Likewise, there were no signs of acute poisoning, suggesting none of the black liquid coating the Jiangshi's gauntlet had gotten on me. That was good news.

The bad news was I was exhausted, and there was an uncomfortable tightness in my back from where I'd jerked to avoid the Jiangshi. I tried my hardest to ignore it as I settled back in my seat, and several minutes passed in silence before Tootsie finally spoke.

"Okay, I'm just going to say it. What the heck *was* that thing?" She peered back through the rearview mirror.

"That was Jiangshi," Brother Kim answered, straight and to the point.

Tootsie snorted, then immediately wished she hadn't, raising one hand to cup her injured nose. "I'll say. Did you see that back there? How the heck did he jump like that?" She glanced at me. "And how many rounds did you fire? Six? Seven?"

"All of them," I said.

All of a magazine's worth, anyway.

Tootsie hesitated, then slowly closed her mouth. She looked like someone had punched her in the gut. "Is it always like this?"

"No," I said. "This was bad. This was…"

"This is what you face when you pit yourself against a Jiang-shi," Brother Kim said as he peered out the window. "Pull over please."

We'd reached the edge of Chinatown, and Tootsie pulled up to the next curb. Brother Kim got out and closed the door before stepping up to our window. "Thank you for your assistance, officers, but I must see to my people's safety."

"How do I reach you?" I asked.

"Call the temple's number and leave a message. I will respond as soon as I am able."

"Be careful," I said.

"You as well." Brother Kim bowed, bringing his hands together in front of him. Then he hurried off down the street and disappeared from view.

"Guess it's just us again," Tootsie said.

"Guess so." I shifted in my seat and gave myself a shake. "Drive."

We pulled away from the curb and crossed over the border of Chinatown and into the Financial District. We took our time, now that the threat of being chased had passed. Unfortunately, even traveling at a modest pace didn't change the fact that we had no place to go. We weren't welcome at the police station, and I seriously doubted that Forensics Division would allow us back into our headquarters anytime soon. We were homeless, stranded and adrift in the sea that was downtown Boston.

"Sergeant?" Tootsie asked.

"Yeah?"

"What do we do now?"

I sighed and shook my head, biting back my initial reply which was to confess that I didn't have a clue. Admitting it aloud seemed wrong.

Transferring to Blue Moon hadn't been my idea, initially, but I'd made peace with it in the months since. More so, I'd accepted the sergeant's badge and the responsibility that came with it. If I was going to lead the division, then I needed to keep a cool head when the going got tough. So instead of answering in the negative, I blew a long breath out through my nose and forced myself to think.

The memory of the Jiangshi sent shivers down my spine, but I forced the fear aside and told myself it was just the aftereffects of the battle that had shaken me. The Jiangshi wasn't real. He was a man, no different from any other. Dangerous, yes, but not immortal.

That being said, I wanted him gone. In a prison cell, preferably, but in the ground if necessary. How could I make that hope a reality?

The answer came quickly. I couldn't afford to face the Jiangshi head on. Doing so would see me outnumbered and outgunned. Instead, I needed to lure him out. Force him to come to me. Put him in a situation where I had all the advantages and make him dance to my tune.

The pessimistic side of me wondered how the heck I was supposed to do that, but I told myself that I already had my answer. Find the one thing he wanted more than anything in this world, his wife's vase, and dangle it like a carrot to bring him out into the open where I could take him out.

And afterward?

See to the safety of Chinatown. Starting with Satoru Doku, although, that was a problem I might not have to deal with. Or, at least, not yet. Much as it felt wrong to admit, I had serious doubts about his ability to survive the Gray Fox. He'd done it once, but only because Tootsie and I had been there to protect him. That likely wouldn't be the case next time, and unless something changed on his end, I suspected his days were numbered.

Unfortunately, that still left one problem. The Gray Fox. Much as I didn't want to admit it, some things couldn't be left for another day, and a ninja running around assassinating people wasn't the sort of thing that I could afford to brush under the rug.

I'd already put a bullet in him back at the furniture store. Once the Jiangshi and Satoru Doku were sorted, I would need to turn all my attention toward catching him. Chinatown was going to have to find its way without the aid of a shadowy ninja in its corner.

And afterward...

There was no afterward.

That was as far as I got, because while I'd been thinking, I'd leaned back in the seat and inadvertently closed my eyes. I hadn't meant to fall asleep, but everything I'd endured over the past twenty-four hours finally caught up with me. I can't speak as to whether passing out in the wake of a firefight is very inspiring, but at least I could never be accused of not giving it my all.

I passed into unconsciousness and time skipped forward. I woke up when Tootsie patted my shoulder.

"Eh?" I mumbled, slowly blinking myself awake. "What's going on?"

"We're here."

Realization slowly returned, and I straightened in my seat. "Here where?"

"Old Harbor Storage."

"Eh?"

"It's a self-storage facility in North Charlestown. Not too far from the Bunker Hill Monument."

"Okay," I said, drawing out the word. "What are we doing here?"

"I called Detective Wei." She shrugged. "You needed to rest, and I wasn't sure what our next move should be. He suggested we could meet him here. Felt like the right thing to do."

I nodded, fighting against the flash of panic that surged inside my chest. Our foray into the Sacred Pine Temple had gone badly, but I couldn't definitively say that was Detective Wei's fault. He was following the clues, same as we were.

That said… something about it felt off. Call me paranoid, but the hairs on the back of my neck don't lie, and right now they were standing at attention.

I stifled a yawn with the back of my fist and checked my pistol, loosening it in its holster before I exited the car. The cat nap, brief as it was, had done me good. Although I could have used a few hours more. I rolled my shoulders and twisted at the waist. All of the aches and bruises I'd accumulated over the past two days were catching up with me. I felt swollen and stiff, and I longed for the feeling of a hot shower. Unfortunately, that would have to wait.

The summer ocean breeze swept past me, tinged with sea salt, motor oil, and rusted metal. Peering around the self-storage facility, it was clear the place had seen better days.

The three long buildings were painted the color of sea foam, and although the doors had once been blue, tying them together in a tacky nautical theme, they'd faded long ago, and bits of orange rust lined the rails on either side. The concrete beneath our feet was cracked along the edges, and tiny sprouts of summer green poked out through the crevices.

"It's this way." Tootsie took the lead, and I followed, scanning the walkways as the wind pushed against my back. We passed down the first aisle and turned the corner to find Detective Wei waiting for us. He was holding a large bolt cutter in his hands, balancing it with his crutches.

"Ladies," he said. "How was the temple?"

"Enlightening," I said. "And dangerous. This Jiangshi is a real problem."

"You're just figuring that out now? I would have thought the bodies would have clued you in beforehand."

"Hush and tell me what we're doing here."

"Remember when I told you I'd found where Xuanming Fei's boat was docked?"

I nodded, flashes of blood and death inside an unkempt apartment rising to the forefront of my mind. I squashed them down swiftly and forced myself to focus. "Yes."

"I went on board for a sneak and peak. No one was around. I searched top to bottom, but unfortunately there wasn't much there. Just a lot of grime and neglect. Then I found this."

He reached inside his jacket and drew out a folded piece of yellow paper. Printed on one side was a receipt that matched the name of the storage facility. It was paid up front for the next three months, and the unit number listed matched the door in front of us.

I took the receipt and gave it a once over before handing it back. "Any idea what's inside?"

Wei shook his head and raised the bolt cutters. "I know one way to find out."

"Pretty sure some might view that as breaking and entering. Last I checked it was illegal."

He gave a half-shrug. "Some might also say we have a moral duty to bring a killer to justice."

"Some might."

"Guess the question is are we among those some or the other some?"

It was a fair question but not one that I could rush to answer. Following clues wherever they may lead was all well and good, but I couldn't afford to lose sight of the fact that we still needed to prosecute this case once the killer was in custody. To do that, I would need to be able to explain every step of our investigation to a jury, and experience had taught me that if there's one thing juries hate, it's the police taking the law into their own hands. Even the slightest hint of impropriety could be enough to see a murderer walk free.

Of course, none of that would matter if I couldn't prove who'd killed those men. Perceived improprieties don't matter when there are no arrests, and by extension, no trial to prosecute.

Detective Wei read the struggle in my features. "It's up to you, Sergeant. This is your case. I'm just presenting options. You say the word and we'll fall back. I can make some calls. Try and secure another warrant."

I didn't know what my odds of getting a warrant for something like this were, but I suspected they weren't good. Maybe if I were assigned to Homicide Division, I could have pulled some strings, but that's one of the drawbacks of being the smallest division in the department. You don't have a lot of room to leverage favors. Mind you, that was changing, but it was a slow process. And we needed to be careful, because while we were building up our goodwill one drop at a time, it would only take one screw up to see it all leak right out the bottom of our proverbial bucket.

I gave myself several seconds to consider, allowing the thoughts to play themselves out. At the end of it, I came to a hard stop on one undeniable fact.

No matter the circumstance or obstacles, I had a duty to the citizens of Boston to ensure they were safe, and my gut told me that trying to navigate the political challenges associated with securing a warrant would only get more people killed. My people. I was here now and if there were answers in this unit, I wanted to see them for myself.

"Tootsie."

Tootsie accepted the bolt cutters from Detective Wei and brought their teeth around the padlock. The muscles in her forearm tensed and strained for about five seconds before the teeth bit through the arm of the lock, and separate ends fell to the floor with a metallic clang.

Tootsie let out a self-satisfied huff, then handed over the bolt cutters, seized the steel door handle and rolled it up into the ceiling. For a brief moment her form blocked my view. Then she moved aside, and I felt my breath catch.

The inside of the unit was filled to the brim.

With *electronics*.

Floor to ceiling shelving units lined the three walls, filled with open top plastic bins. It was like being in some sort of dystopian Best Buy. There were boxes of old cell phones, along with routers and internet modems. Circuit boards the size of my hand that looked like they'd been pulled from old appliances or maybe large printers. One box contained a dozen credit card scanners, the same as you might find at any retail store, along with hundreds of blank credit cards.

"Man," Tootsie said, her voice breathless. "The guys down in Identity Fraud would have a field day with this place."

She wasn't wrong on that one. "Wei, didn't you say there were some rumors about a Chinatown gang dealing in stolen electronics?"

Detective Wei nodded. "Yeah. Couple of us suspected it might be part of a money laundering scheme. But it was thought to be pretty petty."

"This is more than petty crime."

Peering around, I asked myself if there was enough value in here to be worth killing over, and I concluded there probably was.

"Brace yourselves, because it's about to get worse," Tootsie said. "Look."

I glanced at her over my shoulder, but she was peering past me at something inside the unit. Following her gaze, I saw what had entranced her, and my stomach did a quick flip-flop.

Sitting atop the top shelf, nestled between two computer hard drives, was an antique vase. A lone piece of art amidst a sea of modern fare, and once seen, it stuck out like a sore thumb.

"Tootsie," I said.

She nodded and stepped inside the unit, placing her back against the shelving unit and locking her fingers together to form a foothold. I placed my foot in her hands, and she hoisted me up, allowing me to reach the top shelf.

The antique vase was cold to the touch, but it was beautiful, its turquoise body enameled with cranes, butterflies and dragonflies, all dancing in flight above lotus plants and flowering chrysanthemums. My hands shook when I touched it, but I forced myself to exhale, and in one swift motion, yanked the top free and peered down inside.

Someone is Lying. Friday, July 25th 1907hrs

"I am so confused," Tootsie said.

"Same here," I said. "But stick with me and we'll figure it out together."

We'd retrieved the vase, and I'd placed it in one of the plastic bins, dumping the former contents of cell phones out onto the floor and padding the edges with cardboard. Once finished, we'd closed the unit and replaced the broken lock with Tootsie's old locker padlock. She'd taken it with her when she was transferred to Blue Moon. It wasn't identical to the one we'd cut to get inside, but hopefully no one would notice. And if they did, they'd have to break the lock to get inside, so we'd know someone had been back.

We retreated back to my car, and I placed the bin containing the vase into the trunk alongside the bolt cutters before turning to regard Tootsie and Detective Wei.

"Where to now?" Tootsie asked.

"I need you to drop me off at the Oyster House." I said. "Then I'm going to need you to go back out again."

"Where am I headed?"

I told her.

"Okay," she said, frowning.

"I'm working on a theory, but I need a few more pieces to fall into place before I'm ready to place any bets on it. Speaking of which." I turned to Detective Wei. "How friendly are you with that judge who gave you the warrant?"

"He's my cousin. So, there's that."

"Can you call him and ask for another favor?"

"Don't see why not. What am I asking for?"

I told him. "Send the information back to Tootsie and then meet us back at the Oyster House. We've got a lot of work to do and not much time."

He nodded, and the three of us parted ways. Detective Wei called for a ride from patrol, while Tootsie and I headed back toward downtown. Traffic wasn't good, but we made fairly decent time. She pulled up along the curb, and I exited the vehicle.

The scent of butter, salt, and lemon extended through the doorway and I passed through the dining room and made my way up to the second floor. Pongo was seated at the table, his chin resting on the edge of a thick leather-bound book whose title contained the words Massachusetts State Law followed by some Roman numerals. He glanced up as I entered, his eyes widening at the sight of me.

"Oh, my God, Sergeant. What happened to you?"

He started to rise, but I motioned him back down. "Bad guys. Where is everybody?"

"Uh, Officer Mayfield, Cambrie, is attending a law enforcement fundraiser. She thought about canceling, but there wasn't much she could do here, and most of the division heads are going to be in attendance, so..."

"So she's out schmoozing them." I rubbed my eyes but couldn't really be mad at her. Cambrie didn't have enough experience to be much use as an investigator. Her talents were better spent drumming up support for Blue Moon within the other divisions. Even a blind man could have seen that.

JADE ENCLAVE

"What about Robbie?"

"Called away. The Department of Transportation was having some sort of computer issues. Their own IT team was struggling, so Lieutenant Kermit sent him over to see if he could lend a hand."

And hopefully earn us a favor down the line. It was smart, although inconvenient. I reminded myself that Blue Moon Division was bigger than any one case, no matter how dangerous it might be. And besides, I wasn't actually alone.

"I need help, Pongo."

"Okay, what can I do?"

"Are the computers working yet?"

"Yep. Since this morning."

"Good. I need you to print something for me. Then I need you to put it in a manilla folder and slap one of our letter heads across it."

"I can do that," he said. "Anything else?"

"Yeah, I need a bowl of clam chowder. Hot as you can get it without scalding. Load it up with those oyster crackers. I need to eat, then I need to sleep." My brief catnap in the car had helped, but only so much that it had highlighted just how tired I really was.

I'd sent Tootsie on an errand, but I had no way of knowing how long it would take for her to return. I could sit here fretting, twiddling my thumbs and pulling my hair out, or I could do something that might actually help me, and get some much-needed shuteye.

I didn't hear Pongo's response, but a few minutes later I found myself sitting at a booth with a large bowl of said chowder in front of me. True to my request, it was hot but not scalding, and I took it down fast, shoveling large bites into my mouth until I reached the bottom of the bowl. Once that happened, I tore a couple of strips of soggy bread and chewed them thoroughly before fatigue finally won out.

I laid down right there in the booth, and no sooner had I closed my eyes then I fell into a heavy, dreamless sleep that lasted until Tootsie showed back up.

She woke me by tugging on my foot, and something between a moan and a growl slipped out past my throat before awareness asserted itself and I straightened into a sitting position, blinking clear my vision.

Pongo had cleared my dishes away as I slept, and the requested manilla folder with our letterhead sat on the table in its place. I checked the contents inside, then closed it back up and slid out of the booth.

My back had stiffened while I slept, and I clamped my teeth together to stop the groan that threatened to spill up from my throat as I forced myself to stretch. Everything hurt, from my hair down to my toes. Especially my toes. I'd been wearing my shoes for more than a day by this point, and I didn't want to think about what my feet must look like. Probably all pruny, like a marathon runner.

Tootsie cleared her throat from beside me, and it suddenly hit me that I'd been staring at my feet for a good ten seconds. I exhaled and lifted my gaze, rolling my shoulders and forcing myself to focus.

"Did you find her?" I asked.

Tootsie nodded and motioned to the far side of the room. "She's in the private dining room. Figure it's as close to an interrogation room as we were going to find here."

"Did she give you any trouble?"

Tootsie shook her head. "She was staying with friends. Cell phone trace led me right to her."

"Wei?"

"On his way here."

"Make sure he eats when he gets here," I said. "That goes for you too."

"Is Blue Moon picking up the bill?"

I sighed. "Just tell them to put it on my tab. I'll settle up later."

"Cool."

I left off the unspoken second part of that sentence. That if this went badly, what little money I had in my bank account would likely go toward paying off my funeral costs, rather than any outstanding food bills. No use dwelling on the negative. I had more important things to worry about.

I made my way across the dining room and paused beside the doorway leading into the private dining room. Once upon a time, this room had belonged to Titus Broggart, the leader of the Sons of Liberty. He was a lecherous little guy, and I always felt like he was trying to scam me somehow, but standing in the doorway I dearly wished I would find him waiting on the other side. I imagined the Jiangshi's face when confronted with muskets, or even better, a cannon, and felt the corner of my mouth twist up into a smile.

The feeling didn't last.

Titus wasn't here, and there was no cavalry coming to my rescue. It was just me, and if I didn't play this next part just right, a lot of people could get hurt.

I drew in a long breath and let it out over the course of several seconds. Then I squared my shoulders, seized the doorhandle, and pushed through into the room as if in a tremendous hurry.

"Stand up!" I snapped before I'd even cleared the doorway. "We've got to go."

Hui Lan's head snapped up from the table, and her mouth formed a surprised O before she stumbled up to her feet. I took a second to study her. The dark circles under her eyes were still there, suggesting I wasn't the only one who hadn't been getting any sleep, and the edges of her fingernails were red and swollen along the edges where she'd continued to work at them. Any defense attorney worth their salt would have explained those away as stress from leaving her home to attend MIT, but the cop part of my brain told me there was more to it than that. I could sense I was on the right track, but I still needed to know for sure.

Sometimes, to find your way to the truth, you have to start with a lie.

"W-where are we going?" Hui Lan asked.

"Massachusetts General Hospital."

"Why?"

"We found your roommate, Ru Yee. She's there now. We've been trying to get in touch with her family but you're the closest we've come to." I removed the top form from the manilla folder and slid it across the table along with a pen.

Hui Lan blinked and peered down at the form, her expression turning confused. "What is this?"

"I've spoken to the District Attorney, and, given the circumstances, he's agreed to grant you power of attorney over her."

"Power of... what? I don't understand. What circumstances?"

"There's no easy way to say this. The Jiangshi hurt her. Badly. The doctors are doing everything they can, but she's fading fast, and she's in a lot of pain. Signing this form will grant you the power to remove her from life support."

"*Remove* her?"

I nodded without meeting her eyes. "The hospital is committed to rendering aid, but once it becomes clear that they're only delaying the inevitable, the merciful thing to do is to allow the patient to pass in peace. But that's a decision you'll have to make."

She blinked, her face flushing. "Me? Uh, Sergeant. Hold on. I don't think I can make that decision."

"You don't have a choice. Not if you want justice, anyway. We're going after the Jiangshi, but we need your testimony to do that."

"You mean, if I don't sign this paper, you can't arrest him?"

"Let's just say it becomes infinitely more difficult. And an innocent woman may die for nothing." I motioned to the bottom of the form. "Sign, print and date here. And print clearly. The DA gets itchy when they can't read a signature." I slapped my hands together in front of her face. "Quickly now, we've got to get to the hospital."

"Uh... I... Um..."

"We don't have time for umms. Sign and date."

"Okay, okay." She lifted the pen and signed the form, dating and printing her name before sliding it across the table. At the last second, she seemed to realize her mistake. Her eyes widened, and she jerked across the table toward the form, but I shouldered her hand aside and snatched it off the table before she could get her hands on it.

"Too late," I said and pointed to the chair. "Sit."

There was a long moment's hesitation. Then Hui Lan slowly sank back into the chair. I waited until she was down before I looked at her signature. A surge of recognition flashed through me, and the pieces surrounding the mystery started clicking in my head.

"Sergeant, I can explain—"

"Actors struggle with this too. There's a scene in The Office where the guy who played Jim had to sign a cast, and he couldn't help but write his real name. Can't blame him. Most people learn to sign their name when they're just children. By the time you're grown, it's so ingrained in your muscle memory that writing anything except your real name takes a conscious effort. And that's all but impossible when someone is rushing you." I lowered the form. "There was no roommate was there? Ru Yee? She isn't even real."

"Sergeant, I—"

I held up a finger. "Think hard before you answer. I've got a few more tricks up my sleeve, and if I catch you lying again, we'll be having the rest of this conversation through a prison window."

Hui swallowed, and leaned back, drawing in on herself. "She's real. She went home for the summer. Left a couple weeks ago."

"And all that stuff about her and the Jiangshi?"

"I made that part up."

I nodded, having hoped that was the case. The last thing I wanted was to try and organize a well-being check for someone in China. "I met your family. Your brother, your sister, your nephew, and your grandmother. Nice people. They mentioned you. Or rather they mentioned they had a sister studying at university. I didn't make the connection at the time. But ink doesn't lie." I turned the form over and pointed toward her printed name. Hui Guai. The same as the owners of the Lotus Garden restaurant where we'd first encountered the Jade Fangs.

A restaurant which, I now believed, was operating as a front for an electronics money laundering business. It must have been doing reasonably well too, at least in so much that they'd sprung for the tuition to allow their sister to attend one of the most prestigious technical colleges in the country. Likely she planned to use those skills to expand the family business. The *real* family business.

"Let's start at the beginning. How long have you been here?" I asked.

Hui hesitated before answering. I could see her weighing her options, but no matter how she turned it over in her mind, she couldn't escape the fact that I had her dead to rights. Filing a fake police report might seem like a small thing, but I could use it to keep her detained until at least tomorrow morning. Her only hope of walking out of here and making it back to her family this evening was to speak with me, and she couldn't risk lying again.

Which meant I was about to have something of a rarity in law enforcement.

An honest conversation.

"My grandma brought the three of us over here when we were just children. Claimed we were refugees. She worked her fingers raw in that restaurant, and when the former owner died, he left it to her in his will. She practically raised us there."

"How long have you been running the electronics scam?" She didn't answer, but I read her face. "Right, all of your lives. Or at least, some version of it. What was it first? Watches? Rings? Jewelry? You fleece the tourists who come in, those too stupid or drunk to keep their guard up. And then what? Stash the money somewhere for a rainy day?"

"You don't understand," she said.

"What's that?"

"The work my family does. It is not for our own sake. It is for the people. We take from those who seek only to exploit us."

"Is that so?"

She nodded. "The men who come into Chinatown. They care nothing for our culture. They want all our women to work in massage parlors. 'Can I get a happy ending?' they say and laugh as if they were the first to think of it. They view us as disposable. To be used and cast aside. They don't care if we go hungry, or if we sleep in the street."

"That doesn't give you the right to rob them."

"No? And what do they do to us? Those with money seek to buy our buildings. They gut them from the inside, rebuild them, and charge us double the rent. Triple! They force us from our homes and care nothing for those who cannot pay. They would see us sent back to China in boats. If we make it, okay. If we do not, that is okay too. Because we are not them." She drew in a long breath, the rage burning in her chest. "We do what we must in order to survive. We take care of our community. We protect it. That is why I came to you. Why I told you a story about the Jiangshi. You have seen him, yes?"

"Yes."

"Then you know why I sought you out. We cannot fight this enemy. He and his followers will take everything from us. Even our lives, if we resist."

"You could have asked for help."

"And who would have answered? The police care nothing for Chinatown. Why do you think you are the only one investigating the murder of three of our people? Most refuse to even look at us."

"We could have helped you. We could have done *something*."

"And then? Suppose we were successful? We would expend all our strength facing this Jiangshi. And then Satoru Doku and his men would simply come in and pick up the pieces. Instead of a vampire, we would be slaves under the Triad. Different master, but not so different for us."

"You should have started with the truth. I would have helped you."

"You cannot even help yourself," she snapped. "The only hope for the people of Chinatown is the Gray Fox, and now, thanks to you…" She snapped her mouth shut, furious and looking as if she wanted to bite someone.

I stared at her, allowing her words to sink in. I could explain away her knowing about the dead ship captain and his first mate. Like Brother Kim said, word travels fast in Chinatown. But knowing that I'd put a bullet in the Gray Fox? That could have only come from two places.

JADE ENCLAVE

The first was from Satoru Doku. But since most of his men were incapacitated when the shooting occurred, it meant it would have had to come from him directly, which didn't seem likely.

The second option was that it had come from the source itself. The Gray Fox. But what were the chances Hui had spoken to the Gray Fox directly? Pretty slim. Unless they knew one another. Unless they were friends.

Or family.

Hui Guai watched the realization dawn in my eye, and she rose from her chair as I turned and fled the room.

"No! Sergeant, wait!"

I didn't wait.

I had more questions that needed answering.

And now I knew where to find them.

The Lives We Leave Behind. Friday, July 25th 1953hrs

"Keys!" I snapped as I came through the door

Tootsie dug through her pocket before producing them and tossed them across the room to my waiting grasp. "Do you want me to come with you?"

"No." I motioned toward the room behind me. "Stay with her."

I raced down the stairs and out of the Union Oyster House. My car was parked along the curb. I brought it to life and pulled out into the street. Rush-hour traffic had been over for hours, and

JADE ENCLAVE

I was able to weave my way through the last remnants, arriving in Chinatown only a few minutes later.

I parked in the side lot near the Lotus Garden and exited the car. There was some foot traffic on the street, but it was to be expected during the summer. I walked at a brisk pace, forcing myself not to jog.

The Lotus Garden was empty, with a 'Closed' sign hanging from the doorway. I cupped my hands around my eyes and peered through the windows. There were lights on inside, but I couldn't be sure if they weren't on all the time. I debated a moment, then turned and made my way around the side of the building, drawing up beside the back door we'd used to flee from the Jade Fangs during our last visit. It was locked, but the door was aged and rickety. I debated a moment, then returned to my car and retrieved the bolt cutters, pointedly ignoring the curious looks they drew as I returned to the door.

The lock was a deadbolt, but I wielded the bolt cutters like a hammer and smashed the heavy teeth down onto the doorhandle until it broke away and fell to the pavement. Then I used the cutters as a makeshift pry bar, applying force until the deadbolt snapped free of the wall. Once the door was open, I dropped the bolt cutters and rested one hand on my pistol as I stepped inside.

The restaurant was in disarray. The Jade Fangs had smashed the plates and glassware and sliced gaping holes in the booths. Most of the chairs were broken, and the swinging door leading into the kitchen had been torn from its frame. Past the broken doorframe, heavy dents lined the kitchen stove, where someone looked to have played whack a mole with a heavy frying pan. The more I saw, the more I could see that the Jade Fangs had taken our escape personally. Which, given what I now knew, wasn't hard to imagine why.

One thing had been bothering me about this entire affair. Why had the Jade Fangs come to the restaurant in the first place? They claimed to be looking for the boy, and at the time I assumed it must have had something to do with the murder of Haoran Hei and Xuanming Fei. I'd been wrong though. Or, at least, not right, which when it comes to law enforcement is basically the same thing.

The Jade Fangs' presence here did have something to do with the murdered men inside the apartment, but only as a peripheral afterthought. They were like dogs, hunting for their master. And what they sought was the vase.

The Jiangshi knew the vase had made its way to Boston. He must have believed the Gray Fox was involved. Heck, Satoru Doku had outright told me that the Gray Fox had killed the ship captain and his first mate. Likely the Jiangshi had heard the same. And with the two men dead, he must have assumed the Gray Fox now had the vase. Which is why his Jade Fangs had come seeking the boy. They were following the same trail I was, hoping that the boy would have seen or heard something that would allow them to track down the Gray Fox.

Unfortunately, they were right.

I walked past an open freezer door, glimpsing the smashed thermometer before reaching a door that led into a small room. In practice, it should've been a dry storage room, but someone had converted it into a small bedroom. Almost reminiscent of a mother-in-law suite.

Physically the room was little bigger than a jail cell, tucked away at the end of the dim corridor in an aging restaurant. That said, the inside was surprisingly tidy. Every surface was wiped or swept with almost meditative care. The scent of green tea hung in the air, intermingling with a chemical, medicinal smell that reminded me of tiger balm. An aged sleeping mat lay rolled in one corner of the room, deep lines creasing its face like old scars. There was a small portable stove with a tea pot on its base, and an antique storage chest sealed with a brass clasp. A lone, narrow window overlooked the alley, allowing a touch of silver moonlight to peer through onto a small shrine situated in the opposite corner of the bedroom.

A neatly trimmed bonsai tree stood in the center of the shrine, alongside a chipped ceramic bowl filled with incense sticks that had long since burned to ash. There was a photograph beside it, depicting three small children. The photo was yellowed with age, but the tape holding it in place was fresh.

As I stood there, my nose detected another scent, faint among the tea and incense. A baser, more metallic smell. Blood. I followed it over to the antique chest, hesitating at the last moment with my hand just above the clasp. Visions of an Indiana Jones style trap ran through my mind. Poison darts or something worse. I told myself that I was just being paranoid. That if what I suspected was true, then the Gray Fox couldn't have resorted to such traps knowing that either the boy or one of the restaurant patrons might inadvertently find their way back here. It sounded good, in theory, but no matter how confident I sounded in my head, my hand remained hovered above the clasp. After a moment I reached a reluctant compromise and lowered it down to my belt.

Warman's Blade came free from my belt sheath with barely a sound, and I used the edge to unlock the brass clasp, then leaned back as far as I could and forced the top open.

My nose hadn't lied. The first thing I saw was a tangle of bloody bandages. The sight of it filled me with dread, fear that someone must have surely bled out. Then I took a closer look and my eyes started to pick up on the different shades amidst the red. Someone had been bleeding but there was evidence of clotting among the bandages, suggesting their owner was still alive.

And more likely than not, still dangerous.

I lifted the bandages out and laid them on the floor before delving deeper into the chest. Situated below the bandages was the Gray Fox's shinobi shōzoku, his ninja outfit, darker near the shoulder where blood had soaked the cloth surrounding the bullet hole given by yours truly. The fabric was aged, dozens of sewn threads and touchups serving as a roadmap of scars that must litter the wearer's torso, but for all that it had seen it still held firm.

Beneath the garb I found a variety of small containers and leather pouches. The first one I opened contained half a dozen smoke bombs. The next: a handful of shuriken throwing stars. There were handgrips used to scale buildings, along with a curved blade connected to a hand grip by a thread of metal wire as fine as human hair. One of the smaller chests contained vials of colored liquid whose purpose I couldn't even begin to guess. A folding wallet was filled with multiple currencies as well as multiple passports, all in Mandarin script with photos of the family, including the boy.

Footsteps sounded out in the hallway before I could give them more than a cursory glance. I dropped them back into the chest, then took up position beside the doorway, waiting until the footsteps drew closer before rounding the corner.

Yichen Guai let out a startled curse and jerked back. The male half of the Lotus Garden restaurant owners was dressed in slacks, a white shirt with the sleeves rolled up, and a dark neckerchief wrapped around his throat. He started to retreat, but I dropped one hand to my pistol and raised the other with my palm out. "Stop!"

He froze.

"Don't run," I said. "If you do, I'll have to do something about it."

His gaze dropped down to my pistol and stayed there for a long moment before rising. "What do you want?"

"Peace," I said. "And a two week's paid vacation to someplace warm where they serve drinks in coconut shells."

"I don't understand."

"You're under arrest, Yichen. Turn around. Walk slowly back out into the dining room."

He complied after a moment, and we made our way back out of the kitchen, passing through the broken doorway and into the dining area before he turned to face me.

"May I speak?"

I shook my head. "First turn around and place your hands behind your back."

His mouth tightened, and he reluctantly raised his hands into the air. "Please, Officer. I have done nothing wrong. This is, as you Americans like to say, one big misunderstanding."

"Not sure a jury is going to buy that one, Yichen." My non-pistol hand dropped to my belt and drew my handcuffs from their case. "You're facing some pretty steep charges."

"What charges?"

"Seriously? How about murder? Battery on a law enforcement officer? Some more murder. Prancing around the city dressed up like some sort of Ninja Turtles villain?"

"Please, you do not understand."

"Oh, and did I mention you broke my new trainee's nose?" I shook my head. "As hard as this may be to accept, jail is probably the safest place for you right now. I figured out who you are, and it's only a matter of time before Satoru Doku does the same. He'll have his people gunning for you, and with your injuries…"

My voice trailed off as realization slowly dawned.

The Gray Fox was injured. I'd shot him clean through the shoulder. I'd seen the torn cloth and the blood. But if that were true, how was it that Yichen was standing there across from me in a white shirt with his hands in the air?

The answer: Yichen wasn't the Gray Fox.

In that moment I was reminded of a lesson one of our instructors had tried hard to impart on us back during my police academy days. The thing that gets most officers killed isn't lack of training, but lack of awareness. Complacency. And the number one thing that will draw you into feeling complacent?

Fatigue.

Fatigue makes you dull. Causes your eyes to gloss over. Makes you miss things that you would have otherwise caught. Fatigue lulls your brain to sleep while the rest of you continues to walk forward into danger.

I was so tired.

But not too tired to realize I'd made a mistake.

JADE ENCLAVE

Yichen wasn't the Gray Fox. He wasn't old enough. Satoru's words came back to me, reminding me that the Gray Fox had ruled over Chinatown for three decades.

Practically since the moment she'd arrived with three small children in tow.

Lian Guai. The grandmother who'd greeted us at the door. The matriarch of the family. The Gray Fox wasn't hiding in Chinatown. *She* was living here. And had been for some time. In the blink of an eye, it all clicked into place.

Working as an assassin for the Triad, I could only assume, was a dangerous endeavor, especially with family. It made sense, why she would fake her own death, move here, and spend the next three decades quietly overseeing the neighborhood.

She wasn't ruling from the shadows with an iron fist, killing anyone who dared to stand against her. She was building a safe haven for her grandchildren, cultivating a reputation that would ensure the Triad never sought to follow her.

A footstep came down from behind me, and I instinctively started to spin, but it was too late. Something crashed against the back of my head, and the world flashed white.

I hit my knees as a hollow, whooshing sound filled my ears. The white flash receded into dark stars, and I tried to move, but just ended up toppling over. I landed on my side, and glimpsed Yichen's sister, Mei, holding the broken ends of a heavy ceramic casserole dish. Fear flashed through my being, and I tried to speak, but all that came out was a soft moan which the siblings ignored as they stared at one another.

"Is she dead?" Mei asked.

Yichen's eyes met mine, and he shook his head. "No."

"Should we?"

"No!" His face turned dour, and he conceded after a moment. "At least, not yet."

"Then what do we do?"

Yichen considered it for a long moment before he answered. "We cannot stay here. Not anymore."

"But what about grandma?"

"Here. Help me."

He bent down and seized my wrists, while his sister did the same with my feet. They hoisted me up and carried me back through the kitchen and into the broken freezer, dropping me down onto the floor which still clung to its cold temperature.

JADE ENCLAVE

"Seal the door," Yichen said. "That should buy us some time, and then—"

Whatever else he was about to say was cut off by the sound of breaking glass coming from the front of the restaurant. Mei drew in a sudden gasp, and she jerked around, inadvertently knocking the freezer door and causing it to close ninety percent of the way.

"At last, we come to it," a voice said. Not one of the siblings. There was something familiar about it, but it wasn't until I heard the footsteps that I realized who it belonged to.

Through the crack in the freezer door, I glimpsed Cicuta as he stepped into the kitchen, slowly making his way down the aisle. The siblings cried out and tried to retreat, but more Jade Fangs appeared, blocking their way. They ended up back-to-back, with Yichen facing the head of the Jade Fangs.

"Stop," Yichen said, spreading his arms in a gesture of protection. "We have nothing you want here. Tell your master, he is wasting his time."

"Time," Cicuta said, savoring the word in his mouth. "What does an immortal care for the passing of time? An age begins and ends in the blink of an eye, and yet, we live on."

"For your master maybe," Mei said, pushing past her brother's arm. "But not you. Not any of you."

Cicuta's hand flashed, and the back of his knuckles struck the side of her face with a resounding *crack*. She let out a cry and fell back toward the stove, but Yichen caught her, turning her around to shield her body with his own.

The cold from the floor was seeping through my clothing and into my face. I tried to move, but none of my limbs were working properly, and one sound would alert them to my presence. Much as I hated to admit it, I had no choice but to lay there, watching as Cicuta loomed over the pair.

"Insolent girl," he hissed. "You will soon learn the proper respect for addressing your elders. I may even see to your training myself. First though, there are other matters to attend to."

Two more Jade Fangs entered the kitchen. Cicuta motioned them forward, and they strode forward holding something between them. I recognized the chest from Lian's room, the one containing her Gray Fox tools. They flipped the lid open, and Cicuta smiled.

"Ah, at last, all becomes clear. Tell me, children, where is your grandmother hiding?"

The siblings refused to meet his eye, but I could see the fear coursing through them. Cicuta waited for several seconds, then he sighed and removed a throwing shuriken from his belt. He held it gripped between his fingers, allowing the tapered point to slide through his knuckles. "Seize her."

Two Jade Fangs seized Mei around the arms and lifted her up to her feet. They gripped her hair and forced her head back as Cicuta reached out and gently stroked her face. He trailed his finger down one cheek, then brought it up to trace the line of her eyebrow.

"Tell me now, child, or prepare to embrace the darkness forever."

Panic surged within me, and I tried to move, but my belt shifted, and the handle of my gun hit the freezer floor. From where I lay, the noise sounded earth shattering loud. It caused me to freeze, but none of the Jade Fangs so much as glanced my way.

"Last chance, girl," Cicuta said.

"We don't know," Yichen said, his voice pleading. "Please. I swear to you. We were never involved in any of… that. She insisted on total secrecy. We were never even allowed to ask questions. She claimed it was for our own protection."

Cicuta considered this, and several seconds passed before he accepted it as the truth. "A prudent decision on her part. Unfortunately, if you cannot lead us to the Gray Fox, then we will have to give her a reason to come to us." He stepped back to the cabinet, and hesitated over the spice rack, eventually choosing an orange powder I didn't recognize.

"Your hand," he told the boy.

Yichen extended his arm, and Cicuta dabbed his finger in oil, then dipped it into the orange spice. "Write exactly as I tell you."

As far as messages go, it was brief. A location and a time. Long Wharf. Midnight tonight. God save us from bad guys wielding overused cliches. At the end, he dabbed the sibling's hands and forced them to leave orange handprints on either side of the message. Something any mother, or grandmother in this case, would recognize.

Once the message was written, Cicuta motioned toward the doorway, and the Jade Fangs dragged Yichen and Mei through, carrying them out the back and into the alleyway.

I stayed where I was, the memory of their cries lingering in my ears until long after they had faded from reality.

Prepare for Battle. Friday, July 25th 2153hrs

I focused hard on not passing out on the freezer floor, and gradually over the next fifteen minutes or so, feeling returned to my limbs, and my twitches became less... twitchy.

Eventually, I was able to gather myself into a sitting position. It wasn't pretty, and I only made it up to my knees before the chowder I'd consumed back at the Oyster House came back up, splattering the floor and my sleeves. Once my purging was complete, I wiped my mouth on my jacket sleeve and pushed my back into the wall, using it to steady me as I struggled up to my feet.

The lights inside the kitchen seemed brighter, sharper. I absorbed the information and concluded that I most likely had a concussion, but since I couldn't do anything about it at the moment, I filed it away in the back of my rattled mind and slowly limped out through the back door and over to the side lot where my car was parked.

The cop part of my brain warned me that I shouldn't be driving, but I didn't have time to sit back and wait for a ride. It was less than two miles back to the Union Oyster House, and I opted to stay off the highway, making my way north along Lincoln and High Street before turning onto Congress.

I parked along the alley in the back and made my way into the Oyster House through the rear entrance. The stairs took longer than they should have, but I made it without falling, and once I stepped inside, Pongo and Tootsie took one look at me and hurried me over to one of the booths.

The next two hours is a bit of a blur, but it involved aspirin, a *lot* of aspirin, an ice pack on the back of my skull, and a cold Coke which I used to wash away the taste of vomit. There was movement and distant conversation happening around me, but I couldn't focus on it. I'm not sure if I slept, or just sort of drifted, but whichever it was ended when something shattered near the doorway.

Images of the Jade Fangs coming through the door flashed through my mind, and I bounded out of the booth without thinking. I was uncentered and off-balance, and I stumbled on my first step and crashed into the far wall, using it to hold me in place as I jerked my gun from its holster and pointed it toward the door.

Pongo stared at me in wide-eyed shock.

A long second passed before my gaze dropped to the shattered teacup at his feet.

"It's just a cup of Earl Black," he stammered. "It's getting late. I needed the caffeine."

I swallowed and holstered my pistol. Then I limped back to my booth as Pongo cleaned up the shattered teacup. I dropped into the seat, but didn't lie down.

"Where is everyone?" I asked.

"Here," Tootsie answered, as she and Detective Wei came through the opposite doorway, evidently drawn by the noise. "We're both here."

"Okay," I said. "Team meeting in five minutes."

I forced myself up to my feet and made my way to the nearest bathroom. The lights stung my eyes, but I kept my gaze low and removed my jacket and shirt. I splashed water on my face and used the dispenser soap to give myself a quick wash. The scent of the soap, soft as it was, still made my head hurt, and I breathed through my mouth as I dried myself with paper towels.

It wasn't much, but I felt better by the time I'd finished, and I stumbled back out into the upstairs dining room to find Pongo, Tootsie, and Detective Wei seated around the table. The kitchen had closed over an hour ago, but one of them had snagged a basket of hush puppies, along with some cheddar biscuits and a pitcher of Coke.

I helped myself to a biscuit and a couple of hush puppies, setting them down on a plate in front of me before turning to regard the table. "Everyone acquainted?"

A round of nods answered me.

"Good." I looked around and frowned. "Where's Hui Guai?"

"Right where you left her," Tootsie said. "Poor thing was exhausted. Fell asleep not long ago. Want me to wake her?"

I considered it then shook my head. I doubted she had any more information with which to share. "Let her sleep. I suspect she'll need her strength for what's to come."

Tootsie nodded. "You're the boss."

Something shifted in my chest, responding to the truth of her words. Being in charge is easy on easy days, but today wasn't one of those, and I realized in that moment I had some decisions to make.

"Well, about that," I said. "We need to get one thing clear. None of you have to be here. This is not a normal case. You've already gone beyond what's expected of you. Anyone can walk out right now and I give you my word there won't be any repercussions to your career."

I waited for a long moment, but nobody moved.

"Alright then. Know you have my thanks, for whatever it's worth." I drew in a deep breath and let it out in a whoosh. "Here's the situation. We're in a bad spot, and things are about to get a whole lot worse for the people of Chinatown unless we do something about it."

Pongo raised his hand. "Sorry to interrupt. I'm not sure how much help I can be until someone explains to me what's actually going on."

"Right," I said. "In a nutshell, there's a free-for-all about to go down, a real Royal Rumble type of thing, and the winner gets Chinatown. In one corner, we've got a bunch of kung fu vampire nut jobs searching for an old vase full of ashes."

Pongo frowned. "Is it an act, or do they actually believe it?"

"All signs point toward the latter."

"Wow."

"Brace yourself, because it gets worse. In the other corner, we've got Satoru Doku, a Triad gangster on his last hurrah. This goes south and he might as well commit... what's that thing where they commit suicide in order to repent for disgrace?"

"Seppuku," Detective Wei said.

"Right. That. But don't let it fool you. A cornered rat is the most dangerous." I bit into one of the cheddar biscuits and chewed before swallowing. "In the last corner, we've got a retired assassin. A real ninja, if you can believe it. She's ruled Chinatown from the shadows for three decades, and she's not about to give it up now. She may be old, but Tootsie and I have already seen her take down an entire convoy of Triad gunmen. We can't afford to underestimate her."

"That all sounds horrible," Pongo said. "At least there's no one in the fourth corner, right? Silver lining?"

"We're in the fourth corner," I said, my voice quiet. "And the referee is about to ring the bell."

"Oh," Pongo said.

"What are our options?" Detective Wei asked.

JADE ENCLAVE

"Our first priority has to be rescuing Yichen and Mei Guai from the Jade Fangs. Regardless of their grandmother's past, they're innocent until convicted. We need to get them out of harm's way before we try to bring any of the others down. Anyone got any ideas on how to do that?"

There was a round of shared looks at the table.

"You're thinking we should launch some sort of rescue operation?" Detective Wei asked.

"Depends," I said. "Is it doable?"

He considered it. "Potentially. We know where they're going to be and when. It's just a matter of taking advantage of that information."

"We *think* we know," Tootsie countered. "The Jade Fangs might keep them stashed away in reserve to make sure the Gray Fox doesn't try anything."

Detective Wei considered it, then glanced at me. "You think they're going to try and double cross her?"

"I think they're going to do whatever's in their best interest. Which, under the circumstances, would mean having Yichen and Mei where the Gray Fox can see them."

"Why would they risk losing them?" Tootsie asked.

"Because they're not actually after them. They want the vase, and they've come too far now to risk the Gray Fox fading away into the shadows with it."

"But we have the vase," Tootsie said.

"True, but they don't know that. They think the Gray Fox does, so they'll make sure she has plenty of incentive to come to the meeting."

"What about a hit and run?" Detective Wei asked. "Could we create a diversion, snatch them, and be gone before they catch on?"

"Maybe," I said. "But do we want to hedge our bets on being able to get the drop on a bunch of wanna-be vampire ninjas?"

"It does seem like kind of a tall order," Detective Wei admitted.

"Could we bargain for them?" Pongo asked.

Three sets of gazes shifted his way, and he flinched, and straightened in his chair. "I mean, we have the vase, right? That's what they want? Why not offer it to them in exchange for the siblings?"

"It's a good idea," I said. "But there are some problems."

"Such as?"

"For one, we don't know how to get in contact with them, and we have zero time to figure it out. Second, even if we could get word to them, they'd never believe us, and if by some miracle they did, they're more likely to try and kill us rather than bargain." I sighed. "Third, we all know what's in the vase."

Pongo raised his hand again. "Actually, I don't."

"Suffice to say nothing that's going to help us. For now, let's assume diplomacy is off the table. What else have we got?"

Detective Wei shifted in his seat, adjusting his outstretched leg. "As much as I enjoy the comradery of our little group, have you considered calling for backup?"

"Thought about it, but it's risky." I raised my hand and counted off three fingers. "Jiangshi, Triad gangsters, and ninja assassin. Any of them see us coming, they'll assume one of the others went to the authorities. They'll scatter, and most likely kill the siblings at the first opportunity."

"What if they don't see us coming?"

"Still could end badly. The Jade Fangs are setting a trap for the Gray Fox, but it could just as easily be us that falls into it. Anyone want to ask themselves what might happen if our patrol officers find themselves facing off against the Jade Fangs in the dark?"

Tootsie and Detective Wei considered it for a minute, and then slowly nodded. They'd reached the same conclusion I had. It would be a massacre. One the police department might never recover from.

"So what do we do?" Tootsie asked.

I swept my arm up into a fist. "Our only chance of resolving this tonight is to catch all three of them in one fell swoop. And in order to do that, we're going to have to give each party exactly what they want, and then pull the rug out from under them at the last minute and send them toppling over onto their butts."

"Sounds good in theory," Tootsie said. "Do you have a plan?"

"Matter of fact, I do," I said. "But I'm going to need help from each one of you. Now that we know what we're up against, is everyone still willing?"

Tootsie spoke first. "I'm still finding my footing with all of this, but there's no way in heck I'm going to wash out on my first day."

Detective Wei followed. "If it helps the people of Chinatown, I'm in."

Pongo nodded. "I have to stop by my house and get my gun first. I kind of stopped bringing it into work."

"Don't worry about that," I said. "Your job is going to be to stay here and coordinate everything." Experience had shown me that Pongo in the field could only end in disaster, but if things went south, and let's be honest, they probably would, we'd need someone to start waking people up. Although, come to think of it, there was something he could do in the meantime. "Are you able to get inside the police station evidence room?"

Pongo nodded. "Sure."

"July fourth was only a couple of weeks ago. How many pounds of illegal fireworks did the department confiscate?"

Pongo frowned. "I don't know. A lot."

"Bring me some. As much as you can carry."

He nodded.

"What about me?" Detective Wei asked.

"I need you on the phone," I said.

"Who am I calling?"

I told him, and even though he didn't like it, he understood my reasoning.

"And what about me?" Tootsie asked.

"You're coming with me," I said. "If this goes down how I think it will, I'm going to need someone to watch my back, and maybe crack a few skulls."

Tootsie smiled. "That part I can definitely handle."

"Thought so." I looked around. "Everyone clear on their roles?"

A round of nods answered me

"Okay then." I clapped my hands together. "Work fast, people. We've got a meeting to get to, and we can't afford to show up late."

The Meeting.
Friday, July 25th
2355hrs

THERE WERE A LOT of ways we could have gotten to the Long Wharf.

In the end, we chose to drive.

Traffic was nonexistent at this time of night, and we wound our way through the eerily quiet streets. It was only my imagination, but I pictured the residents of Chinatown taking cover inside their apartments, drawing down the shades and waiting apprehensively to see how their lives might change come morning.

I hoped it would be for the better, but in order for that to happen, we would have to play things just right.

The Boston Long Wharf was a historic waterfront area located on the eastern side of the city. At one time, it had stretched nearly a third of a mile out. A combination of construction projects and landfills had seen it shortened, and these days it served as the departure point for ferry and sightseeing services traveling to nearby islands and whale watching destinations.

I saw the first Jade Fang when we were still several blocks away. They had sentries aligned along the streets and rooftops, communicating with flashlights and hand signals as they trailed our vehicle. I called them out to Tootsie, but neither of us had an answer for what to do about it save to keep going.

We drove past the Atlantic Avenue intersection and the Boston Marriot, where the street turned to red cobblestones. The wind came sharp off the Atlantic, carrying the scent of brine, diesel, and seaweed. To the south, the ferry boats rocked gently in their moorings, their hulls creaking as they swayed in rhythm to the ocean's breath. A low fog had begun taking form in the distance, softening the edges of the city's skyline. Out here, it was easy to imagine that we had passed into a different world, one connected to but also separate from the city.

Tootsie maneuvered our vehicle between the concrete pillars, pulling over roughly two hundred feet from the dock's edge. An open-aired pavilion stood to the north, and the Jade Fangs were already present to the east, gathered around the famed Compass Rose embedded in the granite stones.

We parked and exited the car. I kept my jacket edge pulled back, displaying the badge on my hip. I held a manilla folder filled with half a dozen printed pages in one hand and kept the other on my pistol. Tootsie exited out the passenger's side. She had a duffel bag slung over her shoulder, one hand hidden down inside its folds. It was impossible to discern whether she was gripping a shotgun, a short-barreled rifle, or something else, but the angle of her hand, as well as the slight bulge protruding from the side of the bag, spoke louder than any verbal threat, inviting any would-be enemies to try their luck and find out.

More than a dozen Jade Fangs stood scattered around the Compass Rose, with more waiting in the wings. At their center stood the Jiangshi, and to his right, literally beside his right hand, was Cicuta.

I closed my door and forced myself to take a hard look around, peering beyond the Jade Fangs to the surrounding wharf. It was a good thing I did, because it allowed me to spot the siblings, Yichen and Mei. They were being held in an animal cage, forced to kneel in the center of the open-aired pavilion closest to the water. A rush of cold swept through me at the sight of them, huddled and shivering behind metal bars meant to hold a dog. Someone had wrapped barbed wire, like the kind they use for prison fencing, around the cage doorway. Likely as a means of dissuading them from seeking escape.

My feet started forward of their own accord, and Tootsie followed three steps behind. The Jade Fangs eyed us, some warily, others hungrily, but it was Cicuta who intercepted me before I could set foot on the rose.

"Insolent cow," he snarled. "This matter is of no concern to you. Leave now and be grateful that I do not—"

I stepped around him and kept walking, not even bothering to acknowledge his existence. Whatever response he'd been expecting, it wasn't to be outright ignored. He spluttered angrily, and dropped his hand toward the sword at his belt, but Tootsie cleared her throat, and motioned with the duffel bag, miming the action of shooting.

Cicuta glared fire, but a second later his gaze shifted back to the Jiangshi.

The immortal vampire lord considered me for a moment, then raised one finger a fraction of an inch, and Cicuta relented, releasing his sword grip while continuing to glare balefully.

I stopped just short of the rose and forced myself to meet the Jiangshi's eyes. "You've got a lot to answer for, but I'll make you a deal. You and all your friends. You take a swim right now.

Paddle your way out of my city, never come back, and I'll let you go without a fight. Otherwise, this will end badly for you. I promise."

The Jiangshi tilted his head to the side, regarding me the same way you might a particularly rambunctious insect. Interesting, but only for a moment, and ultimately not worth responding to.

I gave him a slow ten count, then nodded. "Don't say I didn't warn you." I mimed looking at my watch. "You might want to take a second to adjust your makeup. We've got company coming, and they should be arriving right about… now."

Every once in a while, a plan comes together perfectly. As I turned and gestured back toward downtown, the first of three pairs of headlights shone through the fog. The sounds of the vehicles' engines reached us a second later, and I took a pointed step back as the vehicles made their way down the Long Wharf, parking not far from my car.

Mr. Zheng got out first, his expression bland as he buttoned his coat. The better part of a dozen Triad gunmen followed, exiting from every door with pistols on their hips and rifles slung across their chests. They spread out in a loose formation, and only once they'd taken up position did Satoru Doku emerge from the second vehicle.

The Triad leader was dressed in a three-piece suit, but there was a hurried, scattered slant to his demeanor, and a hint of glassy redness around his eyes. From the looks of it, he'd been drinking, likely trying to take the edge off in hopes of winding down for the night. Detective Wei's phone call, one of two I'd had him make, must have taken him by surprise, which is sort of what I'd been betting on.

I didn't doubt for a second that Satoru would elect to make an appearance tonight. Men who sought positions of power couldn't afford to stand aside while events that would shape the future went down.

Satoru came out of the car and made his way over, his gaze hesitating on the caged siblings as he came up beside the rose. Mr. Zheng and two gunmen came with him, sticking close to his side while the others spread throughout the wharf.

"What's this?" he asked the Jiangshi, anger shining through his voice. "Killing children is not why you were brought here."

"Isn't it?" The Jiangshi asked, his voice dry and dusty. "I know why I am here. Do you?"

Satoru swallowed. "You promised to bring me the head of the Gray Fox. That was our agreement."

The Jiangshi snorted. "Was it? A pity, immortals do not make agreements with men. You seek to rule, but what matters when your reign is but a lifetime? I tire of your petty squabbles and endless complaining. I am here to recover my beloved. To do that, I will kill the thief who has her, and then return to my rest."

"The Gray Fox," Satoru said, urgency in his voice. "He has her. As I told you."

"Actually, *she* doesn't." All eyes turned toward me, and I shrugged. "Never did, point of fact."

"Be quiet!" Satoru snapped.

I shook my head. "No, I don't think I will. I don't like these vampire ninja idiots any more than you seem to, but I think we all know you haven't exactly been playing straight with them."

"Sergeant..."

"Silence," the Jiangshi said and raised his hand. The nails from his green-scaled gauntlet caught the edge of the moon's caress, seemingly absorbing the silver light. "I would hear her words."

I pointed toward the Jiangshi. "See, he's interested in what I have to say. Of course, it's difficult to know where to begin. Or better said, where the lies started." I pretended to think about it for a minute. "I guess we should start with Xuanming Fei. He was a boat captain, here in Boston. He and his first mate died in blood and noodles, but I'm guessing everyone here knew that already."

Their lack of reaction told me I was right.

"Prior to their death, you might have heard that they took possession of a certain vase, and transported it from China to Boston. It was a heck of a trip. Or at least it would have been, had it actually happened." For the first time since the conversation began, I took my hand off my pistol, and opened the manilla folder, pulling the first page forward. "We found this inside Xuanming's boat. It's a shipping log. According to this, they took possession of the vase off the coast of Zhoushan and sailed it up through the Bering Sea. From there, they crossed the Beaufort Sea and the Northwestern Passage, eventually rounding the eastern edge of Canada and sailing into Boston."

"And? Why should we care what route they took?" Satoru asked.

My hand disappeared back inside the folder and reappeared holding a picture of Xuanming's boat. I handed it to the nearest Jade Fang, who brought it to the Jiangshi. "You take a look at that vessel and tell me that it could have survived that trip. It's basically an overgrown tugboat. I wouldn't trust it to ferry me to Martha's Vineyard, much less across multiple seas."

JADE ENCLAVE

"This is absurd," Satoru said. "You are no sailor. You have no idea of his ship's capabilities."

"Maybe not," I said. "But I know one thing. Every ship needs a captain, and Xuanming wasn't on that journey. He was in county, booked in by our patrol officers on a Drunk and Disorderly charge for at least two of those days. See for yourself." I handed a printed copy of his booking photo to the Jade Fang, who carried it back to his master. The Jiangshi's mouth tightened, and even though I didn't think it was possible, his eyes darkened.

I turned to regard Satoru. "Before they threw him in the drunk tank, he said something about celebrating. Kept talking about his big payday."

"A shame he is not here so we could ask him," Satoru said. "As it stands, you have no proof of any of this."

"Actually, we do. You see, one of our officers knows a friendly judge, and he was willing to sign a warrant allowing us access to the victim's bank statements. Now, granted, there are no names anywhere, but we did note a large payment that came in from the Red Sun Trading Company, which is known to have ties to China, and more specifically, the Triad. You wouldn't know anything about that, would you?"

Satoru glared at me.

"Right, I didn't think so. In any case, it's not what anyone would consider concrete, but we did some more digging. You know New York Customs Office runs a pretty tight ship, no pun intended. You came through there a couple of weeks ago. Did you know they catalogued every item you brought into the country with you? I had a peek at the logs. Fascinating stuff, especially on the second page, where they listed, and I quote, 'one antique vase, blue in color.'" I lifted out a copy of the declaration form, allowing the Jiangshi and Jade Fangs to see it. "Now, there are plenty of antique vases in the world, and one could always argue that one has nothing to do with the other, but lucky us, in addition to cataloguing everything, the customs agent included colored photos." I raised the photo, showing it around with forced enthusiasm.

The Jiangshi peered at the picture, and his face darkened. If his eyes had been black before, now they positively radiated fury.

"Look familiar?" I asked. "I'll bet it does. The cranes and dragonflies are particularly lovely. And hard to replicate. Of course, I know what you must be asking yourself. How does this tie back to our murdered boat captain and his first mate? Well, I have a theory to propose to the class." I motioned to Satoru. "You bought them off. Paid them to doctor the fake shipping log. Paid them pretty well, too, but not well enough, because once they sobered up, they started hearing some rumors about a certain Jiangshi who might have a vested interest in such a vase. Didn't take them long to realize they'd been played. Way I hear it, they set out to make amends, but by that point he was already on his way, weren't you? So they went to the monks for help. They asked for protection, and they got it, for all the good it did them. The monk assigned to guard them ended up dead not long after. Beaten to death." I fixed the Jiangshi with a hard look. "I'm guessing that was you. Mark my words, you'll answer for it before the end."

The Jiangshi's face remained stoney, giving away nothing as he waited for me to continue.

"After you were done with the monk, you made your way inside the apartment. Problem is, the two men were already dead." I glanced at Satoru. "You were right before. The Gray Fox killed them. Snuck inside and ended them without anyone being the wiser. But I've learned a thing or two about her, and I have to ask myself, why would she do such a thing? After all, they were part of the community, right? There's only one thing I can think of that would warrant a death sentence." My voice hardened. "Treason. These men sold out to you. They betrayed their own community and helped you concoct your scheme to bring the Jiangshi here."

"How dare you!"

"Don't try to deny it. You played this all up, orchestrating the fake antique theft, and then leaving a trail of breadcrumbs designed to see the Jiangshi kill the Gray Fox for you. What was your plan after? Send him on another wild goose chase? No, too dangerous. You must have had something else in mind. I'm guessing you were planning to sink the ship so you could claim the vase was lost at sea. Problem is, Xuanming and his first mate got killed before they could play their part. You've probably spent more than a few sleepless nights wondering what happened to that vase. You couldn't go looking for it yourself, too many eyes watching your every move. But you must've been hoping against hope that the Gray Fox took it." I shook my head. "Spoiler warning, she didn't. Likely she didn't know anything about the vase until after the captains were already dead, and by then she was too busy avoiding the Jade Fangs to mount any sort of search."

"You talk much, but say nothing," Satoru said. "There is no proof, especially since, as you have pointed out, the vase remains lost."

"Sure," I said. "Except it's not. You see, I have it right here."

Tootsie withdrew her hand from the duffel bag, revealing the Ming vase. The Jiangshi let out a soft exhale, and involuntarily leaned forward, his eyes never blinking as she handed it over to me.

JADE ENCLAVE

"This thing must have cost you a pretty penny," I told Satoru. "I mean, I'm no historian, but antique vases don't come cheap. It's a shame what's about to happen next."

I didn't toss the vase. Tossing would have implied a looping arch. I was too afraid that the Jiangshi or one of the Jade Fangs might be quick enough to catch it. Instead, I spiraled it down the way you would a football, sending it on a straight shot down to the granite stones.

The vase hit near the Jiangshi's feet and shattered, black dust spilling out onto the ground. The cry that emanated from the vampire's mouth was one of genuine pain and overwhelming despair. He hit his knees, spearing his hands into the black dust and bringing them up, watching as the sea winds blew the powder from between his fingers. He started shaking, and a long moment passed before he turned his head and fixed me with a look of murderous rage.

"I will kill you for this," he said. "You and everyone you hold dear. After tonight, none will dare speak your name again, save to beg mercy for the misery you have brought down on them."

"Keep that energy," I said. "Only problem is, those aren't your beloved's ashes. Its fireworks powder."

Tootsie upended the duffel bag, dumping the torn wrappings of dozens of fireworks down onto the cobble street.

"We had to fill it with something," I explained. "Otherwise, it would have been empty inside. Like it was when I found it. Like it was when Satoru brought it into the country. I know, because the custom's official marked it as so. You can see it there in black and white." I motioned to the customs form. "Capital E empty. Sorry to be the bearer of bad news, but if there really is a vase out there with your beloved's ashes, it's most likely either at the bottom of the ocean or somewhere in China. It's not here. It never was. Satoru lied to you. He played you, tried to use you to do his dirty work, all so he could live happily ever after in New England. Isn't that right—"

Satoru went for his gun before I finished speaking.

But as fast as he was, the Jiangshi was faster. He whipped his arm across, and the knife that came from his sleeve caught a flash of moonlight before it embedded itself in the back of Satoru Doku's hand, passing between the bones and pinning his hand to his chest.

And just like that, the battle for Chinatown kicked off.

The Battle for Chinatown. Saturday, July 26th 0005hrs

As far as battles went, the one on the Long Wharf was fast and bloody.

Swords and shurikens flashed, catching glints of moonlight before they found the Triad gunmen. Their suits provided little to no protection, and where metal found flesh, blood poured.

Satoru died first.

Blood squirted from his chest wound, spitting out through his pinned palm. It didn't click with me right away, not until I noted the knife's location, just to the left of his breastbone. The blade had pierced his hand, entered his chest cavity, and struck his heart. He bled to death in a matter of seconds, collapsing down to the granite with his face turned west, toward the city and Chinatown. A final realization flashed, carrying with it the certainty that he would never rule, and then there was nothing.

The Jade Fangs fought with brutal efficiency. I watched one gunman get run through the stomach, the tip of the Jade Fang's blade coming out through the small of his back. Not far away, a second shooter went down, a long line of stab wounds extending from his stomach up to his throat.

It wasn't all one-sided though. The Jade Fangs cut and slashed and kicked, but they were limited in reach, and the gunmen furthest away from the Compass Rose opened fire, blasting the wannabe vampire ninjas. The small arms fire was bad, but the rifles were worse. They tore the Jade Fangs apart, severing limbs and leaving large, gaping holes in their torsos.

Someone detonated a smoke bomb, then another, and within seconds the wharf was encapsulated in heavy black smoke. The Triad gunmen inside the smoke, led by Mr. Zheng, started to fall back, taking up cover alongside their cars.

I dropped at the sound of the first gun shot, hit the deck and low crawled a handful of steps away from Satoru Doku's corpse. I had my pistol drawn, but only as a defensive measure. My first priority was to make my way over to the pavilion where the kidnapped siblings were being kept. Unfortunately, the smoke and blood had me turned around, and I was suddenly uncertain about which way to go. To make matters worse, time was against me, and the pragmatic voice inside my head whispered that the longer I stayed out here, the more likely someone, either a Jade Fang or a Triad gunman, would notice and decide no one would much miss me in this world.

Peering down, I had a sudden flash of inspiration. If I could reach the Compass Rose, I could use it to navigate toward the pavilion. With a little luck, I could evacuate the siblings under cover of smoke, and once they were safely away, I could see about dealing with the Jiangshi and his minions.

Pushing aside the inner voice that thought it was a much better idea to turn tail and run, I started forward, low crawling half a dozen steps before catching sight of the Compass Rose. I headed toward the center, but just before I reached it, a foot came down, stomping the concrete in front of my face and drawing me up short.

Cicuta stared down at me, his mouth curving into a cruel snarl. His foot flashed again and struck me full on in the face. White light flashed across my eyes, and my head snapped back, carrying my body with it. I hit the ground and rolled, warm blood leaking from my nose to splatter against the concrete as I turned my head.

Cicuta took half a step, crunching the remains of the antique vase beneath his feet as he drew the sword from his belt. He brought it around in one swift motion, flexing his knees as he prepared to leap forward and bring the blade down across the back of my neck.

"Sergeant!" a voice screamed from the darkness a second before a pink flame burst to life.

I extended my hand without looking, caught the flare out of the air, and hurled it between Cicuta's feet.

Where the broken vase lay, its pieces coated in all the inner workings of better than two dozen fireworks.

The flame touched the powder, and the resulting explosion shook the entire wharf, blasting apart concrete and reverberating the entire length of the wharf.

Cicuta went flying into the air. His torso went one way, his legs another, and it rained warm blood down in a long, streaking pattern that passed directly over my head.

Which was, I don't mind admitting, kind of disgusting.

JADE ENCLAVE

Thankfully, I didn't have time to dwell on it. The blast had damaged the bricks around the Compass Rose, but I was able to read enough to get myself pointed north. I decided in that moment to abandon stealth, rose to my feet and took off, moving at a steady jog.

The first Jade Fang appeared before I made it five feet. I raised my pistol and put multiple rounds in him, leaping over his corpse before it even hit the floor. Three more steps and a flash of metal caught my eye. I ducked instinctively, crouching low as a curved kama swept through the space where my head had been. I twisted and fired without looking, blasting the approaching Jade Fang right at belt level. He screamed and went down, but I had no time to reflect on his injuries.

The edge of the pavilion came into view, and I raced up to the edge of the steps just as the last two remaining Jade Fangs dropped down from the ceiling rafters and moved to intercept me. I fired fast, emptying the remainder of my magazine into them. They hit the ground and lay still as the slide from my pistol locked back, informing me I'd just spent the last of my ammunition.

I snapped the slide forward, figuring I should at least maintain the appearance of being armed, and started forward, but a flash of darkness came out of the shadows before my foot came down on the first step.

I started to turn but the Jiangshi's fingers snapped around my throat, and he lifted me from the floor, holding me suspended in front of him. I tried to bring my pistol around, but he caught my wrist, and twisted my arm down, forcing the barrel of my pistol into my own abdomen. A breathless scream tore past my mouth as the hot metal touched flesh, burning a circular pattern in my skin.

"Yes," the Jiangshi whispered. "Embrace the pain. Savor the evidence of your own mortality. This is only the beginning. If you had hoped that revealing Satoru's treachery would save you, then you are sadly mistaken. I will strip away all that you are and feast on your very soul before I allow death to claim you. I will—"

His threats cut off when a narrow wrought blade the thickness of my two fingers tore through his shoulder. He screamed and his hand snapped open, dropping me onto the steps. I hit the ground just as he spun around, noting the ringed loop in the knife's pommel sticking out of his back. A wire chain was connected to the ring, and I followed it back to where the Gray Fox stood, gripping the haft with one hand.

Lian Guai had forgone her usual hood in favor of a simple gray martial arts uniform. There were various pouches along her belt, and a makeshift sling hung from her neck, discarded as she'd prepared to fight.

JADE ENCLAVE

"Get over here!" I whispered a second before she jerked the kunai dagger back. The Jiangshi screamed as the Gray Fox yanked him across the granite stones. She sidestepped his falling form and forced him to one knee as she swept behind him.

The Jiangshi was shaking in pain and rage, but the Gray Fox paid it no mind as she looped the chain wire around his throat and pulled it taut. A breathless gasp slipped past the Jiangshi's mouth, and the veins in his eyes turned red, bleeding into the darkness as he clawed at his throat.

Inside, a part of me cheered, urging the Gray Fox on even while acknowledging that I might be her next target. I'd deal with that when it came. For right now, all I could focus on was that I wanted the Jiangshi off my wharf and out of my city. The morgue would suffice, or else we could just dump him into the icy waters of the Atlantic.

For a brief moment, it looked as if the Gray Fox would prevail. I watched her strangle the life from the Jiangshi, saw the inky black light fading from his dead eyes. Then, in the final moments, he brought his hands up and raked his green-scaled gauntlet nail down the length of the metal chain.

There was a hissing noise, and the smell of burning flesh and cloth rose to fill the air. Whatever he'd used to coat his gauntlet burned through the chain, severing it into separate ends and sending the Gray Fox falling back with a startled cry.

She hit the ground, the broken haft of her weapon clattering against the concrete as the Jiangshi rose, casting his shadow across her downed form.

The Gray Fox leapt to her feet without using her hands, and threw a roundhouse kick, her leg striking against the right side of the Jiangshi, right where his liver should have been.

He didn't flinch.

Her next blow struck him across the jaw, the third in the meat of his hip. I could hear the sounds of impact, and I felt the resounding *whacks* with every strike, but the Jiangshi's face never changed.

As she wound back for a fourth strike, he lashed out with his arm, striking the Gray Fox along the side of the face. The impact from the blow reverberated in my chest, sucking away some part of me, or so it seemed, as she went flying backward through the air.

The Gray Fox hit the ground and slid along the cobblestones, rolling twice before coming to a graceless halt. A low groan emanated from her mouth as she rolled over on to her stomach, bracing with her knees and forearms.

JADE ENCLAVE

"I imagine you believe yourself brave," the Jiangshi whispered. "Strong. Possessing a warrior's heart. The truth is that you are nothing. You, and all those you love, will vanish from this world like flames blown to the wind, your names and memories swiftly forgotten. All that you care for will crumble into dust, and when next I awaken, nothing which you hold dear will remain."

"I would not hold too closely to that belief," a voice said from the darkness.

The Jiangshi's head snapped up, and Detective Wei's second phone call appeared.

Brother Kim walked out through the granite stone Custom House building and onto the wharf. Half a dozen monks flanked him, armed with long bamboo staffs.

"Chinatown will survive," he said. "Those of us who call it home will ensure it prospers. But you." He shook his head. "Your time is past, Jiangshi. To cling to life such as you have is to deny the natural order of this world. If you lack the courage to accept your fate, then that is your burden, but we will not allow you to corrupt our home or our people."

The monks surrounding him let out a fierce cry and snapped their bamboo staffs down in a warrior's pose. Behind the Jiangshi, more Jade Fangs appeared, coming out of the darkness with weapons at the ready. A low hiss ran through their number, and then, as if passing unspoken, both sides rushed one another, coming together in a vast melee of swift strikes and kicks.

Brother Kim struck first, flying toward the Jiangshi and whirling his staff in long graceful arcs that struck against the vampire's head and shoulders. The Jiangshi tried to shrug them off, but there were limits to his invincibility, and the cracks shown through as he winced and covered.

Brother Kim's onslaught never relented, and moment by moment the Jiangshi's desperation grew, until at last he had no choice but to act. He hurled himself forward, and even though Brother Kim had expected the assault, he'd underestimated the Jiangshi's reach. He brought his staff around, but the Jade Fang leader managed to slip inside its reach, absorbing the blow on the forearm and seizing Brother Kim around the throat.

Brother Kim's eyes widened, and a breathless cry escaped his mouth as the Jiangshi lifted him into the air. He brought his other hand around, centering his palm above the monk's breastbone, and drew it back, as if pulling on some unseen force. Chi, I suppose, though I saw no evidence of its existence.

Brother Kim, however, winced and jerked, every muscle taut, as if the Jiangshi had attached an invisible string inside and was tearing it free like a careless fisherman whose catch had swallowed his hook. His mouth peeled back in a pained cry, and he began to shake as the Jiangshi moved his hand back and forth, pulling from the monk with every beat of his heart.

Right up until the moment the Gray Fox took his head.

She appeared behind him wielding a curved sword, identical to the one Cicuta had held before I'd blown him sky high. Crouched as he was, the Jiangshi stood at the perfect height as she brought the sword around in a blindingly fast strike.

There was a flash of moonlight, a wisp of metal passing through flesh, and the wet sound of bloody droplets hitting the cobblestones.

The Jiangshi froze, and the next moment lasted for a subjective eternity before he collapsed into a boneless heap. His head bounced twice before rolling onto the cobblestones. It wound up facing me, and I found myself peering into those dark, dead eyes one last time before one of the remaining Triad gunmen came stumbling out of the darkness.

One glance at the Sacred Pine monks battling the Jade Fangs told him he didn't care which side won, since neither would benefit him. He raised his short-barreled rifle and the sudden crack as he opened fire startled me out of my trance.

I dove for cover at the same time Brother Kim and the Gray Fox leaped in opposite directions. I hit the granite steps, and bear-crawled my way onto the pavilion, coming up beside the siblings' cage.

Yichen and Mei kneeled inside. They were bruised and dirty, their clothing torn. My eyes noted the padlock on the cage. It was an ancient variety, like nothing I'd seen before. I was out of ammunition, so I turned my pistol around and used the butt to batter the lock. Each strike rang out with a heavy, metallic *crack*, but I ignored everything around me, including the burning in my shoulder as I brought my pistol down again and again.

The antique lock shattered, the pieces slipping free and sliding to the floor. From inside the cage, the siblings pushed, forcing the bent door open and ignoring the barbed wiring that scraped and cut their forearms.

A couple of seconds later they crawled free of the broken cage and came to their feet beneath the pavilion. They started to speak, but a figure emerging from the smoke behind me caught their attention, and I turned as the Gray Fox limped into view.

She was bruised, wounded, covered in blood, some of it hers and some belonging to the Jiangshi. As her gaze locked onto the siblings, tears sprang into her eyes, and she stumbled forward, her hands involuntarily rising toward her grandchildren.

The siblings cried out and raced forward, catching their grandmother in a rough embrace. The three of them dropped to the ground in a huddle, clinging on to one another tightly despite the blood and grime.

"Sergeant!" Tootsie appeared from the opposite side of the pavilion and raced up the steps, coming up beside me. "Are you alright?"

"Fine," I said, unsure if I was lying or not. "You?"

She nodded. "I lost my gun somewhere back there. Pretty sure it went into the water."

"We'll work something out," I told her.

"What are we..." She followed my gaze to the reunited Guai family, and her voice softened. "Oh. Well. That's kind of nice."

"Yeah."

"The Triad gunmen are about spent. I saw Satoru Doku. He's—"

"I know."

Tootsie cleared her throat. "Same goes for the Jade Fangs. Someone took the Jiangshi's head. And as for Cicuta—"

"He's done for."

"Bit of an understatement, but yes," Tootsie said. "I guess that about does it then."

"Almost. Not quite."

She followed my gaze over to the Gray Fox and her grandchildren. "Still determined to bring her in, huh?"

"I have it on good authority that she murdered two people."

"Seems like maybe she had a good reason."

"Maybe." I sighed. "But that will be for a jury to decide."

Tootsie considered it for a long moment, regarding the family with a soft, regretful expression. "Maybe we can give them a minute?"

"Yeah," I said. "I'm hoping she'll come quietly if we ask nicely."

"Probably." Tootsie was quiet for a moment before she said, "I sold pictures of my feet online."

I blinked, not sure I'd heard her correctly. "I beg your pardon?"

"Before I started working. I got sponsored through the academy, but it wasn't enough to live on. I needed some extra money, but no one was hiring part-timers. Things got tight, so I posted a few pictures. Nothing dirty. At least not in the traditional sense. Just… feet."

"Just feet," I repeated.

She nodded. "A couple of weeks in and I was making more than I made going through the academy. Heck, even as a patrolman. Everyone told me I should quit and focus on that full time."

"Why didn't you?"

"Because I didn't want to be a foot model," she said. "I want to be a police officer. To serve my city and my community. Someone my son can look up to. A role model." She shrugged. "I did what I had to do during the time I had to do it. And when I graduated and moved into full-time employment, I stopped."

"How did the brass find out?"

"I told them," she said. "Back when I had to do the polygraph test. At the end, they ask if there's anything the department should know about. I didn't want to risk being accused of hiding anything, so I laid it all out. I guess someone read it after the fact and word got around. You know how much of a boy's club this place can be."

"Tell me about it."

"So everyone started calling me Tootsie. And then someone found the pictures and started circulating them. The brass couldn't fire me, since I'd copped to it back when I was getting hired, but they also didn't want me around anymore. Not that they much wanted me around to begin with. Turns out, guys don't like it when you can bench press more than they can. So they gave me the boot. Literally. They stuffed my transfer orders in an old boot and left it in my locker."

"Why are you telling me this now?"

She shrugged. "Not sure. It's been a heck of a first day, and I figured you didn't need any more stress added to your plate. So, now you know."

"Well, I appreciate it. And for what it's worth, I don't care how much you can bench press."

"Thanks."

"And I'm happy as all heck that you're here. Maybe now we can finally start getting ahead of these cases, instead of always starting three steps behind and up a—"

A horrid, wailing cry rose from where the Guai family lay huddled. My head snapped around, and I felt my breath catch in my throat as the world took a dark turn.

Yichen was convulsing on the ground, his heels drumming against the cobblestones as bloody pus poured from his mouth. Mei moved to try and help, but whatever affliction he had was quick to claim her as well, and she slumped down beside him, her body twitching in erratic spasms.

For a long moment I stared at the pair, unable to comprehend what I was seeing. Then a horrible thought flashed through my mind, and I turned and stared at the cage where they'd been kept.

I hadn't noticed at the time, but peering closer, I could see faint traces of dark spots lining the barbed wire wound between the cage's bars. Black spots the same color as the poison that had adorned the Jiangshi's gauntlet.

Realization dawned, heralded in just as the Gray Fox let out a horrid, wailing cry. There was a depth to her voice, an anguish that spoke of raw, genuine pain. It stole the breath from my throat and left me feeling very small.

"Oh, no," I whispered.

Yichen and Mei grew still, staring sightlessly upward as blood pooled around their bodies and the Gray Fox howled her grief, unable to stop the cries that erupted from within her

"My God," Tootsie said from behind me. "Sergeant... what do we do?"

I shook my head, unable to find the words.

The Gray Fox's howls cut off with a strangled cry as she forced her jaw closed. We watched as she closed Mei's eyes, then unwound the neckerchief from around Yichen's neck, wrapping it tightly around her hand.

"Um," Tootsie began, but I held up my hand, cutting her off.

"We can't let her leave."

Whether the Gray Fox heard my words or just caught wind of the sound of my voice I couldn't say, but her eyes rose, her haunted gaze fixating on the two of us. I watched her features cloud over, grief giving way to rage, with us as the focal point.

"She seems really mad," Tootsie said.

"Murderous," I agreed.

"You think she blames us?"

The power of the Gray Fox's glare was answer enough. "I think she's going to kill anyone involved in this entire affair, regardless of whether or not they had anything to do with it."

"Including us?"

"Yes."

"Huh," Tootsie said. "We should probably do something about that."

I nodded. "Probably should."

"You still have your gun?"

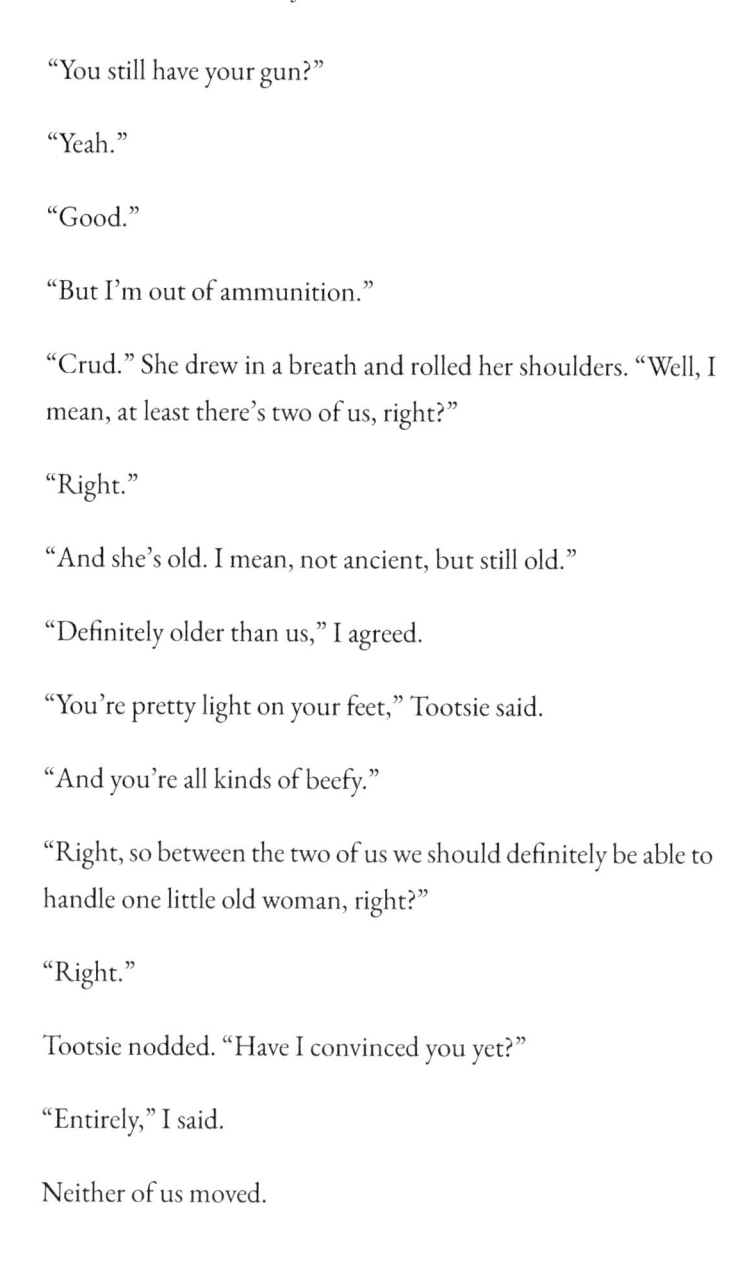

"Yeah."

"Good."

"But I'm out of ammunition."

"Crud." She drew in a breath and rolled her shoulders. "Well, I mean, at least there's two of us, right?"

"Right."

"And she's old. I mean, not ancient, but still old."

"Definitely older than us," I agreed.

"You're pretty light on your feet," Tootsie said.

"And you're all kinds of beefy."

"Right, so between the two of us we should definitely be able to handle one little old woman, right?"

"Right."

Tootsie nodded. "Have I convinced you yet?"

"Entirely," I said.

Neither of us moved.

Tootsie cleared her throat. "Maybe we should try and take her together?"

"Sounds like a good idea," I said.

"Now?"

The Gray Fox began stalking toward us, her eyes void of light or mercy.

"Now is good," I said.

We stalked toward one another, and Tootsie and I separated, circling to the Gray Fox's side. It wasn't a tactic I'd ever used before, but it seemed appropriate at the moment.

Mind you, appropriate doesn't always mean useful, and in this case, where we stood made next to no difference.

Tootsie struck first. She shot forward and launched a heavy, looping punch. The Gray Fox timed it perfectly, dropping in place and allowing the punch to pass over her head before springing back into the air. She struck half a dozen times while airborne, lashing out with a vicious array of brutal kicks, every one of which found a home before coming back down to the ground.

Tootsie groaned and teetered, but remained standing as I shot forward, winding up for a punch of my own. It was a feat that sounded easier than it was to pull off. Trying to fight the Gray Fox was like trying to fight the ocean. She was always two steps ahead, adjusting her stance and ducking beneath blows I hadn't even thought to throw yet. No matter how I angled my punches, I caught only air, and she battered me back relentlessly, breaking me down with feet, fists, and elbows.

I tried to get my arms around her, hoping I might be able to force her to the floor, but she turned and seized my outstretched hand, twisting me around and sending me flying head over heels. I hit the granite stones hard, and she stomped my already bleeding face once before Tootsie seized hold of her.

The muscles in her arm flexed, but it was like trying to hold an eel freshly plucked from the ocean. The Gray Fox wiggled and wormed and did something with her shoulders that caused her chest to cave inward. It only bought her a fraction of an inch, but that was all she needed to slip free from Tootsie's grasp.

Tootsie cursed as the Gray Fox dropped, bending at the waist and sweeping her leg around as if it were a vicious whip. The back of her heel struck Tootsie on the side of the jaw, and the force of her blow sounded throughout the pavilion. Tootsie's body crumpled, her head dropping a split second before she crashed to the concrete.

A pained cry burst up from my mouth and I jerked myself over, getting my feet beneath me. I threw myself forward and caught the Gray Fox just as she finished her rotation, wrapping my arms around her torso and sending the two of us crashing to the floor. She hooked her knee beneath my leg as we landed, and the next thing I knew I was being rolled over onto my back.

She came up on top of me, and something flashed in the moonlight. I caught a glimpse of Warman's Blade and realized in that moment that she had pulled it from my belt as we rolled. Fear shot through me, and I brought my hands up, catching the wrist holding the knife.

Physically, I might have been bigger than the Gray Fox, but she had a lifetime of studying martial arts, and she understood leverage better than I ever would. She shifted her hips and worked her arm, twisting the knife around so that it was directly above my face. Then she pushed, forcing the blade down. I gripped her wrist with both of mine, but it was only a moment before my arms started to shake. I could feel my strength fading. Any second now, my guard would collapse, and the blade would come down. I needed to do something.

With a cry, I jerked one hand free, driving my finger deep into her shoulder, where the bullet wound she'd taken earlier had only just begun to heal. My finger slipped between the ragged ends of her flesh and found its way into the soft warmth. The pain broke through her rage, and she screamed, momentarily relenting before she redoubled her efforts.

Which is what I'd hoped might happen.

I might not have been some martial arts master, but I knew a thing about leverage too, and when she doubled down on her knife strike, I didn't try to fight. Instead, I let the blade fall, pushing aside her wrist and jerking my head to the side.

The blade slipped past my face and struck the granite stone with a sound like a gunshot.

For a brief second I thought I had imagined it. Then the Gray Fox went limp, and her eyes rolled in her head, the light vanishing as she toppled off me. Confusion surged, but I pushed her limp form aside, scrambling out from beneath her as another figure stepped onto the pavilion.

Detective Wei had cast his crutches aside, dragging his wounded leg behind him. He was gripping his pistol, and I noted the thin trails of smoke coming from the barrel.

"Sergeant?" he asked, his eyes never leaving the Gray Fox's crumpled form.

It took several swallows before I could answer. "Present."

Detective Wei nodded, relief flashing across his face. "Just stay put. Area's all clear, and the cavalry is on its way."

As if to lend credence to his words, I heard a familiar whirling siren sound in the distance, and red and blue strobe lights appeared, shining through the fog as they raced in from the city proper.

The Aftermath. Saturday, July 26th 0800hrs

THE POLICE ARRIVED AND secured the scene, evacuating the wounded and then holding firm until Homicide could get here. I glimpsed Mackleroy from a distance but made sure to give him a wide berth. No pun intended. Eventually, things quieted down, and I made it back to the Union Oyster House, where I caught a few hours of sleep in a booth. I woke with the arrival of the morning cleaning crew and gave myself another sink bath before meeting Lieutenant Kermit at eight o'clock sharp to debrief.

It didn't take as long as I thought, considering everything that had happened in the last twenty-four hours. Although to be fair, some of our questions wouldn't be answered for weeks to come, and some never would.

It was a cluster anyway you cut it, but once Satoru Doku's body was identified, the brass seemed more than happy to chalk the whole thing up to some sort of internal strife amidst the Triad. The headlines went wild with talk of fighting ninjas for a while, but for once the police department received nothing but praise. Even better, no one was blaming Blue Moon, and that's a win I'll take any day of the week.

Mr. Zheng saw to Satoru and the other fallen Triad members' remains. He sent me a bouquet of flowers before they left. They were simple and understated. Just like the man himself.

We were never able to discern the Jiangshi's real identity. We tried with his fingerprints, dental records, even ran a DNA sample through every database we could find, including the international ones. In the end, we came up with diddly squat. Who he was or where he came from remains a mystery, and likely always will.

We had better luck with Cicuta. His fingerprints came back with a positive match. From what little I gathered, he was a chemical engineering student who dropped out of Kansas State University during his exams more than a decade prior and disappeared after telling his closest relatives that he was going to become a monk at some monastery no one had ever heard of in China. They assumed at the time he was just having a nervous breakdown, but none of them had ever spoken to him again.

JADE ENCLAVE

Tootsie took a couple days to heal up but has since settled in nicely. It's nice to have someone else to help balance the load. I have high hopes for her.

The Lotus Garden restaurant closed its doors soon after that night, and the last remnants of the electronic theft business collapsed over the coming weeks under Detective Wei's investigation. Hui Guai took a leave of absence from the university and moved to California with Mei's son in tow. I don't know if she will ever return to complete her studies, but I doubt it.

For a while there, Chinatown was swamped with funerals. The Gray Fox. Yichen. Mei. Xuanming Fei. Haoran Hei. Brother Dai. Their funerals were understated but elegant affairs, paid for in full by Brother Kim and the Sacred Pine Temple. I attended all of them but was careful not to overstay my welcome.

To this day, I still don't know who placed Brother Dai's body in my ceiling. I've narrowed down my list of suspects to those who would have had the motivation and the knowledge of how to circumvent the nearby security cameras, including Blue Moon's own. It couldn't have been easy. Lifting a body into the ceiling like that has got to be hard on your back, and even worse on your knees. It's a short list, but I haven't been able to bring myself to ask yet. Not because I fear the answer. More so because some battles just aren't worth fighting. And this was one of them.

The Sacred Pine Temple continues to operate in Chinatown. It doesn't advertise itself, but it's there for those who know how to look.

As for me, I stayed clear of Chinatown for a while, not sure how the fallout would go. I needn't have bothered. Chinatown continued on as it always has, its residents going about their lives with quiet dignity in the face of overwhelming adversity. I was never certain how much word of my involvement had spread, but the next time I ordered my beloved chicken noodle soup, it showed up piping hot, with a note saying it was on the house.

I took that as a sign that things were going to be okay.

The End

What is Next for Chloe?

There's Dangerous Business afoot, and it's about to land rightoutside Chloe Mayfield's front door.

JUSTIN HERZOG , STEVE HIGGS

A wizened wizard with tales of slumbering gods and secrets nolonger safe. Two gardeners in need of rescue, pursued by ghostly wraiths whothreaten more than just their lives.

Dark forces threaten the whole of New England, and while Chloe isno stranger to danger, she's never tackled anything like this before.

Woodwind songs ripe with elven melody carry rumors of a brokenfellowship in need of mending, and stories of a lone ring, forged in fire atopa summit's peak, destined to bring ruin to them all.

An exciting addition to thebest-selling Blue Moon Investigations written by Steven Higgs, fans of theseries will be overjoyed to see familiar characters as well as to meet a fewnew ones in this thrilling spin-off *series.*

A Note from the Author

Dear Readers,

And so we come to the end of another novel. This makes eight in less than two years. Not a bad bit of work, if I do say so myself. As always, I hope you've enjoyed the ride so far. Rest assured there is still plenty more to come for Chloe and company.

I was lucky enough to spend two years living in Boston, with a high-rise view overlooking Chinatown. It truly is a unique place unlike any other. The sights and smells remain in my memory to this day, and it was a pleasure to be able to return (even if only in my own mind) for the writing of this book.

What's next? Book 8 will be titled Dangerous Business, and it will see Chloe handling a case unlike anything she's encountered before. It's impossible to say more without giving too much away, but this one is going to be a little different from our standard fare, and I sincerely hope you will be delighted.

If you would like to read some FREE short stories from me which tie into my other series, follow this link -

https://books.bookfunnel.com/Justinherzogbundle.

My sincere thanks as always,

Justin Herzog

More Books by Justin Herzog

Fairy tale legend Goldilocks is all grown up and working for the US Forest Service.

The newest member of the agency, she spends her days patrolling the Divide, guarding the bridge points that separate our world from The Land and the descendants of the Native American tribesmen who reside there.

When a daughter of the Thunder Song Tribe is killed on our side of the forest, Goldilocks sets out to learn the truth. The chiefs want answers, not to mention her boss, and Goldilocks means to find them, preferably before the tribesman declare the Cabot Accords void and cross The Divide themselves.

When the evidence names her oldest friend as the murderer, she finds herself in a race against time, searching to find the truth and catch a killer whose murderous actions could set the whole forest ablaze and see her burned along with it.

JADE ENCLAVE

My name is Patrick Bannon, and I'm a demonologist.

Most people would agree that the study of demons isn't a practical area of research. Lucky for me, Miami has never been a practical kind of city.

With more reported cases of demonic possession than any other two cities combined, the jewel of South Florida can be a dangerous place for those who don't respect it, and when trouble strikes, it falls to me to set it right.

Now a renowned Catholic reverend is dead, and the church wants to know if it was suicide or murder.

Simple, except when it isn't.

To make matters worse, word on the street is that Tiberius, the demon responsible for my brother's suicide, is trying to claw his way back up from the Void.

One guess who sent him there.

Free Books and More

Want to see what else I have written? Go to my website.

https://stevehiggsbooks.com/

Or sign up to my newsletter where you will get sneak peeks, exclusive giveaways, behind the scenes content, and more. Plus, you'll be notified of Fan Pricing events when they occur and get exclusive offers from other authors because all UF writers are automatically friends.

Copy the link carefully into your web browser.

JADE ENCLAVE

https://stevehiggsbooks.com/newsletter/

Prefer social media? Join my thriving Facebook community.

Want to join the inner circle where you can keep up to date with everything? This is a free group on Facebook where you can hang out with likeminded individuals and enjoy discussing my books. There is cake too (but only if you bring it).

https://www.facebook.com/groups/1151907108277718

Printed in Dunstable, United Kingdom